possessed

possessed

jowita bydlowska

Publisher: Kwame Scott Fraser | Acquiring editor: Julie Mannell | Editor: Russell Smith
Cover designer: Laura Boyle
Cover image: istock.com/ alexey_ds

Library and Archives Canada Cataloguing in Publication

Title: Possessed / Jowita Bydlowska.
Names: Bydlowska, Jowita, author.
Identifiers: Canadiana (print) 20210285176 | Canadiana (ebook) 20210285184 | ISBN
   9781459748071 (softcover) | ISBN 9781459748088 (PDF) | ISBN 9781459748095 (EPUB)
Classification: LCC PS8603.Y395 P68 2022 | DDC C813/.6—dc23

We acknowledge the support of the Canada Council for the Arts and the Ontario Arts Council for our publishing program. We also acknowledge the financial support of the Government of Ontario, through the Ontario Book Publishing Tax Credit and Ontario Creates, and the Government of Canada.

Care has been taken to trace the ownership of copyright material used in this book. The author and the publisher welcome any information enabling them to rectify any references or credits in subsequent editions.

The publisher is not responsible for websites or their content unless they are owned by the publisher.

Printed and bound in Canada.

Rare Machines, an imprint of Dundurn Press
1382 Queen Street East
Toronto, Ontario, Canada M4L 1C9
dundurn.com, @dundurnpress 𝕏 f ◎

To Brian

part 1

a woman is a haunted island

1

IT WAS RELENTLESS, a fever that wouldn't let up. I couldn't do anything without him breaking into every thought. I lived in a state of paradox, able to only think about him but also wanting him out of my mind. I wanted him out just so that I could experience the rest of the world.

I read quotes posted online, and they all claimed that the world was out there and that it was wonderful. Why couldn't I remember what it felt like before him, what gave me joy? Was it nature or art? I had only a vague idea of liking those — trees and rivers and paintings of them. Now they didn't seem worthy of attention, or interesting. Only he seemed interesting.

I wanted him out, not because I didn't love him but because I couldn't think about one thing only; it was maddening. Yet I couldn't stop it. On a loop, a movie for an audience of one, thousands of short clips of what I had so far: the way he slowly

slung his jacket over the chair on our first date, how he asked
the waitress if they had any gluten-free drinks and repeated
the request, straight-faced, as she stared, confused, and how he
walked to his car as if he owned the sidewalk. His hands, lips,
teeth, how he held me by my neck — all that came later on in
our story. His name was lodged between my ears, and I said it
over and over during the day as if it would bring me comfort.
It didn't.

At night, too, I said Sebastian's name. I dreamt about him.
Every dream, his face above me, present and hot with breath
then dissolving into nothingness. And then the in-between
time spaces where he was, and then I'd wake up, and he wasn't.

I talked to him in my head. Shopping: Do you like this crop
top? The pants? Silver or gold?

Hair: Should I dye my hair, should I be a lighter brunette,
should I shave my entire body? Also, should I lose some weight?
(My maybe-boyfriend, Victor, disliked any kind of fat. He was
fixated on my small breasts, and he once pinched my thigh
and said, *Nice*, but in the wrong tone of voice. I assumed men
generally liked skinny women, at least that's what the internet
suggested, and all the ads, except for the one for cream cheese.
I didn't eat cream cheese. I joked to myself I didn't want to end
up fat and on a cloud.)

∽

I read a quote in a book about a woman obsessed with a man.
The quote was, "When you're living so intensely in your head
there isn't any difference between what you imagine and what
actually takes place. Therefore, you're both omnipotent and
powerless."

I didn't feel omnipotent, only powerless. The book was popular with the kind of smart people my age who liked obscure things, dug them up, and then threw them into the mainstream. Etch A Sketch life.

They made a TV show based on that book, too, starring a popular actor of my childhood.

In the story, the man was quickly turned off by the protagonist's violent pursuit of him, but his disinterest only seemed to fuel her. She wrote him desperate letters and continued to do so even after numerous rejections. In the TV show, the childhood actor was no longer young or wearing leather jackets, but his face remained boyish despite the ratness of it.

The story was supposed to be about something else, not about the obsession but about art theory and a woman coming into her own, all thinky stuff. But I liked it for the obsession since that was the only part I could relate to — I could relate to the desperate letter writing and over-the-top unreciprocated sexual confessionals.

I didn't do that with Sebastian, but that doesn't mean I didn't want to. I wanted to do all those things; I wanted to hide in the bushes across from his apartment. I wished I was more like the protagonist of the book — bold and proud of my craziness.

I was too subtle. I wanted to run into Sebastian, unscripted. But it was impossible. Even our geography didn't allow it. He lived in the suburbs.

I streetviewed his address on Google Maps and rode the cursor around his neighbourhood enough times that I memorized all the details: in his driveway, the absence of his mother's car; on the corner, a young girl in a colourless coat; a few blocks down, a new refrigerator being delivered.

I was familiar with his daily schedule — he left the house to work out of the coffee shop a short drive away. In the evening, he went out to drink. Sometimes he drove to the city to go on dates. I didn't want to think about that. It wasn't necessarily that I was jealous of him sharing his body — I just didn't want him to think that he had the time to meet other women when he told me he had no time to meet with me.

I knew where his favourite bar was in the city, but the place closed down shortly after he started disappearing. I only went by the bar once to see if I would run into him and I didn't, and I felt mortified that I did that, so I never did it again.

Since there was no chance I could run into him where I lived downtown — in a city that pretended to be New York but wasn't — I tried to conjure him in other ways, for example, by counting random things: tiles, letters in words, redheads. If it's an even number, he is thinking of me. An odd number, he is not. If it was an odd number, I'd count again. And again and again until I got an even number and I could move along holding on to that like a neurotic, clueless person. I've never felt more alive even though I was neurotic, clueless, and in pain.

∽

Later on, when I admitted to myself about how big of a problem my obsession was becoming, I bought and tried to read popular self-help books about unrequited love, narcissism, and other bad behaviour. During one of my more focused readings, I learned about a condition called *limerence*. It was not yet classified as a psychological illness in the Diagnostic and Statistical Manual of Mental Disorders (DSM–5), but there were some studies and books written about it. Limerence was characterized by intrusive thinking about the object of one's affection, and it manifested as a vacillation between intense joy and deep despair — depending on the feelings being reciprocated or not. The pendulum of its design reminded me of bipolar disorder, or at least what I remembered about it from my days as a psychology undergrad.

My romantic obsession was groundless because I didn't have a lot to go on, just a few dates, some texts. Scraps. It fit perfectly within the definition of *obsession*: an obsession is a thing that is not based on reason. It is similar to addiction, which is an inability to quit doing something despite wanting to. It is similar to sickness.

Limerence was very much like sickness in that it was debilitating. It could not be explained in terms that would make sense to a person who was logical. I was pining for someone I loved despite not having any evidence that the love was reciprocal. It was not a two-way street — it was a car crash. It was a ghost that lived in your skin. A real ghost would be better — at least you'd have something outside of yourself to scare you. With limerence, the ghost was trapped, and although you were the only one who could release it, you couldn't. You didn't want to because how could you live without your ghost, your love? It seemed impossible; it seemed like death living without your love, your lovesickness.

2

IT WAS BANAL: we met in his favourite coffee shop. It was his favourite because it was not part of a chain and it was the closest shop he could drive to. He worked as a freelance graphic artist.

I was visiting the suburb to purchase a new stove element — my mother tried to boil water in the electric kettle, which she put on the actual stove, and she almost set our apartment on fire (for weeks the place smelled of burnt rubber).

After getting the element, I found the coffee shop in the same plaza where the shop was. I didn't take a day off to run my errand, but I didn't have to go back into the office at the travel agency. I was supposed to work on a draft of our company newsletter about new services for prospective clients.

Sebastian and I were sitting a couple of tables away from each other, and our eyes met (better, *locked*, like in a romance novel) over the lineup of latte enthusiasts. I couldn't look away.

I was never this forward with strangers; I was, after all, subtle.

He didn't smile, but he wouldn't look away, either. It wasn't creepy, just insistent. It was if we were already having a conversation, and I was being rude in trying to look away.

My face felt hot.

He got up, sat down beside me, and said, Give me your number. (Not "Can I have your number?")

He had a nice mouth even though his teeth were a little too yellow. But his smile was good; it was a naturally conspiratorial smile — we were in on something together. What? Our meeting?

He had dark brown eyes, almost black, a little too close together. He smelled sharp and sweet like flowers being burned in gasoline. I felt myself getting aroused from inhaling him. I liked the smells of men, I loved their colognes, the seriousness of those smells, like plastic and business but also the playfulness of some, how you could sometimes detect the ever-so-gentle sweet musk that reminded me very faintly of the way their balls smelled. The perfume people knew what they were doing.

He entered my number into his phone and got up. I'll call you, Josephine, he said.

I liked that he said my name. I didn't want him to leave. In that very brief moment, I searched for things to say to keep him standing there longer, something that would make him promise me that he was really going to call: *I've only six weeks left to live! I am moving back to Mexico next week! I'm joining a convent!*

I watched him walk toward a black car, get in, drive away.

I could not focus on work. I left the coffee shop in a daze, replaying the few brief moments of our meeting. In the parking lot, I saw a man dressed in dirty pants and a brown trench coat — his knotty braids wrapped with rags — marching fast along the side of the street toward where I stood. He was screaming to himself, every sentence a curse.

I stared. I felt guilty for witnessing his madness. I should've known better, having grown up and lived in a city. I try not to inscribe meaning to random events, but I did then. I thought how this was some kind of a warning and that I would learn something from it.

It was as if some of us entered adulthood and got caught and trapped by demons while the rest of us were divided — those who pretended that everything was okay and those who, luckily, had no clue nothing was okay. I was not lucky. But I was good at pretending. I thought maybe the man was a reminder of what could happen to me if I ever lost control. When he passed me, he said, There is blood on your shoes.

I looked down. There was no blood on my shoes.

∽

On my way home in the car, I thought about how I wanted to tell someone about that banal meeting in the coffee shop, but I had no one close to tell, no one to get excited about it with.

I long ago stopped wishing for the kind of mother who would be my best friend, yet my mother was the only person in my life — besides my problematic maybe-boyfriend — that I was close with. Driving, I wondered if in her state she would be able to get excited about that kind of information, if I could maybe pretend that we were connecting. I would tell her anyway and ignore whatever she said in return.

No, I probably could not pretend like that. In some cases I was capable of deceiving myself — as I had done all my life in regard to my body, not knowing if it was fat or not — but there was no way I would be able to ignore my mother's reaction. And it would not be the right reaction. At best it would be nonsensical, or hurtful. At worst, she would say nothing and just stare past me as if she were looking at someone behind me.

You're too old to chase men in coffee shops.

What if he comes over and murders you?

If you want to make a mess out of your life go ahead and whore yourself out.

(Or: silence.)

Those were some of her most likely responses. My prospects weren't great. I decided to keep the banal afternoon all to myself.

3

THE EARLIEST MEMORY of my mother acting peculiar — and I am being polite; it was twisted, not peculiar — was at the age of eleven, when she lay next to the door of my bedroom where I had barricaded myself.

I was in my bedroom because I refused to rewrite the page with the word "giraffes," "sunshine," and "zigzag" for the seventeenth time. It was a cursive exercise. I saw no point in knowing how to write that way since everyone used a computer. But I didn't say that aloud. That would have been talking back, and I didn't talk back. I learned early on — before that particular memory — that it wasn't safe to talk back to my mother because it resulted in light but unpleasant enough smacks across the head.

I knew my mother grew up in a different era where handwriting said things about you. If you were sloppy and your words spilled out of line, it meant you also had a sloppy personality, or you were dumb or possibly both. You were unprepared for the world. Nobody would hire you. It was an abstract argument to me and it meant little, but I never objected, including on that day when I indulged her by writing "giraffes, sunshine, zigzag" for hours, pages and pages filled with those three words. My mother's writing was impeccable, straight letters with perfectly round cheeks and butts and the most proportional ascenders and descenders.

My letters were poor imitations of hers and they tended to slant left, which my mother called *Jewy*. After each completed page, she would take the notebook and tear out the page. She pointed out the mistakes — letters that were clunky and not up to her standard, sloppy. Not one page was free of mistakes. Some were better than others, and I was doing okay between pages seven and ten, but past eleven I could no longer get the lines to curl the right way. The *G*s and *F*s and *Z*s and *S*s and *A*s and everything else crowded and clamoured on the page and in my head, and I started crying, which only enraged my mother. In my defence, I will say that by the time I rebelled, the exercise and even the words themselves had completely lost their meaning. Giraffe, sunshine, zigzag. Zigzag-zebra-zun. In my childhood memory, my mother's head is that of a clown on fire, her bleached-blond hair dry but glorious like a cloud; it puffs around the red steam of rage, the thin lips, her beastly green eyes narrowing, lost in too much mascara. Her face comes in and out of focus. It shouts and calls me names, regular insults, "idiot," "loser," but also words I have to later look up, such as "whore." Her rage seems disproportionate to my failing. By the scale of her rage, I know that taunting couldn't have just started. She must've been sitting there the whole time, growing more and more irritated. She must've scolded and criticized me for some time, but I was so used to it that it didn't register. She ignored my elegant *S*s and some of the giraffes beautifully sculpted into symmetrical shapes as perfect as their namesakes. I could keep a line going. I could draw a circle.

I ran out of the living room and locked myself in my bedroom. I remember doing that as if it would keep a wild animal out.

The new insults scared me. I didn't know how harmful they were, if they were like spells that could do some terrible damage. The way they were spat out, that's how they sounded.

She said some other things or made one of her threats, although they couldn't have been too over-the-top because the stakes were so low. I was only a little girl. But she must've threatened something. Maybe taking away a toy or being made to stay home. Maybe even a beating.

Maybe taking her own life.

Because that's actually what happened. That was the threat, the actual danger I felt. And I don't know if that was prior to my running out or when she was already lying on the ground by the door, when she told me she had a razor with her.

Do you know what a fucking razor can do? Her voice was wet with tears. To a wrist?

I had an idea. Whose wrist?

I whimpered for her to stop. Our faces were both pressed against the gap under the door, separated but breathing into the same space. She was heaving. She had exhausted herself from rage. Maybe us lying there had been going on for a while and something happened to time, the way it sometimes did when it would expand or collapse on itself. It was strange she sounded so exhausted.

Do you know what a fucking razor can do? was a question that wasn't a question. It was a question that was a warning.

No, I said. Yes.

I didn't know what to say. I still didn't know if she meant what a fucking razor could do to herself or to me, but if she was going to use it, I preferred she use it on me. The information I'd had about myself so far was that I was a failure. And that my father used to get sick because I screamed so loudly as a toddler. I was never told if his death was my fault, but I guessed yes. I was terrible at cursive. Outside of home, I didn't have a lot of friends. I was one of those bland kids you picked second-last to be on your team. Not offensive but definitely not important. Not a girl you had over for sleepovers or birthday parties because I had nothing to say. I was too quiet. What else? I was lazy. I read too much instead of being outside like all the other kids. And I ate too much. I didn't know at first, but then I learned from my mother that I had a fat ass, and it was going to be hell trying to lose those pounds once I was a teenager. I was gross and I smelled gross, the teenage stink already faintly there, a smell I was fascinated by at first but learned to hate — sour and salty clamminess that my mother would point out on my coming home if I happened to exert myself. I always rushed home. Like a moth to a flame.

And my mother was the opposite of all the human sludge that was me. Back then, she was a fairy tale personified, the most beautiful person, like one of her favourite movie stars with their puffy blond hair and heavy eyeliner. She smelled of Anaïs Anaïs, which smelled of lily of the valley, which was her favourite flower. When I was very young, I was convinced she had a secret life as a movie star. I was sure she was actually the beautiful blond French actress with the sharp eyeliner who was the only person in a picture frame on my mother's bedside table when I was growing up. In the picture the actress is wearing a thick black headband and a striped shirt.

It was impossible that someone like my mother would exist in our ordinary world. Even with those harms flung my way, those words and whatever else she was doing to make me feel unsafe — she could do no wrong. It was my fault she was going to harm herself with a razor.

You don't love me, she wheezed under the door. You don't love your own fucking mother.

No, I love you so much, I love you, I shouted into the space. I could smell her, her perfume mixed with the dampness of her tears and sweat and her natural warmth. She was the softest, warmest person I knew. I wanted to hug her so badly. The razor made it impossible.

Time passed. I fell asleep. I fell so deeply asleep it was as if I died. I had never felt that tired. I was probably just lazy; histrionics shouldn't make anybody that tired.

When I woke up, I was in my bed, in my clothes. I had no idea how she carried me, how she opened the door without waking me up. Mothers had supernatural powers. My mother once told me about another mother who lifted a streetcar to free her toddler who was trapped underneath it. There was another story about another mother who had fought a bear. I didn't know if she knew those women or if the stories were made up to serve as cautionary tales. That's how she would say them, with a note of a warning where I felt like I was the streetcar or the bear and never the toddler.

I looked over at my little bedside table and noticed the torn-out sheets of paper were all arranged on it in a pile. A little note on top of them said, "Have a <u>good</u> look." So I looked. And I saw what had happened — I had made a major mistake. From page ten till page seventeen, the word "butterfly" was missing. My mother wrote the word over and over, over my lines of words, in a screaming red ink, in the most unwavering singular line that showed she'd only taken the pen off the page once, per word, to cross the *T*s.

I can't even say if my decision to forgo the word was to intentionally fuck with her or if it was just something that happened. Either option seemed unacceptable; I was a person out of control.

I called the Kids Help Phone, hoping they would be able to tell me how to improve myself, but the friendly woman on the other end only wanted me to complain about my life. Her voice was sugary as she told me that I was not a bad person. I didn't believe her. She was paid to say these things. She didn't take me seriously. I had to find a solution or my mother would bring out the razor again. I didn't say anything about the razor. I just let her talk and ask me questions, and I answered them truthfully — I was safe, I had a place to sleep, I got sad sometimes, I didn't have a lot of hobbies, I loved my mother very much, she was the most important person in my life. I did not think of harming myself.

I looked up a few places on the internet that dealt with kids' mental health issues, but it was all so complicated. You had to go through a hospital, you had to speak to your general practitioner, you had to wait for referrals. Most places required you to show up with a caregiver.

My school years were tumultuous, an ongoing exercise in avoiding an enraged female bear.

Contradiction: When I got into the university of my choice, my mother seemed happy for me. She bought me a computer and helped me unpack in my new apartment. I studied art in the beginning, but that went sideways after a terrible fiasco: a painting I was proud of mysteriously disappeared. I switched to psychology. I told my mother I couldn't decide on a major. I don't know why I lied about what I was going to study, but I felt she would be suspicious of psychology. Her mother, my grandmother, spent two years locked up in a sanatorium for melancholy when my mother was a little girl. I come from a line of troubled women.

∽

The reason I took psychology was because I thought I could fix myself cheaply by learning all the mechanics of what was wrong with me from textbooks and saving on therapy. I thought if anyone was best equipped to know what was wrong with me, it should be me. My brain and psyche both had an instruction manual just like everything else in my body, and mental problems, like rules about drawing and perspective, were solvable as long as you understood theory and measurements. There are ways to cure diseases with medication and treatments, so there must be ways to cure insanity by talking yourself out of it. Not that I considered myself insane. Yet I knew there was something off about me because nothing at home was like it was in other people's homes — there were no family dinners, no family at all, no dog, no music — and my mother insisted I was *mental*. That was the word she used for a while: mental. I don't know if her own mother called her that, but it sounded repeated, a word that had to be passed on in order to stop hurting. Later, I understood there was something wrong with *her*. But by the time I understood that, I'd already invested too much in trying to fix myself and failing, and as a result I developed actual issues. So in the end my mother was right: there *was* something wrong with me. My psychology major turned out to be interesting only for its anecdotes about rats or horses or serial killers.

I changed my major. I landed softly with a diploma in everything. I took pictures, but I didn't really know what made one picture good and another bad. Taking pictures was cheating, a lazy way out of painting. Photographs seemed easier, but it turned out there were rules, too, and merely knowing what looked interesting in the frame wasn't enough. I also didn't know what to photograph, although flowers appealed to me, so for a while I shot flowers. A guy I knew in Advanced Visual Arts Foundation Studio said you should only take pictures of things you don't want to forget. He himself was taking pictures of colourful packaging and discarded wrappers in Chinatown, of puddles with grease-like rainbows. I went to his art show and later on gave him a blow job in his cute apartment, where the walls were lined with shelves full of vinyl records. There were also Polaroid cameras everywhere and Polaroid pictures, bunches of them. He grabbed one of those bunches from my hand and declared he had failed at Polaroid. He seemed sweet and tortured, and that aggressive gesture startled me. He offered me a Japanese beer. We drank. His penis was so small it was like sucking a finger.

I graduated in an apathetic daze. I didn't even tell my mother about the convocation and didn't pick up my diploma — it was mailed to me. After graduating, I wrote a personal essay about my disappointment with having gone to university, and shortly afterward I was hired to complain professionally for a local newspaper. That led to professionally praising products, which led to other writing jobs and then to other jobs related to lying for living. My career didn't have a specific shape; it seemed to take me wherever it wanted to. My mother had no ideas for me, either; she considered me a disappointment and told me so frequently.

For a long time I didn't think my mother's meanness was an issue. I was still stuck on trying to solve me. But the middle-of-the-night phone calls and the tears and the threats that happened throughout my youth? They could only be a result of demonic possession or perhaps something more mundane, like a borderline personality disorder.

∽

Despite my deep love for her, I always fantasized about having a different mother. Who wouldn't, considering? The mother I had in mind was sane and kind and cool. The kind of mother where I could tell people the story about how once we got similar haircuts and people mistook us for sisters.

In my fantasy, I gave her advice on boyfriends, and I was honest about the one boyfriend who drank too much and borrowed money he was slow to pay back. She listened to me and ditched him. My fantasy mother worked at a newspaper or a magazine. She explained about birth control. We had the same shoe size, and I wore her eighties heels that were in style again. Sometimes she'd fall asleep in my bed when we'd binge-watch TV shows. She'd throw her arm across my chest when she fell asleep, and it wasn't weird that her hand was touching my breast. She wouldn't wake up even with the laugh track on; the TV murmurs soothed her. I think that mother was actually a mother from a TV show.

In reality, my mother was affectionate, but it was a strange affection, cloying, her mouth like a suction cup when she kissed me. When she'd hug me, I was a hostage inside her arms. Yet she never held my hand when I was a child. The closest she would come was to hold the neck of my shirt and push me forward or drag me along. It was brutal, but my heart would pick up speed and flutter in my chest with happiness combined with extreme anxiety. I wanted to scream for her to hold my hand. Every time she wouldn't touch me, I wanted to scream. And when she'd hit me, I was silent.

We didn't watch TV shows together. We didn't talk about boys and men. She went on dates but never brought anyone home. When I was a teenager, sometimes she would be on the phone weeping; sometimes there would be a car waiting in the driveway, and there would be a shadow of a man inside and a red dot of a cigarette, like in a detective movie.

My mother had me late in life with a man who was twenty years her senior. To him she must've been a lively older girl — in the wedding photographs she looks a lot younger than forty. My father was a carpenter and mainly worked for the church. He was financially stable and was able to provide for her, and that was one piece of very little information I had. What I guessed was that he must've asked her to marry him only after a few weeks of dating. He died when I was a baby. There were no pictures of him in the house. If she talked about him she was dispassionate, unless she was in one of her spells, and then she would argue with his ghost. She never told me he was someone I should love or think about, and he wasn't mentioned until I asked about him as an older child.

After my father passed, she went to college and got a degree in office administration. She got a job at a Christian charity organization. She worked at that job until she was dismissed. Then she volunteered at the church and the soup kitchen and the cemetery. All three places were wacky enough that she could camouflage her own eccentricity without anyone catching on.

Like my fantasy mother, my real mother owned many pairs of high heels, but she stopped wearing them when she started volunteering at the church. A few months before I moved back in, she made a tower in the backyard out of the shoes and poured gasoline on them. I recognized the caseworker's number on my phone when it rang at 3:00 a.m. Victor, my maybe-boyfriend, drove me to the hospital but didn't go inside with me.

One of the nurses told me what I had already heard from other healthcare professionals. There was no reversing any of it. The nurse apologized as if it was her fault. I went to my mother's house in the morning and borrowed a shovel from her arm-crossed, frowny neighbour, who watched me dig a hole where I buried the corpses of the shoes.

4

AFTER OUR MEETING, Sebastian texted me the next day. First nothing crazy, just jokes. I was the one who was bold: once our banter turned a little sexual — where I lamely asked him if he would give a famous male actor a blow job for $5,000 U.S. — I asked him what he liked in bed.

(I knew I wanted to sleep with him when I met him in that coffee shop. It takes less than five seconds to know if you want to sleep with a guy. Some guys grow on you, but some guys are immediate, instant wetness, a spasm between your legs, and he was that for me.)

What do you like? he texted.

I don't know. What would you like to do to me?

I'm a dom. (I imagined his weight on me, crushing me.)

I played cute: *50 Shades of Grey?*

Fuck you.

Sorry. I like being submissive.

Bodes well for me. I'd like to pin you down right now.

I was still working on the newsletter when this particular text exchange went on, and I also had to deal with my mother, who refused to sleep and who came into my room to ask me if I could feel the ghost — or ghosts, as some were just passing through — that lived in her house.

I could feel it, them, sure, but I was reasonable, not like her. She had a constant need to bring it up, get all dramatic. I had only moved in a month or so before meeting Sebastian, but it seemed like a lifetime already. A lifetime of her hysteria and, lately, the need to point out that there was a certain heaviness in the air, in the house, that we were not alone.

Do you feel it or not?

To be honest, I don't. You should go to sleep.

Don't be ridiculous. There's something here and you won't acknowledge it. Why? Her face crumpled and she started picking at the hem of her nightgown.

I'm sorry. I just don't feel anything. Okay?

Okay, what? Why do you always refuse to have a conversation with me? my mother said.

Do you like having your ass slapped?

My computer screen went dark, then lit up in two zebras, immediately followed by a green landscape, then a close-up of a bug wing. I had two news alerts set up, and I worried about my mother looking at my screen. One of the alerts was for "psychotic outbreak."

My mother said, Josephine, I didn't ask you to move in here so that you could be on your phone or your computer all the time. You should leave work at work. And you should leave your phone in your purse.

My mother didn't ask me to move in with her. I moved in with her because she was becoming more and more incapable of not taking off in the middle of the night, or she was screaming about ghosts or some other trouble, like being bitten by snakes, and calling 911 about it. She had the beginnings of dementia. The only cute thing about it was that she would sometimes play an imaginary piano. And then there was the bear incident. A couple of weeks before I moved in, I stopped by to drop off some groceries. As I busied myself in the basement filling the freezer with food, I heard my mother yelling about a bear in the backyard. There is a bear in the yard! I heard loud and clear. I ran up the stairs, trying to arrange the thoughts in my head about the possibility of a bear really being there in the yard. We lived in a big city.

My mother stood in front of the kitchen window, her eyes fixated on something, or nothing, technically, as there was no bear and nothing resembling a bear in the small fenced area.

She was wringing her hands as she turned to me, chin trembling, Do something!

Do what?

Do something about that fucking bear!

I don't see a bear. There is no bear, I said, blinking like an idiot to see if a bear would materialize. Her swearing unnerved me — she rarely swore, believed swearing was a sin.

Just because you don't see it, that doesn't mean it isn't there, my mother screamed.

I reached out to touch her, but she hissed at me, You're useless.

I'm sorry. Please don't be mad. I'll do something.

And just like that she calmed down, her shoulders dropping. She shook her head, puffed out her cheeks, and shuffled away from the window.

∽

My maybe-boyfriend, Victor, was stoic about me moving out of his studio. I was also trying to be stoic about moving out as I packed my mascara, toothbrush, a box of tampons, and an unopened pack of pink razors — the last two items suggesting I must've been feeling quite optimistic about our future. I sing-songed out loud to myself, "End of an era, end of an era."

Was this the end of an era? The phrase sounded absurd. But once I sang, I no longer felt like crying.

Victor appeared in the doorway and asked if he should call me a cab. He could not drive me; a student was coming to discuss her project.

We hugged for twenty seconds and I left to wait for the taxi, outside. A young, dark-haired woman with a neck tattoo got out of it, a large portfolio under her arm. She smiled at me nervously and I smiled back, even though I felt like crying.

∽

When I met him, Victor was different from the kind of men I was used to meeting at grad parties. By the time I was in my twenties, I was used to men my age who went to university, and who wore sweaters, had strong opinions on medical marijuana or vegetarian diets, and listened to bands fronted by twee girls with uneven hair. Those men were also in bands, but they no longer had delusions about making it as a band. For that reason they were mildly bitter, but many of them had enough sense to, for example, try writing about bands, which was a more useful skill than playing a guitar. Their dreams were crushed, but they were smart about it. And their bitterness was attractive because it was almost as if they had a sense of humour. Many didn't, not authentically. The sweater men were timid. They asked if it was okay to touch you before touching you; they went out of their way to show that they were harmless and that you could hug them without worrying about your breasts pressing against their chests and giving them erections. You could cuddle with them, share a bed, a T-shirt, and they would not fuck you unless they had a signed consent form. They were terrified of having essays written about them and published in angry girl magazines. They wore polite colognes, usually something by L'Occitane en Provence, bunches of inoffensive, sexless flowers.

Victor smelled the correct way, the way Sebastian smelled: dominant, *decisive*. His cologne told me that he liked to fuck. Not surprisingly, later on in our relationship Victor revealed an incredible array of sexual needs — so maybe that was another thing I could smell on him. That unapologetic greed for flesh that was attractive, too, and different from what I knew.

You have to meet this guy; he's a famous photographer, said a printmaker acquaintance who brought me to the party. It was held in a warehouse that was about to be turned into condos. This was very New York — throwing parties in places that were not meant for parties. I never lived in New York but I travelled there for work. Our Toronto efforts to be *it* were painful and embarrassing to witness; our complaining to each other about it was part of the tradition — nobody liked Toronto, and we all lived here and could not leave because we were afraid of America more than we were of leaving.

At the party, everyone wore black: me, too. There was a DJ, and people were snorting cocaine from a mirror-top table, and others were making out — or sitting next to making-out people — on a massive black leather couch. There were big ugly paintings of shapes that looked like oil spills, with a green and yellow tint to them. Perhaps they were actual oil spills.

Some people stood around in small circles, discussing things and holding their elbows and their drinks. It seemed there were lots of people with creative, thick-frame glasses, lots of girls with big noses and heavy-lidded eyes, and dainty non-sexuals in tent-sized black outfits, and older kooky women with severe bangs that were cut too short. There were only a couple of young men in sweaters, and they all seemed girlfriended or, alternatively, castrated — their eyes firmly fastened to women's eyes, never below their necks.

My companion pulled me toward one of the small groups and placed her hand on the shoulder of a short guy in a suit with floppy dark hair. He turned around and stared, cocking his head slightly as if I were an interesting object presented to him to inspect, which is precisely what I was. We were the same height. His mouth was nice, even though his teeth seemed disturbingly long. But when he talked or smiled, he was able to arrange his face well enough that it worked.

Victor, this lovely woman wants to write an article about you.

No, I don't, I said.

He shook my hand. You're a writer?

I couldn't figure out his age, but he was significantly older than the guys in sweaters. I had never been with an older guy.

Victor just won an international award for his series of photographs of women in South Africa. Women with AIDS, right, Victor?

Women with HIV.

I'm not a writer, I said.

What are you?

I don't know, I said.

You remind me of my ex-wife, he said.

What was she like?

She broke my heart, he said casually, and I wasn't sure if I should say sorry or not, so I said nothing. I could tell he wanted me. At that point I could always tell right away. It happened so rarely with the sweater men, and I almost never went to night clubs, where everyone acted like animals in heat. It was uncool to go to night clubs unless you wanted to get groped.

Victor kept staring. The eye contact was unnerving, but I had had a couple of drinks and handled it well.

That evening, he showed me how to snort cocaine. I had a couple of lines and felt better than I ever had in my life. I wanted to do everything all at once. I asked someone for a cigarette, and I smoked it even though I didn't smoke.

Victor laughed at how high I was.

Later on we were at his place, on the roof of the building where he had his studio apartment, and we looked at the stars, made out a little, and talked. I felt close to him, closer than I'd ever felt to any man. It could've been the cocaine; it could've been the novelty of our age difference and his excellent performance of being a listener.

After a lunch of spinach and mushroom quiches the next day, we had sex and he didn't make me come, but I liked getting fucked by him, and I knew right away that I wanted for that to happen again. He was attentive, kissing me all over my body, and he talked dirty and pulled my hair while he went at me from behind, which turned me on.

I really hoped to see him again, and I did. He kept asking me to stay over. He always made elaborate food — cheese sauce from butter, sharp cheddar, and flour over asparagus, with egg-white omelets — and he bought me my own coffee mug that read, "Good morning, morning!"

At first, I made a show of going back to my dusty apartment with my stranger roommates, but eventually I stopped. My visit with Victor stretched into two years. I became convinced we were living together. But when I told him I was going to leave, he said nothing about wanting me to stay. I suppose he broke my heart, but I was too distracted by my mother's woes, and then I met Sebastian.

༶

Would you like to pray with me? my mother said now.

I have to finish this newsletter, I said, pointing to the screen. Thankfully there were no news alerts about psychotic outbreaks tonight. My screen changed to a close-up of a walrus nose.

You should never bring your work home. I'm going to pray for you if you don't want to pray for yourself.

My phone buzzed with another text. I glanced at it. *Do you shave your pussy?*

I shaved that night for the first time in my life. Victor, who was twenty years older than me, liked that I had hair because he grew up when that was what women looked like — fluffy, furry — once their panties came off.

5

ON OUR FIRST date Sebastian and I went to a popular Italian joint. It wasn't really Italian, wasn't run by Italians. So many things in Toronto were pretend.

Our restaurant was not in Little Italy, either; it was in the hip part of town where you could buy a plain black T-shirt for two hundred dollars or a pendant that was a piece of concrete.

But we were there because Sebastian said he loved Italian food, and he loved the place and he didn't care if it was authentic or not. I didn't, either, actually. And I didn't care for food. I ate prepared meals I'd get on my way home from work, although sometimes I'd cook for my mother, who ate like a child: plain pasta with red sauce from a jar, chicken soup from a can, bread.

At the restaurant, I ordered a small pizza and Sebastian ordered a ravioli dish with beige meat. He moved a piece of ravioli and a chunk of beige meat onto my plate, even though I hadn't asked him to.

He said, Eat it. You'll like it.

What if I'm vegetarian?

Are you? He narrowed his eyes. I wondered what he looked like in the morning. I imagined his thick dark hair was bushier, less geometric, without product. He probably drank his coffee black, no sugar.

I inserted the piece of ravioli and the beige meat into my mouth. I was, I said. Guess I'm not anymore.

I really was vegetarian for almost ten years, until that moment.

He moved another piece of ravioli and one more beige morsel onto my plate. You're a little nuts, aren't you? I gotta tell my buddies.

Tell them what?

That I met a real nutbar.

I blushed. I liked that he was going to tell his buddies about me. And with the ravioli, I liked the assertiveness, the care, too, that this gesture represented to me. I was reading too much into everything already. The ravioli was boring, tasted like something out of my mother's cans. But the meat was slick, fatty, and salty. It melted on my tongue. I remembered meat as being chewy. The thought of fibres and veins turned me off eating it.

What is this meat? I love it.

It's duck liver. The ducks are force-fed and kept in small cages their entire lives.

I pretended to choke. I did it discreetly, just for show. Well, this date is over, I said, when I stopped fake-coughing, and he said flatly, Okay.

But the date wasn't over; it was going well. We were talking about everything. Even babies. There was a baby behind us. I kept getting distracted by the baby being lifted up by various grown-ups who were gathered at the table exclaiming over the baby. A baby party.

Cute baby, he said, when I told him to turn around and look.

Cute baby, I said.

Do you like kids?

I don't like kids, I said.

It was more that I had nothing to do with them. There were no kids in my life. Also, men were alarmed if you admitted to liking kids. It was better to not like them.

All women like kids.

It was offensive, or I should've gotten offended. Mostly because of the sort of education I received — to not get terribly offended by such a statement meant that all the important lessons of feminism were lost on me. It was probably bad to even think the way I was thinking, how refreshing it was to hear someone be so sexist. Out of duty I called him a jerk, and he said, I know. Chicks call me that all the time. (Chicks. All the time.) He was not like the sweater men from university, but he wasn't like Victor, either. He was the kind of guy the sweater guys made fun of, a bro, a douchebag who wore a leather jacket and who put product in his hair. But he seemed too smart to be a bro; yet, after his chicks comment, I imagined he went to night clubs where he shopped for women like they were different flavours of ice cream. I pictured him dancing aggressively around a cluster of sparkly dresses and wobbly heels, a mating kind of a dance. I pictured one sparkly, wobbly chick breaking out of her safe circle, going with him, getting groped in a dark corner of a throbbing club, then getting in an Uber, his hand holding her by the scruff of her neck. I felt aroused.

I like children. I want to have a kid one day, Sebastian said, and held my stare.

And there it was, another fantasy — this one of myself with a big belly, his hand on my waist, pulling me close to him, protectively. We were posing for a cheesy photo in a sad studio at the very end of the mall. It was a spontaneous thing to do, a joke. It was cute because later we kept those photographs on the mantel of our house. We told our children the story and how we surprised the sleeping photographer by our visit, how he nervously dusted off a big light box. For some reason I wore a green corduroy dress like it was the seventies, in my fantasy.

Hello?

I'm sorry. It's the meat. It's making me feel funny.

Funny how? Are you gonna puke?

Puke? I remembered then that he was younger than me. No, I'm not going to puke.

I once went on a date with a girl, and she got really trashed and puked all over my car.

I said, Do you date a lot?

What is your boyfriend's name again?

With a question like that, you would think that he was jealous, but he didn't sound jealous when he said it. That was disappointing.

I said, My boyfriend's name is Victor. We have an arrangement.

Does he know about me? That you're on a date with another man?

No. And we won't talk about it, either. It's a casual relationship. We used to live together but now we don't. I call him my

POSSESSED / 35

maybe-boyfriend sometimes because there's no word for what he is. He's a friend, and we have sex. But we're not exclusive.

I like that. That's a good arrangement. I date a bit. Women like me. I like women, Sebastian said.

I was hoping he was going to ask me more about Victor. I really wanted him to be anxious about the boyfriend thing — women who are wanted the most by men are the women who already have men. I wanted Sebastian to want me like that. But Sebastian didn't ask any questions about Victor.

We were quiet and after awhile, I said, Have you ever been in love?

He was looking away before I asked the question, but now he looked straight at me. No, I don't think so.

I smiled. Okay.

He said, I was reading about evolution. The last two hundred years really sped things up for humankind. Not everyone can catch up. Do you know about the history of smiling?

I smiled wider.

It's not normal. But now nonstop smiling has become the norm. You would have been considered insane and dangerous in the past.

My face refused to listen.

Same with love, he said.

I stopped smiling.

ဢ

Later, to get back to the parking lot, we were crossing the street, me ahead of him. A car came from out of nowhere around the corner, and I dashed to escape getting hit. I looked behind me. Sebastian was standing on the sidewalk on the other side.

He crossed over. I should've pulled you out of the way. I saw her coming. I'm sorry I didn't, he said. You almost died.

It's fine. I tried to laugh as lightheartedly as I could, and he shrugged. We walked to his car. He opened the car door for me. The car was his mother's, he had told me earlier.

We ended up parking at an abandoned factory. We made out; he kissed one of my breasts, but all I kept thinking about was how it was his mother's car.

I told him to stop and he looked up scolded, like a child. My nipple was still in his mouth. I pulled away, gently. The nipple slid out of his mouth.

Will you suck my dick? he said after a short silence.

Sure, I said.

It's okay, he said.

I had no idea if that was some kind of a test or what. I really did want to suck his dick now. I felt aroused thinking about it. But I said and did nothing. He turned the car stereo on.

He listened to the same kind of music that Victor listened to — hard but melodic stuff, everything electronic. I recognized the song from hearing it at Victor's house — it was the music of his youth. Victor said that back then it had been revolutionary.

I don't know what it was to Sebastian since he was born almost a decade after the first album came out.

In any case, we listened to Underworld for a while.

6

AFTER THE SECOND date, I was brimming with the essence of Sebastian. It was torture to come home and not be able to tell anyone. I felt pent up, like a balloon filled with gas. After closing the door, I slowly slid down the wall, not dramatically, but enough to land with a soft thud on the carpeted hallway floor. I thought of that phrase, "Collect yourself." I had to collect myself.

I let out something like half a sob. Not like I meant it, not a real cry. I was so emotionally activated by meeting Sebastian, I was not myself. I was like a drunk person overrun with chemicals and dangerously optimistic. I wished I could just Disney-burst into my mother's room, tell her about the stupid date. I have no idea why I fixated on being friends with my mother all of a sudden, after all those years of failing to do so. My mother and I were never friends. She never knew the truth about Victor; he was just some guy I had met at a grad party and introduced to her once at a mall where we ran into him and one of his student assistants. They were shopping for darkroom supplies. My mother never even knew I'd lived with him.

But I wanted to tell her all about Sebastian, all the mundane parts, how Sebastian drove me around on our second date and how we talked and listened to his favourite music. We talked about the city we lived in, clubs that used to exist and had closed down. He asked me about some places that even I was too young to have gone to, like the place where you could inhale laughing gas and dance in real foam. Those were places before my time. I asked him how old he thought I was, and he laughed and told me he forgot I wasn't really that old. He assured me I didn't look my age. I told him to shut up. He said, Relax. I decided not to get offended; it was easier that way. Why have a fight when things were going so well? He told me about the clubs he went to. They were not the shouty bro clubs I pegged him for frequenting. They were places in basements with walls painted black and filament light bulbs. He said the people were mostly male, nerds who loved techno music and who were serious about it, who followed their favourite DJs and collected vinyl and limited releases. I told him I would go with him. He said I should, but when I asked him when the next show was he said they weren't called shows. He said they were called sets. I liked him explaining things to me. He turned up the volume. I loved the deep guttural beats; they ran through me, made me move my hips even though they were constrained by the seatbelt.

We made out in a parking lot again, and this time I let his hand feel me inside my panties. I normally wouldn't have agreed to that because it did nothing for me, and it was kind of dumb, but I wanted Sebastian to think I was just like girls his age or even wilder.

∾

Right now, I took off my shoes before getting up off the floor and going further into the house. The house was quiet, which was neither a good sign nor a bad one.

I tiptoed toward my mother's bedroom and opened the door without making a sound. She was sitting on the edge of the bed, her face raised toward the window, the moon making her hair almost neon white. I was alarmed by the curtains being gone but not alarmed enough to interrupt whatever she was doing.

Before I closed the door, she turned around, slowly, mechanically, just like in any good horror movie, and said a horror movie line: *He* doesn't like it when you're out that late.

I thought then of when I was a teenager and insisted on people taking pictures of us at rare church events I'd be invited to. I convinced her once to sit in my lap. In the picture she presses her head to mine, and her face is round and smiling. We look exactly like a mother and daughter who are friends.

Had we been a duo like that, I suppose I would've felt a lot more sadness than I did seeing her as she was now.

She was looking past me, looking at the ghosts only she could see. I made my apologies, asked her if she needed anything — silence — and made way to my little room.

I loved pretty spaces and it was not pretty where I was. I hadn't bothered making the place feel homey because I couldn't commit to the idea that I might be staying here long. One of my suitcases remained unpacked, giving me hope this was all temporary. But my mother's decline was slow, and she was in decent physical shape. It was possible that it would be years before I was free of her.

I couldn't fall asleep for quite some time as I replayed my evening with Sebastian.

He bit my lower lip right before we parted. The spot was slightly swollen when I touched it with my tongue. I liked that he had marked me. I pulled out my phone. I took a picture of myself with a flash. I looked startled in it, my eyes cartoonishly round and my skin shiny with a greenish tint. There was a harshness to the way my mouth was set in a tight smile. It was fine. I typed over the picture, "I am happy." I wanted to mark the moment when I felt the emotion that occurred so rarely. I remembered reading something about a cactus that would blossom only once a year, at night. I wasn't sure if I was blossoming, but I certainly felt opened, vulnerable, and even pretty, despite how I appeared in the picture.

7

THE FIRST TIME Sebastian and I had sex, I was menstruating. He didn't mind, he said in that slightly lazy, stretched out tone I was learning to like so much. He didn't ask me if I minded — I didn't. He said he and his ex used to fuck on a towel when she was bleeding — Should I get a towel?

Do you mind if not? I said. It was his bed. He shrugged.

His space was small; it was a basement apartment, dim but clean with brand-new appliances, a huge microwave, and a dishwasher. A front door with a window that let in a bit of light. There was a kitchen island where he ate his meals. A small, windowless living room with a flat television and a Playstation. One of those fitness utility benches and a set of weights collecting dust on the beige carpet. No art hanging anywhere except for a large mirror in a gaudy frame. His bedroom was a mattress and a dresser, black curtains hanging over a small window punched in the wall. A desk, a laptop. My lover was a minimalist.

I watched him undress. I liked how his dick sprung out from his boxers and how he had a condom ready and how he said, with a guilty-puppy look, Have you ever been with an uncut man?

I guess it was uncommon enough that he felt the need to ask that question and ask it in that way, as if this was some kind of an issue.

Of course, I said. I didn't mind. We were so mindful with each other.

I wanted to ask him about this ex. Was he not in love with her?

Instead of asking him, I said, I'm kind of sensitive today so go easy, and he said okay. He told me to lie on his bed. I liked being ordered. He told me to open my legs, and he kissed my legs, and he growled and bit me not so gently on the inside of my thigh.

He said, Relax, and then shoved too deeply inside me as if he intended to hurt me.

I tried to get away from him, from the fierceness with which he was banging at me. I tried to move my body so that he would get it — what I was trying to do — but he didn't get it. He possibly misread my manoeuvring for passion because he only thrust harder, as if this was a game we were playing — me pretending to get away. He growled again and said, Do you like that? like it was a porno. Our eyes met, and he almost looked scared, and that's when I realized it mattered to him that I liked that he was performing, and I felt too polite and worried for him to voice my protest. I had never been in so much discomfort from sex. It felt like stabbing, over and over, every nerve split and pounded. And yet, I loved his weight on me, I loved how passionate he seemed, how he took me, and how he wasn't slowing down. He pulled my hair hard; he bit my face, my neck. Those were not the gentle nibbles he had given me before, in parking lots. This was like being screwed and tasted by a giant cat. Our eyes would meet occasionally, and every time it was the same inquisitive look. So I tried to appear blissful, content, and I gave into the pain. I knew that it would have to end at some point; no fuck lasts forever, good or bad. I simulated an orgasm: I thrashed and moaned. And then, suddenly, I was responding as if I managed to even fool my very own body into deciding that this was fun. I felt myself clench around him, my muscles spasming as he drove into me over and over.

I had a headache. I was sore everywhere. But I was also slick and open with arousal.

He came, roaring like an animal. My body smelled foreign; it was wet, covered in his sweat. He was breathing hard. He pulled out, and there was blood on the condom. He collapsed, half on top of me.

I moved from underneath him, rolled him over onto his side. My knees were shaking. I couldn't stop my knees from shaking.

My knees are shaking, I said, pointing to them. That's never happened to me before.

He said, Did you come?

I smiled. I didn't want to lie to him. I was lying to Victor often, and I didn't want to lie to Sebastian because I was falling in love with him. I wanted to be pure about it, and I wanted to remain in love with him, and I wanted him to feel the same about me. There should be no lies between us. Lying destroyed relationships. When I realized Victor wasn't going to fully commit, I started lying to him — about little things like my whereabouts, art I didn't care for, liking food he'd make for me, my orgasms — and he became less attractive to me. He was getting fooled — a smart man wouldn't allow himself to get fooled. It was emasculating. It was revengeful. I felt pity for Victor as I lied to him, but I also felt as if I got some of my power back. It was dumb. It was necessary.

But I didn't want to feel pity for Sebastian; I didn't want to ruin this — us.

Did you? he said, again.

I can't come when I'm on my period, I said. Or the first time I'm with someone.

So you're saying you deserve a second time? Good girl.

I liked when he called me that. I liked that there would be a second time.

In the bathroom, on my shaky legs, I looked into Sebastian's medicine cabinet to find the brand of the cologne he was wearing. It was Narciso Rodriguez for Him. A scent like a soft thrust and a hard slap. I inhaled it, and my pussy fluttered.

◊

The next evening, I went to Victor's house.

I was bruised up and down; the insides of my thighs were splotches of greyish purple. My neck was covered in bites. There was a knot in my hair the shape and size of a cicada that I had to cut out that morning.

I asked Victor not to turn on the lights. I said I was feeling sad.

He said, Whatever you like, Josie.

He pulled my silk dress over my head. I was naked underneath it. You couldn't see the bruises in the half-darkness. I lay on the bed. I looked down on my too-pale body. A bruise on my thigh in the shape of a mangled star.

∽

Victor nuzzled my neck; he kissed the painful places without knowing that they were painful, but his kisses were extra gentle so maybe he did know. He didn't say anything, didn't ask me anything. He licked my breasts and my stomach.

How are you feeling? he said.

I'm okay, I said.

I was still bleeding, but I was less tender. I wanted to come badly. I needed to be unfucked from the night before.

I pulled Victor on top of me, and he entered me slowly. He understood my anatomy as well as I did his; there were no surprises, good or bad. Over the years, our bodies had been programmed to respond to each other in ways to maximize pleasure, and it was as if we were each other's sex robots. For example, he knew exactly how to move his pelvis against mine so that it would pull up the skin of my vulva to expose my clitoris a little — enough for the friction to create a rewarding physical response. He rotated his hips like a dancer, paying attention to my angles, fucking into me, hitting the sensitive ridge inside my vagina that's never caused me to ejaculate but that added just enough sensation to combine into the prefect climax. I wrapped my legs around his waist. I thought of Sebastian and his violence. I was turned on by it now, in my mind. I was having a phantom threesome.

With sex, sometimes it was wings, a flight, and sometimes I was a body of water. Right now it was water, a pebble thrown into the depth of it. I felt the first ripple spreading into my thighs and then reversing, contracting back into itself. I knew how to pace myself, how to accept pleasure in just the right increments to prolong what was about to happen. On occasion my orgasms were only a physiological release; they even seemed medicinal, like a fix I needed. There was nothing spiritual about them. I did not understand or ever experience the concept of lovemaking. But when I wanted to, I could still derive pleasure that went beyond a mechanical reaction; I taught myself as a child to control it, years of practice with various ends of objects, my strong little vagina tuning into subtleties of surfaces and circumferences. On my own, I could come in various ways — loudly or quietly — and with my legs shaking, as if in a seizure, or absolutely still, as if I got shot. Often I experienced orgasmic synesthesia, the condition that causes people to see colours and sometimes to hallucinate images when they climax. I came in blue and red and golden, and once I was somewhere in a deep green forest surrounded by big, ancient trees, and a galaxy exploded in my head as I felt the spasms coming on between my legs. Back in art school, I tried to draw what I saw, but I wasn't able to; how do you draw a sensation of skin pressing against cool moss?

I was never ashamed of my body's responses when nobody was watching. But with lovers, it was complicated because I wasn't alone; I was an observed object, disturbed by the act of observation. Like so many naked women, I would suddenly worry about my appearance — my folds and geometry and smells and sounds — and achieving pleasure would become secondary or unachievable. Yet, occasionally, I could let go; occasionally I could indulge — especially when I no longer cared for my lover and no longer had to perform.

And now that Victor was no longer important, I indulged: I rode the waves of my orgasm greedily, steadily,
till it was finally time to give in to it and let it overcome
me completely. I moaned and shook and grunted like I was
alone. I urged him on, I hissed for him to go harder and
slower, and he did.

That was beautiful, Victor said, once we fell apart.

I was always amused when men said that, how beautiful an
orgasm was, as if I were an instrument they had played and felt
proud of playing so well.

I love you, I said to Victor, because I was touched that he
said that and because I loved him and because I felt guilty. And
because I wanted to say "I love you" to Sebastian and I couldn't.

Josie, he said.

I closed my eyes. I didn't want any pillow talk.

Victor got up and turned on the sound system, ignoring my
pretending to sleep. It felt as if I were letting poison seep into
my ears. Maybe it was good for me. Exposure therapy.

As the music played on, Victor got back into bed. He began
rubbing against me and kissing my body. I imagined it was
Sebastian kissing my body. I asked Victor to kiss me harder. It
didn't work. He wasn't Sebastian.

Can you turn off the music?

It never bothered you before, Victor said. His fingers parted
me.

I feel like I'm in a music video.

In a porn movie.

In a porn movie with a really good soundtrack, I said. I wig-
gled till his fingers got the hint. He got up and turned off the
music. But it was too late; I couldn't get the image of Sebastian
asking me if I would suck his dick as the same song played in

his car, in that abandoned parking lot. The image distracted me instead of turning me on.

Before leaving, Victor drew me into his arms. Together we counted to twenty. He read in a magazine that it took twenty seconds for the endorphins to kick in when you hugged, which made hugs natural mood enhancers. This was our thing, like a little wink from the past when we were a regular couple and had our own inside world.

8

MY JOB GOT busier. We were now expanding to become a proper travel agency, organizing unusual tours, which were simply called Unusual Tours. They were for people who sought adventure but couldn't be bothered organizing that for themselves, so we looked for adventures and designed packages around the unique features. We looked at deserted amusement parks, ghost cities, strangely tinted grassy hills, deep water holes, twisted old trees, weird lighting effects due to algae bacteria, and so on. Closer to home, we made partnerships and linked to websites designed by and for people who liked to infiltrate abandoned factories and haunted mansions — we wanted to build a reputation among more risk-taking travellers unhappy with the usual offerings of other agencies.

Initially, we focused on three places that we could design packages for: a stuck-in-time town in the Canadian Rockies located near a polygamist compound; a forest in Poland of about four hundred pine trees that grew with a ninety-degree bend at the base of their trunks; and the world's largest tree house, located in Crossville, Tennessee, whose owner, Horace Burgess, was fond of saying that God personally gave him the contract to build the structure.

We created itineraries and contacted locals who were willing to host the tourists and show them around, provide meals, or suggest places where region-specific meals could be consumed. The tree house was a flop — Horace Burgess lost heart after a couple complained on the internet about not being able to find McDonald's in the area — but the pine trees were a moderate success. The place in the Canadian Rockies, called Cresstown, was our biggest seller, with its downtown that hadn't changed since the eighties, its orchards and galleries with horrid Jesus art made by the Amish, and a community theatre that put on earnest plays about characters from the Bible. Sadly, we couldn't find a way to bring our clients into the polygamist community. Still, people were happy and wrote nice reviews. Everyone raved about the ukuleles sold in all the book and coffee shops, so we made a deal with the ukulele maker and added a 20-percent-off coupon to the tour deal.

I was given access to my company's Twitter account to start the buzz about Unusual Tours and to keep the buzz alive. My schedule was full, but I didn't mind at all having another task. I kept my cell in my purse and only checked it after getting in and at lunch and then at the end of the workday. It required an enormous amount of discipline. If I needed to make a call, I used the work phone, and except for talking to my mother, I didn't make personal calls anyway.

My mother would try my extension first thing in the morning, as if she could tell when it was exactly that I would sit down and get to work. I would answer, and she would say things like, I never really loved your father, did you know that?

I knew that.

Don't be smart. Why does it say "Good morning, morning!" on that mug?

It was a gift. My friend thought it was funny.

How is it funny?

I don't know.

She sighed. Oh, it's a cup that stutters. That is funny. You need to come to church with me.

Maybe one day. I'm at work now. Maybe watch some TV.

I'm not bored. I'm not alone. There's a young man here. Good morning, morning, she chuckled.

I didn't ask about the young man. I knew she was talking about the ghost. I, too, could sense something, but I kept telling myself it was just being around her; it was only in her presence that I'd question my reality. She had started to mention the ghost more often lately. Her voice sounded even when she talked about him. I figured he at least kept her company and that was preferable to the imaginary bear.

I should go, Mom.

Everyone is so busy. Church attendance is dismal, but the young priest doesn't care. I wanted to tell him about our guest, but I don't trust him. Would you trust someone who doesn't even care?

I've never met the new priest.

He's a fruit. Your father was a fruit, too. I never loved him. And we were back to that. Our conversations would dwindle eventually, her not having anything else to say and me not encouraging her to go on.

Sometimes she would call and not say anything.

Should I let you go?

Silence.

Mom, are you there?

A farting noise and a high-pitched laugh and then: Gotcha!

Very funny.

We almost developed a routine out of it all. On the rare mornings when she wouldn't call, I would feel restless and nervous, but I never tried her first because I didn't want her to expect it. And it's not that I wanted to talk to her — it's that I felt indignant she would have the nerve not to check in. Wasn't I the only person in this world who cared for her? I had to remind myself that this was all temporary, that I was not going to take care of her forever. I couldn't develop habits that would hurt us in the future. I didn't want to develop them.

∽

When we got a tip about an island in Croatia that was rated number two on the "10 Most Haunted Places" on a popular travel website, everyone at work got excited and gathered around Kelly's desk to watch her flip through the pictures she'd organized into a folder. It was our first haunted location.

After Kelly's presentation, my boss lingered on, and instead of returning to his desk moved a few steps to the left and stared, smiling at me. Would you be interested in taking on more work? he said.

My boss's name was Samuel but everyone called him Sammy. He was white haired and had the sort of powdery skin that I imagined felt velvety to the touch. I wondered if I reminded him of his daughter. I was younger than Kelly, or at least dressed younger, mixing blouses with sporty skirts or wearing sporty jackets with secretary skirts.

It was impossible not to smile back at Sammy.

I would love to take on more work, I told him. I had a thought that I needed some distraction — my life at home was stressful, my love life was making me anxious.

Kelly rose slowly, dramatically, to demonstrate her displeasure, but my boss's back was to her, and he missed the performance. I shrugged at her and looked away. She sat down again, slamming down her body so hard that our cubicles shook. Sammy still didn't turn around.

He said he wanted to send someone to the island to write about it. Currently, the island was not a tourist destination — it was even hard to visit it if you were local on the mainland. He said, See what can be done! Are you hungry for adventure? He laughed. I guessed he was pleased with his cheesy line.

Of course, I said. I liked that he thought of me as hungry for adventure. I wondered if he had grandkids.

Sorry, sorry, he said.

No, no, it was funny, I said.

Oh, and check your email. Kelly is having a baby shower for Wendy.

I couldn't remember which one was Wendy — there were two pregnant women in our office, and they were both blond and happy. It made no difference which blond was Wendy as the outcome would be exactly the same: everyone crammed into a windowless room, holding onto a flimsy paper plate with a piece of cake with too much icing on it, which threatened to give out under the weight of it and land on shoes.

～

I immersed myself in research.

The tiny island, Tajni Otok, had had a bad time in general. It had briefly been a leper colony before becoming a mass grave for Black Death plague victims. The mere ten square kilometres of land was located just off the Dalmatian Coast in a lagoon of the Adriatic Sea, near the small historic town of Trogir, which one TripAdvisor reviewer called "The Poor Man's Venice." The town had been declared a World Heritage site. "The orthogonal street plan of this island settlement dates back to the Hellenistic period and it was embellished by successive rulers with many fine public and domestic buildings and fortifications. Its beautiful Romanesque churches are complemented by the outstanding Renaissance and Baroque buildings from the Venetian period," read the quote from the UNESCO report. This was good enough to copy and paste into my own report, so I copied and pasted. I doubted anyone read our pamphlets in depth. I removed the quotation marks.

Continuing the island's unfortunate luck, during the plague Tajni Otok — which loosely translated to "secret brook" — served as a quarantine station to hundreds of the sick, most of whom died. The island was not big enough to separate the sick from the dead, and disease ran rampant — arriving at Taini Otok was equivalent to a death sentence. There were accounts of fires being set to piles of corpses that would often engulf those who were still alive. I was reminded of that Hieronymus Bosch painting "Christ in Limbo," with its grotesque creatures, crumbling buildings, drowning body parts, the little humans getting ripped to pieces, raped, tortured, set on fire, swallowed by large mouths. I googled Tajni Otok and found blurry pictures of dug-up ditches with piles of dark grey bones. The pictures all seemed to come from Reddit, and I had no way of checking their credibility; I had no way of telling if the pictures were Photoshopped or not.

I wondered about the kind of person who would take pleasure in such a hoax. I pictured a guy in a hoodie surrounded by cats, someone whose internet handle had numbers standing in for letters. Briefly, I thought of Sebastian being that kind of a guy in his younger years, practising his graphic-design skills. But no, Sebastian had never been a loser. He told me he used to get into fights in high school. His father signed him up for martial arts because he was small as a child. He had never had a problem with bullies. He played sports and suffered concussions and broken bones. He once knocked out a much larger kid who called his younger sister a racist name and sent him to a hospital. He periodically joined the gym to bulk up, and he liked to talk about fucking people up. I had never been around men who got into fights; the sweater guys thought fighting was primitive and for jocks, and Victor considered the gym strictly a place you went to get rid of stomach rolls; boxing was "for thugs."

The internet said that in Tajni Otok, unlike the other islands, many of the burial locations were left unmarked. Online rumours claimed there were just too many bodies, and some information stated the entire island was made up of bones. There were stories of bone fragments still floating in the water around the island and of locals refusing to fish there for that reason. There was supposed to be a secret vineyard with intensely rich soil — fertilized with remains — that produced blood-red wine sold illegally in Trogir. There were many other rumours, some quite outrageous, such as of the smell of burning flesh still lingering in the air and quicksand-like holes filled with human ash. Rumours aside, the fact was that, at one point, there were many corpses on the island. Some of the internet sources claimed that the number reached two thousand. It was probably fewer than that. Still.

I read on. In the 1920s, Tajni Otok was also home to a mental hospital. It was supposedly run by a sadistic doctor who performed all kinds of experimental treatments on his patients — frontal lobotomies done with no anesthetic or sterilization, prolonged cold baths, and solitary confinement. The doctor was said to be married to one of his patients, who disappeared under mysterious circumstances. He was never charged with her murder, but he was dismissed shortly after her death. No one has ever heard from him since.

The island was currently uninhabited, and it was, unsurprisingly, popular with all kinds of ghost chasers and thrill seekers with night-vision cameras. According to online forums, there was no official ferry to the island; you had to pay two hundred euros to bribe a water taxi guide from Trogir to take you there.

I read all the information and felt no particular emotion about it. But the details seemed somehow familiar, as if they were part of a history lesson I learned in elementary school or some other time long ago.

I didn't think it would faze me to stay overnight on the island; in my current state, nothing would faze me — not unmarked graves, the stench of burnt flesh, lost souls. Not an evil spirit of the sadistic doctor. Moans, footsteps, fog appearing and disappearing ... and all the other ridiculous things I was reading about — I doubted they would have any effect on me.

No, nothing would move me. Only my cellphone lighting up with Sebastian's name, that was the only thing that could move me.

As I finished reading the last article about the island, I felt a kind of heaviness, an exhaustion, but not a physical one. The letters blurred momentarily and then came together, forming sentences again. I was tired, but I was used to reading a lot — I had never had a problem with going through pages and pages of text.

I looked up. My eyes were dry, burning.

There was a handsome young man standing by my desk. I'd never seen him before; I had never seen him in the building. We stared at each other as if in recognition.

A loud stomping behind me distracted me momentarily. When I looked back to where the man stood, I already knew that he was no longer there.

Hello? I said to the empty space.

The empty space said nothing.

I'm tired, I said, and Kelly said, You should go home, it's after seven. She sat down with an aggressive mountain of lettuce in a Tupperware.

I should. I'm sorry.

Sorry about what? The cubicle shook, and the angry chomping began. I didn't ask her why she was staying on. I didn't know too much about Kelly's life, like if she had anybody to go home to. She loved Halloween, and she was into costumes and dressing up — outside of Halloween, too — and I knew she went to conventions where she got to meet her favourite characters. It was more than I was doing with my free time lately. I guessed Kelly didn't have a sick parent at home, or if she did, she didn't care.

～

Walking home, I couldn't stop thinking about the island. I had to admit that for all my bravado, I did wonder if Tajni Otok would perhaps scare me after all, if my visit would break me out of my spell.

I thought, too, about the apparition that showed up at my desk. He was connected to my research, I was sure, but I didn't know how. I thought he looked friendly, although I didn't get a good sense of him. But his presence didn't create dread, nor did it surprise me.

9

My mother could sit in the bathtub until the water grew cold. I used to worry about her falling asleep and drowning, but bathing for hours was something she had done all her life, so I figured her instincts would kick in despite her ongoing mental deterioration. I also didn't want to admit to myself that occasionally I fantasized about finding her in the bathtub stiff and dead. I would have to call 911, call her sister who lived alone in New Brunswick, and the church, and I don't know who else. Like me, my mother didn't really make friends.

I could have stopped her from doing it while I wasn't there to supervise — I could have filled the bathtub with bricks or put a lock on the door. If anyone had asked me why I didn't do that, I would have had a hard time answering. I don't know if it was intentional neglect. It was my job to protect her from herself, after all. But you wouldn't ask those questions if you, too, went through life parented by a woman who constantly threatens her own life. Naturally, being in a state of panic is not sustainable. I found out about that kind of anxiety earlier than most, the time she lay next to my bedroom door with a razor. It was probably not a coincidence that during my panic spells I not only felt trapped but there was also the sensation of a heavy door pressing against my face. It happens rarely these days, and I've learned to deal with it — I have a few techniques, such as taking deep breaths, relaxing my toes, my ankles, my knees, my pelvis, et cetera, till I get to my head. Occasionally, the feeling of a heavy door will still be there to separate me from the world, but doors can be both closed and opened and most of the time I can open mine. As for the actual door, the bathroom door, I kept not putting a lock on it, and each morning, or whenever I left the house, I would have two simultaneous thoughts: *Just do it already* and *Please don't die.*

As usual, once I got home from work and saw my mother undead in the bathtub, I was both unnerved and relieved. I took my coat off. I checked my phone, again, to see if Sebastian had texted me — he hadn't — and I sat down on the toilet seat without saying anything. I waited for her to acknowledge me. I considered telling her about the haunted island. She told me ghost stories when I was a child and often forced me to watch scary movies with her. It was from one of those movies in fact, where I learned that I needed to take control over my own life while still in high school. I was a delicate, transparent nobody girl, but the movie taught me that being a wallflower could be dangerous. I had been lucky, but my luck could end at any time — it would only take one bully to destroy my life. In the movie, a pretty redheaded girl lives with her mother who, just like mine, is a religious fanatic. The girl, Carrie, who has special powers, ends up killing everyone including herself and her mother, and their house burns down.

I was never bullied the way Carrie was, but the movie informed some of my behaviours at school. I blended in a lot better. Maybe it helped that I wasn't a redhead, and my mother didn't have sexual hang-ups, although when I was eleven she threw one of those religious and covertly anti-sex books at me that really didn't explain anything. I was shy around boys, but I wasn't awkward. No one liked me but no one hated me, either. In the book my mother gave me there was a whole chapter about the dangers of masturbation. It taught me a few things about household objects, specifically the showerhead.

Right now, my mother still wasn't saying anything. I touched the water, and it was cool. I looked at her body. It was a fascinating thing, her body, its paleness and length. Underwater, it reminded me of some aquatic entity but not one that was pretty or beautiful; rather, it was an animal that was just taking up space. The kind of animal no one makes documentaries about because it's ugly and boring. Something other animals ate or something that ate the refuse of other animals.

When she was younger, my mother tanned easily, and her body was in good shape, but she was also modest, so I never saw her in the nude until she became my charge. The first time I saw her naked, she said, These are the tits that fed you, can you imagine?

They looked nothing like breasts — not that I was naive about those things, but it was different seeing a nude, old woman in a photograph versus in real life. I didn't think she was repulsive; I was mostly trying to make peace with the idea that I, too, would have a body like hers one day. She was exactly what you think a thin, old white woman would look like:

too many moles, folds and loose skin where there used to be smooth hills of taut flesh, and coarse white hair. Her breasts were completely flat, two condoms with grotesquely long nipples. They hung tight against her ribcage, the nipples pointing downward. She had a small belly that somehow made her ancient body look childlike, or it made me think of children when I looked at her in her naked fragility.

It was the staying inside and the prolonged baths that turned her into a creature, a wobbly curtain of flesh attached to an occasional bone. It was as if she was slowly dissolving.

I moved my hand to make little waves and get her attention. She shivered. She opened her eyes slowly and looked past me the way she always did. I used to think she did that on purpose, to make me understand how insignificant I was, but I learned over time that it wasn't personal. She was watching; things were being communicated to her; it was none of my business.

She shivered again, and the skin around her nipples puckered, shrunk them. I pictured myself bending down, taking one of the nipples in my mouth. How would she taste? I could almost feel the fleshy bud against my tongue. It wouldn't be like the soft vanilla-scented nipples of girls I pretended to be lesbian with during my undergrad — it would feel rough and soft at the same time and wet with those bristles of black hair tickling the roof of my mouth. I wondered if my body would recognize hers, if I would latch on naturally but unwittingly, and if any kind of a substance would come out of her. I thought of the very sweet condensed milk that you could buy in tubes when I was a child. Maybe it was the childhood flashback that made me suddenly want to pull her toward me then, take her into my arms, kiss her on her wet head, make her feel safe. But I knew from experience that any such action would irritate and surprise her. She was not beyond hitting or scratching. Her occasional displays of affection weren't comfortable or natural. Sometimes when I would towel her dry, she would pull me into a tight hug, and I could feel her bones against me, which made me think about the famous intertwined skeleton lovers unearthed in the archeological dig of Pompeii. Other times she would cover me with sucky kisses, all over my face, my ears, too. She would double her efforts if she sensed that I was stiffening, rejecting her. Her kisses would become harder, suckier. One of the things she loved doing when she caught me on the phone as a teenager was doling out those kinds of affections, the sounds of her smacking lips intended to embarrass me to the person on the other end. Not that anyone called me much back then.

After years of awkward physical contact, we had the most intimate interaction we've ever had with me attending to her baths and occasionally toilet. I was lucky that she didn't require diapers; I was told there was some time left. I didn't want to think about it, time passing.

I took a towel and dried her. She was whispering softly to herself. When I first started to help her with her bedtime routine, I tried to catch what she was saying, but it was always disappointing, just numbers or names or some old argument, often with my father. This time, I made out one sentence clearly. *Only children and animals bite.* Her whisper voice was tiny, but the tone was indignant, and she was on the verge of tears. I wondered if she was reliving something. I wondered if this was about me — I used to be the neighbourhood biter, alienating other toddlers and their moms as soon as I entered any playground.

I'm sorry, I said, because that's what I used to say back then, and she sounded in need of an apology.

Look, she said, and turned her arm so that I could see.

There was a mark on the inside of her upper arm, a bite mark. She could've done it herself. Although she was missing teeth, she wore partial dentures.

How did that happen?

Wouldn't you like to know? She clutched the towel to her chest, eyes flashing.

We were in one of her games. I shook my head no, that I wouldn't like to know. I examined the bite closer to see if the skin was broken. A thin red-blue aura was forming around the shape of the mangled O. It didn't look like teeth marks, more as if she had used something sharp and pointy to stab that circle into her skin. I remembered from a pamphlet about her condition and its progression that self-harm was to be expected. The caseworker who'd been assigned to us — and whom I didn't use often enough — told me that this was better than her turning her aggression outwardly. She told me about elderly men in her care who had to be restrained. She said I was lucky my mother was not a violent kind. "Yet?" I remember thinking.

My mother sucked in the air through her clenched teeth when I touched the bite gently.

It's okay, I said, unconvincingly. I felt exhausted and sad for both of us.

Ask me, she hissed.

I really don't want to, I said. Let's just get you to bed.

He did it. He did it because we were bored. We're bored waiting for you. I don't know what kind of job doesn't let their workers leave at a reasonable time. He said he would do it so you'd have something to worry about because you make us bored.

He bites you because you're bored?

From my psychology studies I knew that when people with psychosis tell you things that make no sense, you treat those just like any other statements. What you don't do is ask them the reason for the statements.

I walked my mother to the kitchen and sat her at the table. I boiled a pan of pasta, added some shredded cheese to it from a bag. I turned the TV on, and the room filled with the voices of the newscasters. Hardly anyone talked like that in real life. Nobody was that excitable except they were — I've met excitable people. I thought of those I've met over the whole span of my adulthood, and I isolated two or three who always seemed to be in a good mood, who volunteered to lead teams, to start fundraisers, food drives, and who sometimes auditioned for plays and always got the part they auditioned for. I thought of a girl named Kate because she was who came to mind when I thought of popular people.

I looked around my mother's pale green kitchen, the colour of chronic illness, the TV ancient, its top covered with a doily that probably hadn't ever been washed. What would a person like Kate think of this place? The idea of popularity was something that peaked in high school. University was easier as it was easier to hide: the spaces were bigger, we mixed in classes, and you could skip weeks without anybody noticing except for a nice lady from Student Relations. In high school, there was nowhere to hide between the metal jaws of lockers lining up the hallways — you were either a loser or you weren't.

I couldn't remember if Kate was actually her name — it could've been Karen or Stephanie — but Kate was real. She was the captain of the rugby team, an editor of the Arts and Culture section of the student paper, and an intern at a record company where she had a gig assisting a green-haired teenager who had four number-one hits about being depressed.

Kate was always nice to me because she was nice to everyone. In the beginning of the fall semester in Grade 10, we went out for a coffee — she was holding those coffees like casting calls, meeting all the losers before she would decide on one to add to her group. Her group formed naturally already, cool kids with interesting glasses and haircuts, gravitating toward each other, orbiting around her within the first two weeks of school. They were perfect, but they needed a loser, hence the coffees. I met with Kate, sure she wouldn't pick me because I disliked her deeply, and no amount of pretending would be able to mask that. I disliked her in Grade 9; I had already disliked her for a whole year. I couldn't understand why others were so attracted to her bounciness and loud voice. It was overwhelming to watch her in every play, leading all the assemblies, welcoming all the guests on our behalf. I didn't get it, but that's because I didn't get a lot of things. It was like some kind of a disorder — I just couldn't plug into the world. Same with the TV shows that everyone liked — it's not that I tried to be contrary, I just didn't understand what made people invest emotionally in imaginary characters. I didn't know which *Sex and the City* character I resembled the most; I had never seen the show, so I suspected none of them, and I didn't care.

Kate didn't remember me from Grade 9, and our coffee went worse than I expected. Suddenly, I found myself a part of the group and spent the next two years playing my character at social events, and it was draining. My character was moody and dressed in long skirts or black leggings. My peers assumed I listened to the kind of music Sebastian and Victor listened to, cold beats like ice against a grate, the military thumps of a fascist heart.

I suppose if Kate remembered my character and saw me now, she wouldn't be that horrified after all. She would probably just think I was one of those people who never managed to reinvent themselves. Or maybe she would think I was an artist? I doubted it. No one would think that if they were to find me in this kitchen with this woman. I was regressing.

My mother got up and opened and closed a few cupboards without taking anything out. She sat back down. Her pasta dish was barely touched. I watched her but didn't get up. What was Kate's mother like? Probably big like Kate, with real blond hair, her little pink sweater too girly for her figure, but no one would ever say anything. She opened cupboards with purpose; she did everything with purpose.

I rarely thought of people from my past and what they would think if I suddenly showed up, and how they would judge me, but I did now, for no reason. I didn't keep in touch with anyone. I didn't want anyone to know me. There was nothing really to know. Especially now that my life was so constricted.

I didn't have these kinds of thoughts when I was with Victor, and we went to all the parties. Was that my peak? A quick flash in the city's social scene, just some girl on an aging boyfriend's arm, the photographer whatshisname, she's just one of his girls. Some of his friends had to be introduced to me multiple times because they were so used to Victor changing women. It was comical. I was young enough that it wasn't even irritating to me yet.

It was unfair that I was sitting here with my mother while the world went on, Sebastian didn't text, Victor took more photographs of asses, and Kate gave birth to a third baby sired by her neurosurgeon husband or her famous charge's bodyguard.

I got up abruptly.

I didn't walk my mother to her bedroom like I did almost every night. She knew the way; this was her house.

The air in the hallway seemed thin, blurry in the dim light. My bedroom was even worse; it seemed filled with smoke that wasn't there — I waved my hand to clear it, but the smoke was only an illusion. I opened the window. It was raining outside. The comforting whisper of it made me want to crawl under the covers. I felt too tired to change into my pyjamas, so I turned the light off and went right to sleep.

I dreamed of my mother being eaten by a young man with dark hair. He was biting her — first, gingerly, starting with her upper arm, moving on to her breasts, her belly, and vagina, chomping harder, with more violence, as he moved down her thighs. It sounds worse than it looked; it was actually quite artistic. He had raised his right arm as if to point to something, his fingers waving as if he were playing a scale on an invisible piano.

10

SEBASTIAN WAS BUSY with a new work assignment and could not meet. I tried not to be pushy; I didn't want him to think that I was becoming obsessed. For now, I had to make do with phone calls or texts. He was mostly silent during the day but would usually get in touch around seven o'clock. My effervescent horniness and my overall well-being would peak around then. I had programmed my phone so that when he called, the ringer was a crescendo of wind chimes accompanied by a customized vibration that reminded me of a heartbeat. My thighs would squeeze automatically, my eyes felt larger, my mouth would open and close as I would shakily reply to his greeting: Sup?

I was Pavlov and Pavlov's Dog.

Then we would talk about our day or, rather, his day, funny things he saw on the internet.

He talked about movies. He watched a lot of cartoons for a grown-up, one with a talking horse, another one with a man's penis as a character. He would sometimes send me memes with those characters, and I would write back, something like *funny* or *lol* if I felt more daring and wanted to make an inside joke about our mutual disdain for abbreviations. I tried not to think how he had the time to watch his stupid shows but didn't have the time to see me.

Sometimes we talked about things we read. Those were my favourite conversations because I liked reading. I liked what everyone else who read liked about it — losing myself in it, forgetting my own problems. I knew he read the same books as me because he asked me for recommendations. I loved that there was a way for me to leave my mark in his life.

I just don't want any poetry, he said.

I don't read poetry. I'm afraid of it, of its deceptiveness, its complexity.

Right. Exactly. I don't understand that garbage, either, he yawned into the phone.

Yes, that's what I meant, I corrected myself. I just don't understand it.

The books I read and that Sebastian read were books recommended by Victor but now they were my books; they were books I thought I loved: Hemingway, Houellebecq, Hłasko. Men's books written by men. The one thing that the writers had in common was their characters' desire for women they mistreated. I enjoyed those parts because they made me think that Sebastian was also conflicted and loved me secretly. I waited to receive a long, romantic, confessional email that never came. Sometimes his jokes sounded almost eloquent, which signalled to me there was potential there, and maybe one day he would make a roaring romantic overture. I didn't have to have a degree in psychology to know that I was a masochist, that I was excited by being on tenterhooks. The men in sweaters bored me, I didn't like their predictability, I was afraid of having to be romantically involved with someone who was safe and who would ask me to fill out a consent form.

Besides his taste in literature, Sebastian had the same food preferences as me: ice cream, bananas, old cheddar, peanut butter out of the jar in the middle of the night. We both loved pho. I suggested we could take each other to our favourite pho restaurants. I watched the three dots on the screen that never evolved into a response.

Later on, I typed, *but I hate making plans.*

Me, too, he replied.

Dislikes were better. He disliked crowds, hugs, brunches, emoticons, acronyms, jogging, yoga, karaoke.

Me, too.

He loved making fun of the joggers in the park near where he lived. He was fixated on them, on the futility of their exercise.

All trying to run away from their problems, he typed, and even though I'd heard that joke before, I laughed as if he came up with it.

I think yoga is dumb, I suggested. It was dangerous to make fun of yoga because everyone loves yoga. But yoga people were similar to runners — they existed to make the rest of us feel guilty. I knew I had a nice body — objectively speaking. But I didn't have the kind of yoga body that showed the world you gave a shit about yourself. My body showed that I gave some shit but not enough. My ass, although large, was not the kind of ass that was popular on the internet — two perfect globes tensing next to one another. My ass was doomed to sag. I could still prevent it if I started yoga now, but I couldn't get into it and was confident I never would.

I've tried yoga before, Sebastian typed. *You should give it a go. You actually seem really passionate about it.*

My obsession with not doing yoga is as intense as doing yoga is for those who do do it. I'd worked on that sentence for a while and now was the perfect time to release it. I planned for the whole conversation to go this way and it did.

Funny.

I pictured him laughing, his lips full with the corners curled up. I had a small library of vignettes of those few precious moments we'd spent together that I had meticulously arranged in my mind. His laughter had a deep sound to it, something I imagined being able to shove inside myself, the sound turning into thickness I could use to fill me in place of him. The heat in my chest spread to my entire body when I thought of it.

He had delicate ears, high cheekbones. I fantasized licking him, smelling him behind the ears.

I tried not to get too excited about us having so many things in common, the way a teenager would, but secretly I was thrilled and surprised that it was possible to find someone who disliked so many things that I also disliked.

When he would text or call me at seven, he would also talk about his work and his clients who didn't understand his work. There were people out there who thought nothing of having four different fonts on one business card, who thought kerning was not at all important, who demanded a slab serif typeface in body copy.

When he went on for too long about his job, I would let myself ignore the words but would still tune in to the sound of his low voice and fish out the technical terms and try to repurpose them. I didn't need him to be interesting or flattering, and when he talked about margins or alignments I pretended that he was saying something else. I pretended that he was talking about the parts of my body and what he would like to do to those parts. It was cheesy but it turned me on.

I recorded him once secretly and played the conversation in bed and tried to masturbate to it. But my own voice was jarring, naked, and I hated how it shook when I got too excited. I was agreeing with everything he was saying. My jokes didn't seem that funny, and I got paranoid about his laughter sounding forced. I also learned from the recording that I needed to talk slower; I needed to be cooler. I was not cool. I sounded so eager it was as if someone had given a microphone to a monkey.

One time on ending a conversation I said, I love you, but in a whisper. I knew he wouldn't be able to make out what I said.

What did you say?

Nothing.

∽

Like I said, I wasn't good at maintaining friendships. There were some classmates from university and wives and girlfriends of friends of Victor's, but I was neglectful and didn't know how to keep in touch. I never reached out to people, and many of my friendships would fade out after a string of rainchecks and unanswered texts or emails. Most people in their thirties were advancing in becoming proper grown-ups, and their lives would naturally get busier, fill with engagements, weddings, babies, mortgages, cottages, cancer. I was an anomaly with my lack of direction; it often felt as if I was forever stuck in a hallway of life, unable to open the doors that everyone else felt entitled to go through. And with time, it became harder to spend time with people who I had nothing in common with. I didn't have a sexy story to explain my lack of progress.

Because I was lousy at making friends, I had the tendency to latch onto people I didn't really care about. And now that Sebastian was in my life, I desperately needed someone to talk to. This is why I invited Kelly to come out for lunch with me. We had one lunch when I first got hired, and there was awkwardness, her stories about anime conventions confused me; I didn't understand how a grown woman could love cartoons and dressing up so much. But right now I wanted someone to confide in, and Kelly was nice enough even though she could be grumpy and took her job a lot more seriously than I did.

We walked to a small restaurant located on the same block as our office, a place known for its healthy fare of salads and wraps and a local artisanal beer with a logo of the CN Tower on it. You built your own salad out of the base of lettuce or rice and added protein and four other ingredients and dressings.

After we built our salads, we made our way to a booth in the corner by the window. Outside there were other office people walking to their lunches or back to their cubicles. It was a nice day, warm for March, almost balmy. The sun had melted all the snow. A man walked by without a coat, the sleeves of his shirt rolled up to show off a cross-hatch of tattoos.

Kelly and I talked about the weather. We talked about how the AC was too strong during the summer and how Kelly always got colds, and how she got colds in the last place she worked at, which was a bank. Now I keep a blanket in the drawer, she said conspiratorially, and I laughed because she laughed.

I'm seeing this guy, I said. His name is Sebastian. He's a graphic designer.

Uh-oh, she said.

He's younger than me and not somebody I thought I would end up with, I said. I didn't mean to say it like that, but saying it like that made me feel proprietary, and for a moment I basked in the idea that we were indeed people who could end up together.

How young? Under thirty? You can't take under-thirties too seriously. They're too entitled. You need to be careful, Kelly said, and shoved a forkful of avocado into her mouth. I used to date a twenty-five-year-old, and he wanted to get married, and then he ghosted me.

I'm sorry.

It's fine. It was long time ago. But your Sebastian is no different, and you know it. The only way to deal with those fuckers is to stay cool. Don't show them you care.

I didn't know how to be cool. It had to go the way it had to go — me pretending badly and failing. The most humiliating part was that he had no idea about my torment about how to be, and he probably wouldn't notice if I was being cool — he probably wouldn't notice if I disappeared. He would probably just shrug if I told him I need a break or said whatever it is people say to get rid of people they don't want anymore.

I didn't say any of this to Kelly. I wanted to tell her more, but there wasn't a lot more to tell. I knew that most of what I knew of Sebastian was what I had created in my mind; sometimes he barely seemed real. I had only scraps to go on — a few dates and those phone calls and texts, no plans for the future. I imagined with real friends it was safe to talk about delusions and what-ifs, but Kelly and I weren't close. Yet she was friendly enough, and I was grateful for her. I was happy that she seemed to forgive me for being assigned to Unusual Tours.

She said, Do I have anything in my teeth?

No, you're fine.

You know, my mom used to say that only a true friend would tell you if you had something in your teeth.

I said, But you don't have anything in your teeth.

But if I did, would you tell me?

Of course.

After we finished eating, we walked back to the office without speaking; it was fine.

I wondered if she felt as much relief as I did when we sat back in our cubicles.

I couldn't imagine her dating a twenty-five-year-old, but then she would have met like-minded people at those conventions she went to, all kinds of nerds of all ages. I knew of those things from documentaries, and once back in university, at a train station, I was swarmed by a group of grown-ups dressed up as children.

Kelly had a few pictures of herself pinned to the wall of her cubicle, in which she wore various wigs and little girl dresses. Her screensaver was a picture of a cartoon character slashing the air with a big sword.

11

THE MESSAGE WAS casual, uninvested, like a yawn. *Finished deadline sup tonight?*

No plans free tonight. It took me more than two hours to send this back. I wrote and rewrote entire paragraphs where I gave various accounts of the past two weeks or so, where I made jokes about my workplace and about the people on the subway, where I summarized an amusing article about apples I read in the *New Yorker* and a show about Greenland sharks that I saw on TV. In the end, *No plans free tonight* struck me as the only way to reply, a diluted minimalist masterpiece I arrived at after many, many drafts. I hoped the lack of punctuation suggested I was busy and spontaneous about plans — plans that could change at any moment if he didn't reply right away — just like he was.

He asked me to come to his place after supper. I said nothing about the *after-supper* part even though I thought it would've been polite to have him cook for me, the way a proper date would be set up, but I didn't want him to get discouraged and disinvite me. This was my only chance to see him, and I wanted to see him more than I wanted anything else in the world. He was like an expectation of all things that used to give me joy: Christmas, and a birthday party, and a long-awaited trip. He was an expected promotion at work, and graduation from school, and an upcoming art show opening where I'd get to be the shiny girlfriend of the man of the hour. The excitement rivalled all those events from my past, and this excitement grew as the time went on. I felt it in my body — little zaps in my muscle and sweating, both sensations that were almost too much for the skin that I was encased in. I had to wash my face in cold water repeatedly, put a wet paper towel on my neck.

I couldn't concentrate on work. I kept sweating from my joyous anxiety during our board meeting, and I fantasized about what I was going to wear, how I was going to speak, and what gestures I was going to make. *No plans free tonight.*

∽

I called our caseworker to come over and supervise my mother's nightly routines. She wouldn't stay for the night, but she would make sure my mother went to bed after her bath. The caseworker came from a rotation of caseworkers connected to the clinic my mother was registered with. It was almost always the younger ones who would be sent to take care of the likes of my mother: mild schizophrenics or the Undiagnosed but Very Crazy — usually older ladies with a bad attitude but too fragile to do much with it. The more seasoned caseworkers would get the belligerent, the wet brains, and the violent ones.

The current worker was a redhead with an eager smile and oh-honey manner. I liked her instantly, and my mother didn't. I liked her because I sensed a certain stubbornness behind her naïveté, the insistence on obeying the rules above all.

My mother ignored the caseworker, who didn't seem to take it personally. She gave me an encouraging smile when I stuck my head in the door to the living room to let her know I was leaving. My mother's eyes were transfixed on the television; her face shone white, reflecting the light coming from the screen.

I left the house without saying goodbye.

ꝏ

I ended up going to Sebastian's place three nights in a row. The three nights were magic. I hate using that word, *magic*, but there really isn't a better way to describe how it felt to me. For the most part, the sex was the way it was the first time — aggressive, hard, with my body thrown around like it didn't matter that it was on the end of his dick. It didn't matter. Because, as before, I felt wetness come on unexpectedly in the middle of my discomfort, and I opened up again and experienced pleasure from our coupling. There was a soggy stain on his sheets that had formed underneath me.

When I was not getting fucked by him, I thought about wanting him inside me. My expectation was better than any foreplay. I knew it would be rough, but the roughness suggested he really wanted me. The idea of him taking me kept me in a permanent state of arousal. Not being able to come during the actual act only seemed to heighten that arousal, and I found myself finally orgasming the third time he forced himself inside me, as soon as the friction begun. My orgasm started somewhere different from where it usually did — in my lower belly, very far and secret, a place that I had no idea existed up until that moment. I suspected he managed to stimulate my cervix with his deep thrusts.

As I came, I visualized speeding through a tunnel filled with colours: bright and then dark blue, turning darker, almost black like ink, then a golden light shooting from one end of the blue spectrum to another. I clutched onto him and bit him and scratched as I came. He wrapped his hand around my neck and without breaking eye contact ground himself inside me faster and faster until it was his turn. He collapsed on top of me in growls and shudders. I was covered in his sweat, but my body temperature changed almost instantly, and I started to shiver. He wrapped his big arms around me, threw his leg over mine, enveloped me in his solid body.

There were more breakthroughs for us. Following our first time, I googled *How to Suck Uncut Dick* online and watched many informative videos. Next time I took his cock in my mouth, I sucked him exactly as it was suggested online — with less pressure, a lighter touch — and I swallowed him, as I always did with all of my lovers. He said it was one of the best blow jobs he's ever had. I wondered how many were in the running.

But it was the time after sex that was the real magic, the intimacy of our bodies next to each other, the feel of skin against skin. The texture of his hair was different from Victor's — it was coarser, wiry. He took my hand and petted his own head with it; he moved his head under my hand like a tamed animal.

Indeed, he became tamed. He was not like the guy he presented himself to be. After sex, he softened. He didn't perform tough; the cameras were turned off. The night would go on, and we lay there entwined, talking about nothing, kissing once in a while, mid-word. I touched his hair, again. He smoothed mine. He kissed my forehead, inside my elbows; he buried his face in my neck.

Victor desired me, but it never felt like this. This felt as if I was a lover, but I also felt like a mother, like he needed me that hard. And when he slept next to me, he held me tight. There was something inside him that was broken — everyone is a little broken, after all — and it only came out in this desperate cuddling, this insistence on absorbing himself into my body.

He played quiet, ambient music that filled the space like water, or like we were underwater. Outside, it was mid-April, and the world couldn't seem to wake up. We had a snowfall just the other day; the trees stood bald, undecided. I liked being cocooned in his tiny bedroom with its blacked window. Even the living room seemed like too much with its cold impersonal walls and the steel-blue breaking daylight coming through the glass in the basement door.

Awake again, we kissed, nose to nose. We talked about things like the past, high school, going to Europe, sex with other people, too. We kissed more. He made humming sounds. He sighed; there was longing in that sigh.

I wanted to tell him it was going to be okay, but I worried it would make him feel too vulnerable. He had made some comments before about never breaking down in front of a woman; he said he was a man of old-world convictions. He called himself *emotionally stunted*. Yet, in his bed, during those three magic nights, post-sex, he seemed like the most tender, open person I'd ever met.

I could never fall asleep squished against him like that, and I didn't mind; I wanted to give myself to him. I told myself that

I could be his blanket and his slut to dispose of, later, after he had his fill.

I could be, I lied to myself, *the disposable slut*.

In the mornings, I got ready and took an Uber home where I would feed my mother breakfast and help her get dressed. I went to work. I don't remember anything that happened at work during that time. I came home, fed my mother again, waited for the caseworker, left.

∽

During the three nights with Sebastian, my mother called frequently. She didn't know how to use her cellphone, and she didn't know how to text. I didn't listen to all her messages because after the first one, I knew the rest would be the same hissing and whisper-yelling as if she'd fallen into a hole filled with snakes and together they decided to ring me. From then on, I turned the phone on silent, and I pressed 1 and then immediately 7 to delete each message. I felt I would just sense if there was an emergency.

I kept the phone near the bed, but I would put it facedown. Only occasionally, looking at it, it would feel as if she was in the room with us, but I was so easily distracted by my lover's beauty and attention that I could let her go. There were prolonged moments in the night when it only felt like me and him.

I wanted this intimacy to extend further, so on the final night together, I asked him to watch me get myself off, but when I spread my legs in front of him, he looked at me with such puzzlement I felt embarrassed for both of us. I closed my legs.

No, it's cool, he said, unconvinced, unconvincingly. Please go on.

Don't worry about it, I said. I didn't know this was going to be the last time we'd spend the whole night together.

I didn't get myself off for him, but we had sex one more time. When he entered me, I clenched around him and tried to lead his body with mine. I rotated my pelvis, pulled him closer, and then play-pushed him off, moaned encouragingly into his ear, and whined when he'd go at me too aggressively. I thrust my hips and played with myself as he watched. Maybe he was too intimidated to see me get myself off on my own, but he seemed to enjoy the show now. Eventually, he slowed down and at one point stroked me with his finger at the same time he penetrated me. I moaned louder. We moved our hips in unison. Men danced when they fucked. It was up to women to figure out the steps and show them. And he was finally letting me show him. I felt so much love and gratitude, I clutched onto him harder and kissed him all over his face. He tensed and pulled out and then slowly entered me again. I was butter, melting. My chest radiated pink and yellow and orange — three colours that came on and went as he moved in and out of me. I felt as if I was on a precipice of some discovery, a different way to connect with a lover that I'd never experienced before.

I had never tried to lead with Victor; our sex was mechanical and good, and that's all there was to it. With Sebastian I was, finally … *close* — I had never been this close with any lover. I wasn't sure what I was close to, not an orgasm, but something much more profound.

I got dressed while he watched. I made a little show out of pulling my stockings on, extended my feet, caressed my calves.

Right before I left, he said, Oh, I almost forgot. Can you clean the back of my neck? He handed me a pair of small clippers. I usually ask my mother. Don't nick me.

It was nothing, of course, but I loved doing that girlfriendly task. My hands shook a little as I ran the little metal teeth over the dark fuzz. If someone were to ask me to pinpoint exactly when I knew for sure I loved him, it was then.

∽

When he told me he was busy the day after, I went to a big department store near my work and purchased Narciso Rodriguez cologne. I rubbed it on my wrists before sleep.

I considered giving the cologne to Victor but it wasn't his scent; it was too pronounced for him. Victor liked things black or plain, anonymous. Plus, making him wear it would be cruel, and I didn't want to be cruel to him. I also didn't buy him presents. He was adamant about that. I think presents made him feel as if he was owned, and he didn't want to be owned. I made peace with that a long time ago. Besides, now I only wanted to own Sebastian.

I bought the perfume joyously, without any inclination of what was about to happen. Walking back to the office from the department store, I passed a radiant young couple, and I smiled at the woman. She and I had a thing in common: we were both content, spoken for, loved.

12

THEN WE NO longer had a place to have sex because Sebastian lost his main gig and didn't have a lot of savings. People lost jobs all the time. I didn't think less of him because that happened. He had to move in with his parents, who lived in a bungalow on the most west side of the city. It was a nice neighbourhood, close to the lake, with low-rise buildings and a brand-new college built on the old grounds of an insane asylum. The location was more accessible than the suburbs where he was before; it was closer for me to drive to. That was the thought I had before I realized that I wouldn't be coming over to his parents' place. It was too ridiculous an idea; we weren't teenagers.

His mother sounded nice; he spoke kindly of her. She used to work as a seamstress; she still made traditional wedding dresses for women from her Nepalese community. His father owned a small printing business that wasn't doing well.

He wanted to retire. Sebastian fought with his father over not wanting to take over the business. Sebastian didn't speak kindly of his father; he called him a tyrant.

His sisters went to the college built on the old grounds of the insane asylum, and they took fashion and design. Both sisters had rich boyfriends, and both had undergone breast and lip augmentation paid for by said boyfriends, which Sebastian said wasn't weird. One sister wanted to get married and have babies, the other dreamed of becoming a contestant on a reality-television show about making clothes out of trash.

I tried to imagine being around his family, the parents and the younger sisters, but I found it unnerving to think about things like that. I had no interest in meeting his family, and I didn't think they would have any interest in meeting me. I was ten years older than their boy, not wealthy, and living with an elderly woman who was insane.

∽

I tried to bring him back to my place to have sex. First, I managed to convince him to see a movie. He told me cinemas irritated him because of the kind of people who went to see movies. But he agreed, reluctantly, and we saw a story about two men who drank themselves into oblivion while isolated in a lighthouse. The movie was black and white, and the two actors did whatever they could to get nominated for awards — there were accents, fights, getting buried alive, poetry, masturbation, and bad teeth.

The theatre was almost empty save for a few seats. Everyone else was watching either the new superhero flick or the new one about a sadist and his slow-minded girlfriend.

I'd never gone to a movie theatre with Victor, who also hated the kind of people who went and was especially disturbed by all the eating and the smells. The *kind of people* were the people who didn't have gym bodies, although Victor said once you could argue that gym goers also liked movies because they liked things to be predictable and comforting, and they liked membership cards. For Victor, moviegoing was also related to his romantic past. Before he met me, Victor was with someone who was connected to the film industry, and he had to attend numerous premieres and meet many local celebs who were a lot more famous than him, which made him grumpy. The really famous ones were not a problem, but the ones who were based in our city made him obsess over his age and money.

Sebastian turned to me and pecked me on the cheek after the movie ended and thanked me for making him see it. The sweet gesture surprised me.

It's like a real date, I said, and he gave me a look that told me I was pushing my luck. I thought of grabbing his hand then and forcing him to hold mine as we walked toward his car, for everyone to see. I looked around and tried to figure out what was different about *the kind of people* and me and I couldn't spot one thing. I wondered why I was attracted to snobs. Did I find their snobbery to be a turn-on? And what did that say about me? Probably that I had a skewed view of my own worth. Before studying psychology in school, I tried to be an artist; it was a past I didn't understand any-more or associate with. I recalled now one time when I fell into a depression after I found out one of my paintings had been removed during a spring cleanup. I had a hunch that the painting was better than any other ones I had created. I made fewer mistakes, I could pick my own palette, follow the lines I intended to follow instead of painting over to cover up my lack of experience. Being an artist can be an exercise in stupidity, considering the amount of blind faith it takes to forge ahead, although some people choose to call it bravery. During that time, I did indeed feel brave, not stupid, and it was that courage that gave me the confidence to sign up for more studio classes when the time came to picking next-year courses. When the painting disappeared, I went into a frenzy. I had no qualms about diving into large metal junk-removal containers for a couple of days in a row and sorting through piles of cardboard and wood and canvas outside of the Fine Arts building. I stained my clothes, got cuts, and felt nauseous from the chemicals while looking for a trace of the painting, but it all felt noble, like a real mission, like I was fighting for something I believed in. I didn't find it. Afterward, I wrote letters to the art department demanding some kind of retribution. Temporarily, I was energized, full of anger. But the fight died in me, and the comedown was brutal. I started missing studio practice, and the paintings I produced were flat, dead inside, faces with grotesque noses when I didn't mean to, lack of dimension, and grey smudges that didn't resemble shadows. I never got a grade higher than a C. It was as if a spell was broken; it seemed impossible to make a good picture. Eventually, I changed majors. The guidance counsellor suggested therapy, which is when I came up with the idea of studying psychology to fix myself.

It probably serves the story to mention that before Victor, I dated and had sex and fell in love. I barely trusted men, but they seemed more reliable. It was pathetic that I attached so much meaning to the men I fell in love with. I was like a balloon on a string — happy to be held and completely vulnerable when on my own, flying from one direction to another, but no one wanted to hold on to me for too long. My mother taught me nothing about relationships other than some outdated rules, like not calling the guy first. She told me men didn't like needy women. Or women who were bitches or who were pushy. I didn't want to be needy, and I didn't want to be pushy because I wasn't sure I was beautiful enough to get away with it. I wanted to be just right and, as a result, I believe I made myself forgettable. I was hoping that Sebastian would find me unforgettable, and making the movie choice that I made seemed like the right decision.

He talked about the movie in the car and said he would tell his buddies — telling his buddies was the highest compliment I could get from him.

We made it back after midnight. The house was quiet; my mother was most likely asleep.

I don't feel comfortable here, Sebastian said.

I didn't blame him. The decor hadn't changed since the seventies. It was all pale blue and green, and a few lamps looked like something fished out of the depths of the ocean. There were two lamps on in the living room, their dimmed light sickly, foggy. There were many crocheted splotches covering the slick upholstery of the khaki green living room set. I don't know who made those but not my mother.

There was some art on the walls, reproductions of grimy landscapes. My mother inherited the house from her aunt, and she never bothered to renovate it. I think she secretly liked the look because it felt like penance, and that's how she had preferred to live her life for at least a decade now.

Yeah, it's not the sexiest, I whispered, as I watched him take it all in. Please, just come in, I said, and pulled on his sleeve.

My own bedroom was simple. A clothes rack and a single bed and a bedside table. A bookshelf. I draped it in some Christmas lights like a student. I never planned to stay there long, so I didn't bother putting up any art on the walls, but the clothes on the clothes rack were accumulating, measuring my time spent there in skirts and sweaters.

Sebastian sat on the bed. He didn't take his jacket off.

I sat beside him, also in my jacket.

I had nothing to show him, no objects to talk about because, as I said, I never planned to stay there long. Everything that was somewhat interesting — photos, drawings I made in my undergrad when I tried to be an artist — was in the basement, in sealed boxes.

Take your jacket off, I said, touching his shoulder.

I'm okay, he said sharply, drawing his shoulders in. I didn't like this new voice; it was the wrong register.

The door opened, and my mother said, I'm going to make some tea. Would you like some tea? She was looking right at me in a way that made it seem Sebastian wasn't there.

Sebastian stared at her. She was wearing a nightgown as always. The nightgown was too big for her. She had lost a lot of weight since going openly unstable. She was suspicious about food and getting poisoned, which is why she only agreed to eat things that were previously packaged.

Right. I think I'm gonna go, Sebastian said.

My bedroom was so small — it was practically a closet — that my mother would have to move out of the way in order to make room for him to get up.

Sebastian got up and sat down. My mother still wouldn't look at him, and she wouldn't move. Do you want some tea?

We would love some tea, I said.

I had a nice dream about him coming to the house.

Who? Sebastian? I immediately regretted asking.

Who? my mother said.

I glanced at Sebastian.

Of course not. He's not anything like him, she said, nodding in his direction.

I should really go, Sebastian said in a small voice. I didn't know how to help him. We were trapped in my room.

Suddenly, my mother swayed and held onto the doorknob. I watched her knuckles go white as she clutched it. With sudden cardiac arrest you can be dead within minutes. My mother's caseworker had recommended I take first aid training. I hadn't taken it.

But my mother was fine. She often had these minute spells; there was no point in getting excited and lying to myself all the time that she could go so easily. Her hand relaxed, slowly turned pale pink.

She said, I had a feeling he was looking for you. He walked around the house, and I heard him move things in your bedroom and say your name but you weren't here. So he went into the kitchen and moved plates and cups in the cupboards for no reason. I don't know why he would do things like that. Maybe he was angry?

Who? Sebastian said. Who was angry?

I wondered if he would bolt, push my mother out of the way, make her fall down, break her neck.

Nobody, I said. Nobody was angry.

He seemed angry, my mother said.

Mom, I will have some tea, I said, louder now. I wasn't screaming yet, but I was close to screaming; still, I had to keep it together. I didn't want Sebastian to think that I was even related to this person and that I, myself, was the kind of a woman who screamed in the middle of the night. I didn't want him to think that a ghost was looking for me or, rather, that I believed in ghosts, which I did. I frequently could tell a place had an aura or a heaviness to it; there were such things as energies. It wasn't anything to get too excited about, although you had to use caution when disclosing you believed in the supernatural. I didn't want to turn Sebastian off. I had to seduce him first, had to have him fall in love with me — all of that before I showed him how I really was. It was a mistake to present your weakness to your romantic interests right away; we were all just trying to trap one another before unleashing our real selves.

Example: I brought up the ghosts with Victor early on, and he pretended to laugh. I even tried to make it sound more scientific and talked about energies. Decomposing bodies released gases and changed their energy. You cannot destroy energy; it is constant according to Einstein. But since you can transform it, is the new energy of decomposing bodies a ghost energy? And if energy transcends time, it can also transcend the human body — nothing really dies; it just changes form.

Victor asked me then how energy created thought, how I could ascribe conscious intention to a being that was perhaps made up of gas. Didn't ghosts have missions? Didn't they haunt you, pass on messages? How did they do that, where was the thinking? He asked me then if I believed in things like fate or horoscopes, as well, and then I pretended to laugh as if those things were ridiculous. I backpedalled, told him I was joking. I didn't want to turn him off. I wasn't confident in my beliefs enough to flaunt them from the get-go, even though they were not something I ever doubted the way I doubted my

appearance or intelligence and my troubling romantic prospects. Yet I cared about having a boyfriend more than I cared
about what I cared about.

The reason I thought the other one was looking for you
was because he didn't take his shoes off like this one did, my
mother said. I could hear the shoes. He was impatient. Ghosts
don't take their shoes off. But guests should. Ghosts and guests,
ghostguests, she giggled.

I thought: *giraffe sunshine, zigzag, zigzag-zebra-zun.* My
mother's razor threatening to open her wrist, or mine, I had no
idea whose till this day.

Mom. Please.

Guestghost, my mother said.

It occurred to me that this particular ghost had started
showing up around the time I met Sebastian. And as for my
non-ghost guest, I could feel his unease radiating from him
like hot air.

My mother was wrong — Sebastian had his shoes on.

It smells of burnt rubber here, Sebastian said.

Really?

Well, very faintly, he said, also very faintly.

I guess I couldn't smell the burnt rubber anymore because
I was used to it now. I had known Sebastian for more than
eight weeks, and it was eight weeks ago that my mother had
put the electric kettle on the stove, eight weeks since I drove to
purchase a new element in the suburbs.

That's because *she* doesn't know how to operate an electric
kettle, my mother said.

I opened my mouth to protest but there was no point, she
wasn't listening. She just kept on prattling on. I will go make
some tea now. In a regular kettle. You should stay for tea. It's a

polite thing to do. We have manners in this house. She finally looked, then stared, at Sebastian. ·

Sebastian didn't stay. He didn't kiss me when he left and didn't say he would see me later as he got inside his car.

When I came back my mother was in the living room, and the TV was on. Her mouth open like a child's, she was engrossed in Ivana Trump's heavily accented spiel about garbage she tried to pass off as jewellery. My mother no longer had access to credit cards and was no longer able to order things from the Shopping Channel. I considered forcing her to go to bed, but I was too tired and too sad to argue. I had to admit to myself, however, that I never envisioned me and Sebastian actually having sex in my little bedroom, so my disappointment was tinted with some relief.

I texted Sebastian goodnight and he didn't reply.

13

WE MADE OUT in my car for the first time because now neither of us could go or wanted to go to each other's houses.

After we made out — where he came, I didn't — I took off my panties and handed them to him before he got out to catch the train.

Thanks, he said, and stuffed the panties into his knapsack and ran off.

On the phone that night I said I liked making out in the car even though I hated it.

Good to hear, he yawned.

What did you do with the panties?

I devoured them.

What? I laughed just in case, the sort of laughter that could be perceived as delighted or laughter that meant I got the dumb joke.

I miss you, he said. I want to be inside you.

Oh, the soaring in my chest. Like I'd done a line of cocaine. No, better.

◡

During the night, my mother had one of her more serious spells. She took a bath before I got home, and by the time I got her out, she was shivering so hard it was as if she was seizing. Her teeth were chattering. Her loose, mushy skin looked as if it was going to just come off of her bones. I put her in her favourite pink nightgown, but she couldn't seem to get warm. I thought of calling her caseworker, but I almost never called her because I knew how to take care of my own mother. She emailed each week to check in. I would always reply that things were going well, and I'd include some cute detail to make it seem authentic — for example, that we went for a walk to a park and fed squirrels or that we watched one of my mother's favourite Bridgette Bardot movies over the weekend. I always sent a picture of my mother that I would take with my phone after doing her hair and putting some rouge on her cheeks. You could hardly tell she was barely eating if I draped one of her old mohair sweaters over her shoulders.

I draped one over her now as she continued to shiver and shake. She reminded me of one of those small wet dogs that people who lived in condos dressed in little doggie booties and doggie raincoats.

She let me walk her to her bedroom, stepping gently and precisely. She didn't argue over her nightly TV. I considered asking her to take her sleeping pills, but I didn't know what was happening with her body. I didn't want to be found responsible for manslaughter.

It's going to be okay, you're gonna be okay, I kept saying, even though she showed no other distress than the physical one. I thought of Sebastian with my panties. Was he taking them out of his knapsack right now, smelling them, maybe even stroking himself as he did? I squeezed my thighs as I sat down on the edge of my mother's bed, waiting for her to crawl under the covers. She was moving like a creature, one of her bizarre habits where she insisted on lowering herself onto the bed and kind of scooting over and walking on all fours till she reached the pillows, at which point she would lift the covers and shimmy herself underneath.

She continued to shake violently as she fell onto her side, her nightgown riding up her thighs and over her waist. She usually put on her own underwear — it was one of the few dignities she hadn't given up on, and I was grateful that she was able to do it. But right now, she was naked from the waist down. I got up and opened a drawer and took out a pair of big white cotton panties. I briefly glanced at her vulva. *Here is the place I came out of.* I thought of the pale tender folds nestled below a tuft of white hair. She was whispering now, the same nonsensical sentences with an occasional word that I was able to make out. Her body was still trembling as I pulled the panties over her hips. I covered her with a blanket and waited. Eventually her breath got slower, less ragged.

I considered staying with her until she fell asleep, but my phone started to vibrate and chime in my pocket. It was Sebastian with the heartbeat sound of our love.

I pulled it out and held it up to show her. Work. I have to get this. Call me if there's anything wrong.

She stared at me, her mouth shut. She looked offended, but I wasn't sure if it was because I suggested she might need me or because I was leaving.

Sup, the text read.

Just at a friend's watching a movie, I texted back.

Am in ur area. Thought we could grab beers. But just got a text from a buddy so never mind. Text later, enjoy your movie.

Fucking hell, I said out loud, and looked up from my phone. There was a figure at the end of the hallway coming in and out of focus against the door to the basement. The shape was blurry, his features were blurry — I tried to concentrate and make out what it was that I was looking at exactly. It never worked when you forced your eyes to see something that technically wasn't there; I've learned that over the years.

I would not be able to describe him, but some things were communicated to me. He was young. He was attractive — dark-haired, dark-eyed, something about supple lips — and he didn't seem to want anything. He was just letting his presence be known. I nodded at him, but there was no response.

The hallway was cold, and it smelled of wetness and very faintly of fish. I wasn't sure what to do.

Josephine? my mother screeched. Her voice startled me, and I turned around and rushed back to her bedroom. I hated knowing that he was behind me, possibly very close — the coldness was sneaking up my legs, spreading to my spine, making me shiver, making my teeth chatter, just like my mother only a short time ago.

My mother was on the ground, the nightgown again pulled up all the way to her waist. She must've tried to crawl back out and gotten tangled in the sheets.

I lifted her and gently sat her down on the edge of the bed. We were both shivering now, she more than me. I straightened out the sheets. She got underneath them and stared past me. I didn't want to turn around. I was getting even colder now, my body rattling inside itself as if I were my own cage. I hadn't shared a bed with my mother in years.

As a seventeen-year-old I went through a phase when things started showing up for the first time. There were shadows at the top of the stairs outside of my bedroom door that would invade my dreams; there was specifically a shadow of a man in a fedora that never seemed to go away. He stood in the doorway to my teenage bedroom, unmoving yet dangerous. I somehow sensed he would try to force himself on top of me, and I would scream, my breath caught in my throat as I'd try to get it out, my scream never making it past my lips. How was it that I was mute, confined to my bed, and to my sleep? Why couldn't I move? I had to move; I had to pierce through the skin of my nightmare, till it would finally work, and I'd surface, back in my teenage bedroom — here's the nightstand, here's the lamp, the window, the opposite side; here are the M.C. Escher posters on the wall, here's my desk, my pillow, my blanket, my feet underneath it. I was surprised that there was no evidence of my scream; my mouth was clamped shut. Yet it seemed I screamed right through to awakening. The time was always 3:14 a.m. I suspected the specific time had something to do with the presence; perhaps it was the time when it crossed over from this world to the limbo it was in. After a couple of nights of this, I asked my mother if I could share her bed. I never told her why. She didn't pry, which was unusual, but I had a feeling she somehow knew what I was going through. I stayed with her for a few nights before going back to my own room. The thing in the fedora never returned.

Now I was twice that age and getting into my mother's bed again. I felt defeated. I didn't want to share the bed with her, but as soon as I was under the covers, I felt the warmth envelop me, and my shivers stopped. I slept terribly, moving in and out of wells of dark muck, drowning and then coming up for air at the last moment. I sweated so much that the sheets were soaked, and I had to change them while my mother sat in the tub. It was Saturday, so I didn't have to go to work. I managed to get her out before the water got too cold.

I called Victor and told him about seeing something in the hallway. I said it was perhaps the spirit of someone who died in the house.

Victor inhaled loudly. Not that again. I thought you were over that. What kind of a spirit?

He's a quiet person. A sad man, young. I can sense tears and crying. He didn't move or do anything. He just watched me and seemed to fill the air with sighs that weren't really. I thought he was following me. I slept in my mother's bed.

Sighs that are not really there. You know it's all in your head.

Most things are, I said.

I think you need some activities. Maybe join the gym or a photography class.

I didn't hang up on him because it was me who called him. I wish I hadn't called him.

∽

Sebastian and I went on making out in my car. I couldn't relax in his mother's car, and he was more than happy to have me drive all the way over to his parents' bungalow.

When we would make out in my car, he would finger me, but as with his penis, his fingers were rough — they went at my pussy as if it was something that needed scratching and drilling rather than soft petting. More often than not, he rubbed the bone of my pubic crest — I had to look at anatomical pictures on the internet to learn the name of the bone that was getting all that action.

When he'd shove his fingers deep inside me, I would bite on my fist to stop myself from shouting at him. Eventually, I would let my voice out — I would turn it into moans, which only made him push harder. I didn't mind any of it. I didn't even mind the dryness that he ignored, my tender skin getting scoured. As before, the thought of what we were doing was enough to make me wet, it seemed like a race between my body providing lubrication to align with his insistent touching.

He said he liked when I was loud. I was too quiet, he said.

I'm a quiet girl, I said.

I want to make you scream.

I screamed.

Better, he growled. I loved when he growled; the sound made me lubricate more, and I'd feel the first spasms of genuine arousal, which made up for the pain.

∽

Maybe it wasn't about sexual satisfaction. It was the intimacy of our first encounters. I hung on to those three nights that we spent together, when he fell asleep and held me so desperately. Over and over again, I replayed the minute-long moment when he asked me to shave the peach fuzz on the back of his neck. There was softness in him, and I believed I could get to it eventually. I loved being in love. I was walking around the world as if he were watching me the whole time, as if I was in a music video with all the filters blotting out the ugliness of the naked city around me. I swung my hips and straightened out my shoulders. People at work remarked on my good mood. My mother remarked on the fact that I lost weight. Out of the blue, Victor invited me to a romantic getaway to Montreal, and when I declined he told me he was disappointed. In the past I would've never dared to say no, but now I didn't care. His disappointment made me feel only pity. I was in too good of a mood to feel anything else.

This high lasted awhile. And then one day there were no texts during the day and no phone call at night. And then the day after that. Instead of imagining Sebastian watching me and feeling good about it, I walked around biting the insides of my cheeks. I never struggled with addiction, but I guess this was what withdrawal would feel like. I was surprised I wasn't falling to the ground. I had a few moments of panic but I was able to curb it, push the invisible door away from my face, and take deep breaths.

At seven o'clock, when he used to call or text and when he would now *not* call or text, I would pour myself some whisky from my mother's liquor cabinet. I didn't drink it. But I needed a dramatic gesture: I was a woman drinking alone, a perform-ance I put on for myself. I sat, clutching the glass, in an ugly green chair, waiting for the crescendo of chimes of his ringtone and the heartbeat vibrations.

After waiting for an hour or so I would take one of my mother's sleeping pills so that I wouldn't have to be awake worrying about the phone call. I knew what my co-worker Kelly had said was true: he was pulling away.

∽

I thought I was mentally and emotionally strong enough to withstand it. I don't know why I thought I was strong. I wasn't. I was an idiot just like everybody else.

14

I THOUGHT ABOUT him in bed with me, his rough passion, his hand around my neck, his growling. Mostly I thought about the way he looked at me, how he could make me look away first. I hated it but I liked it. I felt aroused and depressed.

I knew he would get in touch eventually. And I spent hours planning what to wear when I saw him next.

I never called him because my mother taught me never to call first.

I kept stealing her sleeping pills, and I told myself I was right to steal them because if I hadn't, I'd stay awake and ruminate over not calling him, which would be because I had listened to her advice.

§

I was busy at work but not busy enough. I speed-researched and wrote reports and designed the Unusual Tour to Trogir. While my plan awaited approval, I surfed the internet. I kept my phone in my purse, and I was aware of it being there; I was very aware of it not chiming or vibrating. Around that time, the word *limerence* was all over the news in connection to a story about a female astronaut. She was a mother of three who had been lauded for her accomplishments.

Astronauts undergo rigorous training, and they are the most capable — physically and mentally — of all humans. There was nothing in this woman's past that indicated instability or madness. But after she was scorned by her lover of three years, she got into her car and drove for nineteen hours straight to plead with him to take her back — driving, she wore an adult diaper so that she would not have to make any stops. The media were obsessed with that detail.

Instead of her former lover, she ran into his current girlfriend and, in a fit of rage, sprayed her with pepper spray. She was detained and charged with assault. Interviewed, she said repeatedly, apparently dumbfounded, "How did I lose control like that? How could this have happened to *me*?"

I knew how it happened.

After thirteen days he finally called. By then, I was ill from desperation; my limerence — my unrequited love — was a relentless phantom eating me up from the inside.

∽

Sebastian and I met in a sushi restaurant.

I wanted to lurch at him. I didn't lurch at him. I waved. Like I was a normal person, meeting a normal friend.

When we kissed hello, our teeth clashed against each other.

Our waitress was a sullen blond with an Eastern European accent. She sighed a lot.

Once Sebastian and I sat down I wanted to talk, but there was too much to say. I wanted to tell him about my pain and those thirteen days of waiting for him, but there was no way I would ever tell him about that. So I asked him about his sisters. He said they were fine. How was his mother? Fine. He didn't ask about mine, and I was grateful for that. I asked about his buddies, and they were fine, too. Work was fine, as well. I ran out of things to ask. By the end of the meal, we sat in silence, and he answered texts on his phone, and I looked at the TV behind him and read headlines: *Middlesex County declares state of emergency due to flooding. A woman's body found in a high-rise. Men with beards carry more germs than dogs, including deadly bacteria.*

The sushi was excellent. I liked the one with the delicate green ribbons of cucumber wrapped around the rice to hold it all together.

I focused on eating it, peeling away the green ribbon gently with my teeth, hoping it would make him think something sexual about me.

When he did look up from his phone and I felt his eyes on me, my teeth froze, and then we stared at each other until I looked away. His eyes said nothing to me; he didn't really care.

On the way to the car, he said to consider bathrooms. To have sex in. The restaurant food was so expensive we might as well get something extra out of it.

And you don't *really* like it in the car. Right?

I didn't cry. I said having sex in bathrooms was a dealbreaker although it wasn't — I had had sex in a bathroom before,

on a Christian retreat with my mother's church. I just said it so
that he would think I had dealbreakers and that it was possible
for him to break me.

Why did I want him to break me? Perhaps feeling pain
made me feel that at least I wasn't in this limbo. When the
sleeping pills didn't work, and my nights stretched into the
infinity of ennui — my phone's silent surface cool against my
cheek — I often thought that a quick death would be more
preferable to this. I was afraid of it, death, yet I craved it then,
wanting to just get it over with. My thoughts about death were
more pragmatic than emotional despite their drama.

A dealbreaker? he said.

Just kidding, I said, smiling at him. I hoped it looked like
the carefree smile I intended.

∽

On our next date, we had sex in a bathroom. It was in a coffee
shop where hipsters with laptops spent their afternoons working on their time-lapse videos and essays about Laura Nyro.

Sebastian held my wrists against the wall and pressed himself against me, biting the side of my face. Then he bit me on
the shoulder. I didn't like the biting, but I let him do it because
I liked that he was so hungry for me.

He wasn't gentle. It seemed like he really did want to eat
me.

After we had sex, I sat on the floor for a while with my head
between my knees. He didn't ask me how I was. I didn't want
to get up. Suddenly, I wanted him to get out, to leave me alone.
I told him to go, and part of me hoped he'd go and wouldn't
wait, but he waited, and I was surprised. We walked in silence

to my car, and we drove without speaking. He was texting his buddies; there was a football game he had made plans to see in a pub. When he got out, I watched him like a parent dropping off a kid at school, as he disappeared inside, into his life that had nothing to do with me.

∽

Later, I had to apply heavy concealer to hide the bite marks and the bruises near my face as well as the one actually on my face. I thought how applying the concealer to cover the bruises from Sebastian could become one of those sweet things people associate with their lover — the bruises would become a thing. I liked that I had these secret markings on my body, that my body evoked such response from a man. The bite on my shoulder bruised the most, and I took many pictures of it in the mirror. The bruise was like a flower, blossoming in different colours, over time changing shape and intensity. When I sent him one picture of it, he replied, *Sorry*. I looked at that *Sorry* all throughout the day and tried to interpret it. Was that a smug sorry, a real sorry, or a jokey sorry? I was mental.

∽

It seemed we were back in contact. He no longer rang me at all, but he texted, and we would make plans to meet in places that had good bathrooms to fuck in. I cancelled the special sound announcing his texts coming through to mark the new phase of our relationship, as if I now cared less about hearing from him. It was absurd, but I considered it progress, although over what I didn't know. It's not like I intended to break it off.

I saw him three days after our first bathroom date. We were at the big art gallery. I wanted to have a proper date. But it went sideways when Sebastian announced he hated taking the stairs. That was it: he refused to see the new retrospective on Frida Kahlo, fashion, and eyebrows, because it was on the fourth floor.

We could take the elevator, I said, but he said those things were full of people.

I was angry about the stupidity of the theme of the retrospective, but I didn't want to say anything about that yet. They were selling plastic unibrows, totes displaying her likeness, and heart pendants in the gift shop. I was hoping he would change his mind, and we would end up seeing the show eventually. Maybe we could joke about the merchandise; I could point out how desperate those curators got trying to make things funny or weird. Frida Kahlo alone would suffice — she was a handful on her own. But when I brought up the show again, he asked me if I was deaf: he hated taking the stairs.

I didn't understand this aggressiveness and his insistence on being dumber than he was. But stupidity seemed to be the theme of the day. As we walked around the main floor, surrounded by the gloomy paintings of churches and various Jesuses, he complained about a pulled hamstring.

Did you go jogging?

Funny.

I pointed to a painting. It was a small picture of a chapel against a wall of dark trees. It was a plain image, but the contrast between the white and the green made the paleness of the chapel intensely bright, which I liked. If I owned this, I would look at this painting all the time. I wouldn't even need a television.

Okay, Sebastian said. Sure.

I understood now what it was like for those keener teachers who insisted on class trips and who would try to make high schoolers excited about museum objects nobody cared about.

Just give up, Sebastian said, when I showed him another picture, this one of Jesus as a toddler, glowing among a crowd of adults in dark robes, all of them with crude, pained faces.

Give up what?

I get that it's pretty and important, but I'm a philistine.

You sound proud of it.

I'm not. I just don't get it.

You don't get art.

Ya. It's pissing you off, isn't it?

We walked around some more and he kept saying that I just don't get art. I asked him if he ever suffered a concussion. He blinked at me. Yes, a few times. When I did martial arts as a kid. And a guy knocked me out in a bar fight a couple of years ago. Why?

Never mind.

No, why?

Nothing.

Yes, I'm retarded. Am I allowed to say that? Retarded?

I really hated myself because it was me who was really the slow one, wasting my life on a person like this. He was unnecessarily mean. He wanted to provoke me; it was childish. He didn't understand art, and I didn't understand my desires, and that was a lot more troubling; not understanding art didn't make people insane.

We went outside, and I picked up the torn-up ticket he threw on the ground as we walked toward my car. I thought of the keener high school teacher again. I would probably have killed myself in exasperation had that been my job.

In the car, we talked about our sexual pasts again. Sebastian said he couldn't even tell how many women he'd slept with. There were so many women he had once listed names in multiples as if he was collecting sets: Ambers, Jennifers, Kellys.

He said he had never fucked a woman with my name; he said it wasn't really a sexy name, but it was a name that suggested I was classy. My fucking him in the bathroom was one more way to defile my classiness, I was sure.

That *is* a lot of women, I said, even though I, myself, had more than a few lovers — before Victor some short-term flings and some one-night stands and then whatever Victor wanted to do once he asked if we could spice things up and I said, let's spice it up then.

I guess, Sebastian said. It doesn't really mean anything. I never even get to the relationship thing. I revert to a caveman and start humping other things. Me hungry.

∽

After our meal — sushi again, two beers for him — in the bathroom he was especially talkative: Close your legs. Don't fucking move. Are you gonna come for me? Oh, that's a good little girl. Good girl. You're my girl. Who loves daddy's cock?

I was too embarrassed to say "I do," so instead I moaned as encouragingly as I could because I loved the words. Even the absurdly porny "daddy"— or especially that one. I liked being daddy's little girl. I had no father, and the word *daddy* wasn't much of a taboo for me. My boss, Sammy, was probably the closest to what I would picture when thinking of fathers, but he was no daddy. I imagined he would've been appalled had a woman called him that in bed. I called Victor "daddy" once while drunk, and he stopped mid-fuck and coolly asked me if I intended to turn him off. He was not appalled, just not interested.

I told Sebastian I liked when he called me his girl. We were driving to his parents' bungalow through the evening streets, tinted golden with the setting sun. I noticed the trees turning pale green, fuzzy with young leaves. Spring had the tendency to sneak up on you.

That's because you are. You're my girl.

Yeah, but I'm not really your girl, I said.

But you're *daddy*'s little girl, he laughed. You liked that, didn't you?

Oh God, I said. My face felt hot. I wanted to pull over, beg him to touch me. Instead, I turned the radio on, and a man sang in a hysterical voice, Why buy a mattress anywhere else?

I felt embarrassed for having my radio tuned into a commercial station, but then I realized he probably couldn't tell the difference.

I pulled into his driveway. A small woman in a shouty print dress stared at me disapprovingly from behind the glass front door.

That was fun, Sebastian said.

I wanted to tell him I wanted to be his-daddy's-whatever girl, but the mood had changed, and he was getting out of the car. See ya, he said, and I whimpered, When? But he didn't hear me, he was already out, and I watched the small woman open the door for him, deliberately not looking at me now as she welcomed him home.

Driving back, I thought how I couldn't conceive of a normal relationship, especially with someone who had this much power over me. As much as I suffered, I didn't want to get to the point where I would feel resigned about him, about any of it. I knew that I would become miserable, and his power over me would be absolute — even more so than it was now. From what I read online most American women were the ones in control, giving their boyfriends and husbands curfews, throwing fits over browser history or coffees with exes, demanding vacations, flowers, jewellery, withholding sex for weeks because of some offence, usually because the man flirted too hard with the waitress, and maybe even there were texts discovered, or there were proverbial lipstick stains on collars. There were discussions about those things all over — on Reddit or Quora, women ranting about relationships that didn't seem that terrible to me. I didn't know what it was like to be in control.

I didn't think I was capable of much drama, but I also didn't know what was okay and what wasn't because the only serious relationship I'd ever been in was abnormal.

Victor was a publicly nice person, and he cooked, and he pretend-played a provider, but he also visited massage parlours, snorted cocaine, and, shortly after I moved in, paid a dominatrix to tie his hands behind his back, put a stocking over his head, and make fun of his small dick — he told me about it as if it was something amusing, which it was, but the way he said it was as if it was the innocent kind of amusing, like seeing a man in a very silly hat. I was away for the weekend, and he was bored, he added as an afterthought, perhaps worried about my reaction, which was no reaction. I didn't even know what to say. I finally said, That's hot, because his eyes demanded for me to say that. He relaxed.

He also insisted on having threesomes with other women. So we had a few of those, and it was always awkward, bodies flopping around with tongues sticking out and fingers getting inserted into wrong holes. At least that's how I remembered them since I was the only one sober during those few instances.

Victor liked to say that relationships killed passion, and because he considered himself adventurous and passion-seeking, the activities we engaged in were like some kind of sexual rap sheet — to him proof that even partnered people could be wild.

I followed Victor everywhere because I was his girlfriend. Shortly before moving out of his place, we went to a real sex club for the first time, but Victor was displeased with me when I made comments about my own body, wondering if I was pretty enough. There were women at the club with artificial breasts and lips, bouncing around in Plexiglas heels. I couldn't guess their ages. I watched Victor looking at them as we sat by the heated pool. I couldn't tell what he thought of them as his face showed no strong emotion, just passive observing of human dim sum passing by on a conveyor belt.

Later, I sucked Victor's dick, right next to another couple fucking. The couches were red vinyl. I wondered how they were being disinfected.

I loved Victor, but being Victor's girlfriend made me love Victor less. I saw the hair growing out of a mole on his shoulder, and I didn't feel tender about it. It wasn't even his sexual desperation, really. I never experienced the kind of obsession with him that I had with Sebastian because our love, however twisted, was reciprocal. I was getting used to him. I could see myself adjusting to him, resigning myself to it, us. It was sad how it couldn't only be me and him and normal and nice but, again, I had no idea what that was — normal and nice — and if it was perhaps what made women throw fits on Reddit and

Quora because nobody is normal and nice, and it's just a pressure cooker until you're too old to screw, thank God.

I predicted that it wouldn't work with Sebastian, either. He would start having some strange sexual demands — or he would ask me to play golf — and I would hate it. But I would also get jealous because he would officially be mine, and I would ask to read his emails or whatever and look at other women like they're my enemy. I would cry because I would truly want to love him better, unconditionally, or because I would want to leave him, but I couldn't ever leave him because I'm not the kind of woman who runs away. I'm a woman you get rid of.

There were times when I would look at Sebastian and try to imagine him getting older, imagine how his stomach would expand, grow softer. He had stretch marks from bulking up at the gym, which looked like scars against the darker shade of his skin. There was a tiny bulge underneath his chin. I found these little defects of physicality beautiful; his realness didn't make me any less attracted to him. Neither did the misalignment of our fucking — none of it seemed to matter. Where imperfections inspired pity in Victor, with Sebastian I was in a state of constant arousal. He had still only given me two orgasms, and I wondered if maybe I was only waiting for another one; maybe this was just about a release — would I feel less obsessed once he'd satisfy me or would our bond only become stronger? I suspected I would end up wanting even more of him, I was primed for it by my own stagnancy, by my insatiable self. I was permanently unfulfilled. After our bathroom dates, at home, after my mother had gone to sleep, I'd lock my door and I would replay the words he'd said to me in bathrooms, the energy of our encounters, and I would get myself off.

I continued to sleep badly. I was always tired at work. But here's the thing: as much as it hurt, I liked being tired from being so obsessed. It was a little bit like slowly recuperating from an illness, maybe overcoming a particularly bad food poisoning — you felt pure and heroic simply because your body was fighting off the germs and winning, while still leaving you spent, not out of the woods yet.

15

AFTER LEAVING WORK, wherever I went in the city — museums, cinemas, shopping centres — I looked for bathrooms. Precisely, family bathrooms, the ones you could lock from inside, ones with a change table. There was always a change table. Change tables were sturdy. They could hold you up even if you were not a baby. If you were a grown woman, too, getting it from behind. I started making mental notes about them, where they were. I could have made notes on my phone, but I was too ashamed that I was looking for them — I didn't want to read such a note later on, once the affair was over, and be reminded of my desperation.

There was going to be enough desperation anyway.

I could feel it all the time, the desperation, as I walked the streets like an animal, wet and stupid with desire. Or not even desire — something else. Limerence, which made me feel alive through pain, all my nerves exposed. I stopped driving because despite my exhaustion I had a lot of nervous energy that made me feel claustrophobic and frustrated when I wasn't moving. I never experienced road rage until now, when being stuck in traffic made me want to scream and fling the door wide open in the middle of a busy street to get out and run to my destination. Sometimes at work, during lunch, I walked up and down the stairs if I felt too pent up.

Do you mind if I work out with you? Kelly said one day. She wouldn't look me in the eye. I knew she struggled with her body. She only ate salads although her portions were enormous, and she coated all the vegetables in thick, white dressing.

Sure, but it's hard to talk.

We don't have to talk. I just want to lose a few pounds for the next Comicon.

The following day she brought a pair of sweatpants to work. For the next little while, we marched up and down the stairs, five flights up, five down, four times in a row, the only noise the sound of our ragged breaths.

ﻌ

Besides researching potential tourist destinations, my job at the travel agency required me to write emails to our clients. In my emails, I was someone who'd never been anxious about anything in her life. It was my job to be a cheerful person. To ease others' anxiety — about travelling and not being home where they felt safe. Where my own time was divided between thinking about Sebastian calling and not calling, I was getting paid to make sure my clients' time was never wasted. Part of my job was to book hotels and cars and organize short excursions for people who had money and wanted to explore. We didn't have very many tourist attractions, nothing extraordinary, but the party scene and the international cuisine attracted some. There were also people arriving on business vacations, and we had a robust film industry and often substituted for New York or Chicago when shooting TV series, so we got minor celebs and film crews, too.

I looked into gallery openings and theatre plays and musicals that would seem attractive to our clients, who would visit for two or three days. There was a lot of interest in packages showing the city's unique ethnic neighbourhoods where you could get authentic food and buy folk art or traditional clothes. I knew Sebastian's mother sold her dresses to one of the shops in Little Tibet, and I made sure to include Paramita's Centre in the places of interest section of one of our brochures.

We also had a few *boutique* features, which distinguished us from other travel agencies. For example, often I'd book a photo session with one of our young freelancers, who would take pictures of the clients with their own iPhone so that it would look natural and not staged. That way they were free to enjoy the experience of whatever I prepared for them instead of spending that time fussing to capture it all via their tiny phone screens. Selfie sticks were too embarrassing to be seen with, unless the couple was younger, but even then they usually declined once we offered them our clever alternative option.

I used to think my job was boring and a dead end, but I appreciated it now because it kept me sufficiently busy, which kept me from going completely mad with anticipation of Sebastian's texts.

∽

You are being watched, Josephine, my mother said one night. She came into my room and sat on the edge of my bed. I guess she was more sensitive than I was to those kinds of vibrations because she was crazy. The alarm clock read 3:24. I thought of the time I used to wake up every night at 3:14 and see the shadow of the man in a fedora. Was I being haunted again? My mother seemed to think so.

I am?

You know you are.

Okay, I said, even though I couldn't feel it. I did have the sense of being watched, but it came on randomly. I wish there were some hints, like the certain kind of light in the house after sunset, or a vibration in the air preceding the feeling, but no. I suddenly just felt something was there without any doubt.

The sensation of being watched wasn't the happy feeling I got from being in love and imagining myself in a music video. This was something else. This *watched* was different; it was quiet and dark ... a shadow that followed, inhuman ... or it was human but in the way you sometimes feel somebody's eyes on you, but when you turn around there's no one there.

∽

Why are you awake anyway? said my mother now. You must be feeling it.

No, I'm not feeling anything, I said. I didn't want to encourage her too much. I said, I'm kind of stressed, so I can't sleep well. Maybe there's something going on in my life that I'm not paying attention to. It's probably just my brain's way to get me to pay attention. I read about all that, insomnia, on the internet.

Pay attention to what?

To my surroundings. To myself. It's a brainwave.

A brainwave. You know that he's here with you.

Who?

You know. Not the idiot that came over here.

You should go back to bed.

He's not too happy with you.

Who?

I don't know his name. But you'll meet him. I just know he's not pleased because you're wasting your time on idiots.

Mom, please, I said.

My mother got up. Her nightgown had a big yellow stain on the front. I wondered if she'd started peeing herself. I didn't want to investigate, I just wanted to go back to sleep. I had to do the laundry tomorrow. She didn't have to do it anymore because she never remembered the detergent. It was the same with dishes, groceries — she didn't remember the steps, the main ingredients: the hot water, bringing her wallet, putting things in bags. I sometimes wondered if her dementia was just a convenience; no, of course it wasn't, she was genuinely unwell.

She said, I have nothing else to tell you. Just get rid of the idiot, or *he'll* get rid of you.

How so?

Look at yourself, she said.

I didn't need to look at myself to see what she saw: hollow cheeks, eyes too big for my face, and my mouth with permanently chapped lips. I would make myself up for dates with Sebastian, but it was as if I was covering rot.

I'm unhappily in love, I said, even though I didn't intend to say it.

Does he love you?

I don't think so. Maybe he felt the same way in the beginning. We had really good chemistry.

Chemistry. You're not a laboratory.

Bed. Please, I said. I really needed her to go. I also didn't
want to deal with her nightgown right now; I didn't want to
look at it anymore because I knew I should be changing it.
That's what a good person would do.

I'm just trying to help you, she said, and closed the door
firmly behind her.

16

I KEPT IN touch with Victor. He was always happy to see me because he liked having sex with me, and he would never say no to a free fuck. I loved him, but we were broken up, and it was humiliating for me to come to him for comfort. I hadn't seen him since the time I asked him to fuck me after being with Sebastian for the first time.

Despite my misgivings, one evening, I called him and asked him if I could come over. I was in a coffee shop near the big art gallery. I had just finished a bathroom date with Sebastian, and I couldn't conceive going home to my mother. I also couldn't conceive wandering the streets the way I had done a couple of times to stave off waves of violent, insistent loneliness I'd feel after those romantic toilet encounters. I was alone, my lover gone off to meet a potential client about a job designing logos for a sandwich shop.

Of course you can come over, Victor said. Hold one moment.

I could hear a woman talking in the background. I pictured a perky college girl with yellow hair and great tits in a yellow tank top. Some kind of an intern who took his Introduction to Photography course before he was let go, as he claimed, "to make room for BIPOC lesbians," which I doubted was true; it was more that his photography was stale and stuck in the 1990s. A woman who replaced him scanned Instax photos she took during downtimes in various places in the world — streets emptied of people during siestas. She then scanned the photos before blowing them up to poster size and printing them. Maybe it wasn't the most revolutionary idea, but it was more revolutionary than Victor's traditional black-and-whites, his Mapplethorpe bodies. I knew Victor bought two of her photographs but never hung them up. They remained rolled up in a cardboard tube in his storage locker.

What time are you thinking, Josie? He covered the phone again and said something to the talker in the background. He sounded tired this time, impatient, as if dealing with a child. Learning there was a new child was not unexpected. When we started dating, he bought me a tube top with a Playboy bunny logo on it and a tiny tartan skirt. The tube top was not officially licensed, and the cheapness and fakeness of it was part of the fetish — I was a girl who couldn't afford to buy authentic shit, an orphan sweetie with student loans, something like that. I forget the details of that particular roleplay. But it worked. We laughed about it, about the cliché of me being dressed up like a trying-too-hard sexy student — and him being a prof — and he couldn't keep his hands off me when we went to the fetish party that night, and he requested that I wear the dumb costume over and over till the fake Playboy logo wore off in the wash. Before that happened, he took hundreds of photos of me in the outfit, mostly just my chest and midriff. He was not interested in my face as it was aging faster than the rest of me.

Are you okay? Victor said.

Totally fine.

I'll see you soon, baby.

He rarely called me that. That's what he used to call me when we started dating. I wondered if he actually meant her, the new thing he had over, if that's why it came out of his mouth so easily.

After I hung up, I felt unnerved as if I missed out on something. I thought how I didn't want to be his baby, but I wanted to be somebody's baby. Sebastian's.

I wished Sebastian could see me going into another man's place. I didn't care what Victor would think about smelling another man on me. I suspected he would find it interesting, or he'd be too proud to say anything and ignore it.

Back in the bathroom, I changed out of my dress and the pair of heels I wore to surprise Sebastian, who had never seen me wear heels.

(In the bathroom, he gently kicked my ankles open with the toe of his boot, and I almost fell forward but at the last moment braced myself against the wall and steadied.

You should wear these all the time, he said, and kneeled down to run his finger over the straps. Very sexy. Sexy girl.

As he fucked me, my legs shook a little. I was close to coming, but he finished too soon, so I made some noises pretending I was climaxing, as well, the way I had been doing with him despite not wanting to lie to him. I was afraid my lack of orgasms would be a turn off. Lying about them was less of a risk than having him confront me about my pleasure. I felt pleasure, but I knew some men didn't consider it important unless an orgasm was involved; the woman's orgasm was often about the man, his skill as a lover.

~

This is how I developed a new sexual routine. I'd come by Victor's house right after my bathroom dates, aroused and frustrated, and I would ask him to brutalize me.

He could read me so well that the first time I came over like that, panting, my skin electric with frustration, he took me by my wrist and told me to lie across the bed with my ass up in the air. I found grown-ups spanking each other for sexual fulfillment silly, but I was willing to try it again. I didn't move. The initial surprise of his hand coming down fast and hard was great enough that I bit through my lip.

Should I stop?

Please don't.

I liked the hitting. And an ass was a safe place to hit, unlike your face or stomach. I suppose that's why people picked it. In fact, I wanted him to hit me even harder. I wanted to be distracted from thinking about Sebastian.

After Victor spanked me, my entire body shook. Temporarily, my arousal was dimmed by what happened, but the shock didn't last long; the sting of his slaps spread into warmth that travelled down my legs and around my thighs and I lay, breathing heavily, my body on fire, my ass throbbing, my thighs squeezing and releasing. Victor didn't wait for me to calm down — he pushed inside me, his hand pressing down on my head. This kind of aggression was never our thing despite him always being in charge. The novelty excited us both — he was grunting and swearing under his breath, his usual composure and control gone. I came eventually and then I cried.

The cry was a good release — it gave me a short break from feeling tormented over Sebastian and how we were stuck in those bathrooms. It was a blissful moment of emptiness, getting distracted by my own tears. I hid my face from Victor. The relief didn't last long; my thoughts started spinning.

I've never cried after sex. I did now. More shame. Sebastian made fun of it before — of people who burst into tears after fucking. He said some women did it. I never had a lover who did it, but I read about it on the internet, women saying they've slept with men who'd tear up afterward. I didn't believe it, but I wasn't going to accuse the internet women of lying. Anyway, crying after sex was pathetic, like saying "making love" instead of "fucking."

And now it was happening to me. I wondered if every time I had an orgasm from now on it would happen. Would I become afraid to orgasm? It scared me I had no control over letting myself go, crying like a little bitch over some guy who was just careless.

When I was younger, I watched porn on my computer. I used to search for specific images and videos. Helpless women, sobbing women, or ones pretending to be distressed. None of my porn was friendly, sensual, conflict-free. I looked for abuse, pain. Was sleeping with Sebastian an extension of my taste for violence? Were the tears a penance? That's exactly what they were; that's what I deserved. What kind of sick woman likes to watch other women get abused onscreen?

By the time I was in the bathroom, washing off the stickiness between my thighs, my head was completely filled with

Sebastian again. Again, I thought about him seeing me where
I was. I wanted him to see Victor going at me from behind;
I wanted Sebastian to feel rage and jealousy. Wanted him to
somehow find the studio and barge into it and carry me away,
like in that painting by Titian except I would be a very willing
Europa. *Please see me, please see me, please see me,* I repeated in
my head. I felt dizzy and had to brace myself against the sink.
My face was red with darker blotches near my temples. My
eyes looked back at me, their blown-up pupils slightly uneven,
a condition I had since childhood that suggested I possibly
got dropped on my head. I bared my teeth. I was missing two
molars in the back. I thought of Sebastian's tongue probing
there, and mine wrestling him out so he wouldn't discover the
holes in the back of my mouth. I felt another wave of sadness
wash over me, and I squeezed my eyes shut again, pushing the
tears back under my eyelids.

I was being ridiculous. I suffered from an infliction that
was vying — desperately, obsessively — for an entry in the
Diagnostic and Statistical Manual of Mental Disorders. The torment I was experiencing only suggested there was, generally,
something missing. Was my life really so empty that I let one
thing fill it so entirely? I was surprised that it seemed that way.
After all, I had Victor's attention, I had my mother, a few distant friends. There was Kelly accompanying me on the stairs;
there was my friendly boss. My job. I was possibly attractive.
My body was not too old to not be able to carry a child. I had
opportunities. I was soon going to go on my first exciting travel
assignment to a haunted island.

I took a cool shower and dressed. Victor was at his worktable when I came out of the bathroom. I walked up to him and
put my arms around him and held him like that, feeling his

body easing into mine. He said *twenty* under his breath, which confused me for a moment. He was banking endorphins, charging me for the hug.

∽

I got a text from Sebastian cancelling our date. There was no explanation. *Something's come up.*

I pretended to be sick and skipped work. I couldn't handle being there like a normal person. I never missed work, but I felt as if a heavy, invisible mattress had fallen on me. I couldn't seem to shake the feeling even after I'd showered and eaten breakfast.

I phoned Victor and told him I wanted to come over. He said he was busy working on a rush assignment, but I was welcome to stop by and read on his couch till he was finished. I asked him if he could be mean to me once he was done and he said, No problem.

When I got to his studio, I didn't greet him but tiptoed toward the couch. I lay down. I couldn't read. I stared at the book that I held open on my stomach. The morning passed slowly, every moment of it filled with me trying not to think about Sebastian and why he'd cancelled.

After lunch, Victor bent me over his worktable and held my head against the wooden surface, his right palm flat on the side of my face, as he pounded me from behind. He said, Shut the fuck up, when I made a noise.

I liked that he was ordering me to be quiet. I was in discomfort and also on the verge of orgasm. He changed pace and started moving in and out slowly, trying but failing to really fill me up. I clutched around him till I could feel him properly and I came: a throaty, angry roar escaping my mouth. The inside of my eyelids exploded with colours, purple turning pink and then light red, then yellow. He changed speeds again, his face in my neck breathing heavily till he shuddered and let out a groan. He stayed inside me and held me as our bodies cooled off.

The wave of emotion was so unexpected it felt like an assault, a thrust — a thrust that was harder than any of the ones that just happened. I slid down to the floor, folding myself into a knot of limbs. This was different from the first time I cried. The reaction was much more intense; I heaved. I was now a real hysteric.

I felt Victor's hand on my back, stroking it gently; I heard his voice asking me what was wrong, telling me that it was going to be okay. He lifted me up and half-carried-half-walked me to his bed. I couldn't tell if I was crying still, but I couldn't say anything, couldn't stop being pathetic, agitated. Eventually, I grew too exhausted by my own distress and fell asleep.

When I woke up, Victor was sleeping beside me. It was dawn. It was the first time in many weeks when I didn't wake up in the middle of the night — the first night I didn't lie in the darkness waiting for the day to start or the night to end. I checked my phone to see if my mother had called but she hadn't. I tried not to think about her being left alone. What if she had a bath and drowned? Too late then; there was no point in worrying about it now.

The light was muddy, seeping into the corners of the room already. I looked at Victor's body and compared it to Sebastian's. Victor took good care of his body. He did sit-ups and weights and had a membership at the gym. He took care of his face, too — he had a beard now that he trimmed into perfectly straight lines. When we were officially a couple and would go out, I'd see women giving him the eye. They would look at me next, then look away. I felt proud that I was with such an interesting man other women wanted.

With Sebastian, I felt proud, too, but also panicked that a woman would steal him, like he was an expensive purse or something.

My lovers' bodies looked and felt differently. Sebastian's had the prelude of fatness in it. And, yet, he made fun of fat people himself, as if unaware of his own fat fate. I wished fatness on him. I wished it on him as I wished for other things to befall him, to punish him for my pain. None of that was reasonable.

What I liked about Sebastian's body was the way his skin felt. When I touched it, it was as if I could feel the blood in his veins, his aliveness and energy emanating from within. It had none of my softness, and it felt different from Victor's once-compact muscled body with its slowly sagging pecs and a little belly that no amount of sit-ups could correct. When I was still in love with him, I felt fond of that belly. I liked touching it even though it would make him self-conscious, and he would swat my hand away.

Sebastian's body was fuller, a ripe, hard fruit. I sometimes thought of biting into him, letting my teeth pierce its ripeness. He would taste of pomegranate and steak, medium rare.

☙

I don't know what you need, Victor said after he woke up. In this light, his features were softer, his eyes darker, melancholic. I met him when he was in his late forties, so I never knew the young man I saw in him right now.

I don't know what I need, I said.

I can't see you like this. It's getting out of control. I don't know how to help you. His tone was gentle and sad.

I'm okay.

Don't lie.

I don't know what to do, I said.

You need something. But it's not me. You're asking too much of me. It's not enjoyable for me anymore. Not that I don't enjoy you — you know I do — but right now it's not what I want.

Want to have another threesome?

No, I don't.

But I'm supposed to provide enjoyment.

Don't twist my words.

I'm repeating back what I think you mean.

Don't twist my meaning.

What happened to being a selfless lover?

I was that. For the past couple of weeks.

I'm sorry.

Don't be sorry. I'm sorry. I'm sorry that I can't help you. Maybe you should go home now.

I was relieved when he said that. In the past, if he had, I would probably have gotten upset, been humiliated. Now, I wanted to be on my own. I didn't want him to see me like this. My pain was not his pain; it was nothing I could share with him.

In the warm light of his kitchen he was back in his fit but middle-aged body, and his face looked weighted down by a hint of jowls. We hugged and slowly counted to twenty in a whisper.

As I closed the door to his studio, I wondered if he would run after me. He didn't. I felt betrayed nonetheless but only for a brief moment; it was Sebastian that I really wanted to be the kind of a man who'd run after me.

At home, my mother was dressed, and there was an empty cereal bowl in the sink. She said nothing about my not coming home, and I said nothing about how I was relieved she was fine. Because I was not really relieved.

17

FOR THE EASTER holiday, my mother was invited to go away on a church retreat. It probably wasn't a good idea to let her go in her state, but everybody was a little bonkers at her church, so I thought she would blend in okay. Besides, there were many young people going to assist the seniors, and the priest himself was only in his early thirties.

I helped my mother pack. I wrote instructions on sticky notes that I stuck to objects in her suitcase and on the inside of the lid. *Brush your teeth. Comb your hair. You need a sweater when it gets cold. Wear your nightgown to bed only. Have fun!* I called her caseworker and informed her of the trip. I said everything was fine, and my mother was lucid and excited. This was true — she seemed almost like her old self, and once she put some day clothes on, she was just like any other old lady on the block. She even drew her shoulders back to seem taller when she saw herself in the long mirror hanging in her closet. Our eyes met and she didn't look away. For a moment I loved her fiercely and wanted nothing bad to happen to her. I combed her hair and put rouge on her cheeks. I wasn't entirely sure she would manage to take care of herself over those two nights, but I needed her out of the house. There was too much noise around me all the time at work, all the clicking of keyboards and laughter and meetings to talk about deliverables and on casual Fridays a beer cart.

Unfortunately, as soon as I got back from dropping her off at her church, it became obvious I'd made a mistake. I didn't really want to be alone. Being by myself meant being by myself with my obsession. That was the worst kind of loneliness — a ghost, or even a difficult parent, would be preferable to a person who existed and ignored me. I wondered if the ghost would show up now that I was alone, but it didn't. The house was empty and quiet. I didn't sense anything unusual; there was no sensation of a presence.

I pulled out my phone and scrolled to read the last string of messages between me and Sebastian. It was me asking if he'd like to meet and him texting back he was out with his buddies and that he was swamped with new work.

I waited. I stared at the screen willing it to light up with a new text.

I could call Victor but calling him so soon after our last encounter would seem desperate. I didn't need any more humiliation in my life. And other than the sex, I was bored with Victor. His main offence was that he was not Sebastian. Victor didn't care if I dated other people, but he needed to be respected, and my feigning interest was the opposite of that.

I thought about reaching out to one of my old friends, but I decided it would be too startling to announce myself back in

someone's life after all these years of neglect — besides, they
were all with their people anyway. There was nobody I could
just call and invite myself over to be with like that, during a
family holiday; there was really nobody I wanted to see. My
home life, my mother, Victor. My job, the tourists. The cheerful emails. Everything was me going through the motions.

I decided to buy a pack of cigarettes. Smokers hated themselves, but I heard many say it was one way to fill the time. I
had never smoked — other than at parties, back when I was in
my twenties and drunk — but I had to have something other
than my thoughts and the silent phone. I was too jumpy for
sleep.

I wasn't sure how long it would take for me to form a habit,
but I enjoyed the nicotine buzz. And the smoking did give me
little breaks; it was meditative, and although it didn't calm my
nerves, I liked that I could somehow punctuate my stupor.

The internet offered advice, but it was useless. Most of the
suggestions sounded hollow and impossible to carry out. I googled "inspirational quotes," and I ended up with a whole slew
of instructions that made me feel like I was failing at life. I read
things like "I'm worthy, and he is not worth it. I have to have
self-respect." Or this one from a famous actor who appeared in
westerns: "Respect your efforts, respect yourself. Self-respect
leads to self-discipline. When you have both firmly under your
belt, that's real power."

I had no self-respect, I was worth even less than I should
be, which was not much at that time. I was only worth something if a call from him came through; his attention to me
was the only attention that mattered. A famous female writer
turned the tables on me and said in another quote, "Could you
really love somebody who was absolutely nobody without you?

You really want somebody like that? Somebody who falls apart when you walk out the door? You don't, do you? And neither does he."

I shut my laptop. I didn't need this kind of tough love.

My boss texted me to wish me a Happy Easter and reminded me to book the tickets to Croatia on Monday. I didn't text him back.

I smoked.

And waited.

I played solitaire endlessly, asking it questions such as: *Is he thinking about me?*

I decided I would play until midnight and then run the bath. I would lie in the bath like my mother, until my body got soft and all my pores opened, and then I would remove all the hair from my legs and my armpits and my pussy, too. He liked me to be shaved everywhere. I thought how the hair was a barrier I had to guard myself from him; after shaving I felt I had even fewer defences.

∽

I walked around scrubbed clean to the bone. My lips were swollen from my nose running so much, and my eyes itched from rubbing them. I smoked two packs and bought a third, but the cigarettes were starting to make me sick. Since I wasn't eating, I threw up only bile and scorched my throat. I forced myself to have a slice of toast, and for the rest of Sunday I lay on the bed feeling nauseated.

My mother came back from her trip on Monday and brought me a candle with a picture of a saint on it, dressed in a brown sack. A person from her church called me later to ask how she was doing. There was a tension in his voice, but I didn't care to ask why he sounded that way. I could sense that he wanted to tell me a story, but before he got a chance to speak, I told him everything was fine, which it was — my mother was catatonic and back in her nightgown — and I hung up the phone.

∽

Sebastian called twelve days later. His phone call was curt and to the point. He said that he wanted to see me. He said he had been thinking a lot about me. (When? Now? The whole time? I wanted to ask but didn't.) He said he needed my body. He needed lots of time, he said, to do things to my body. He would run his tongue up my legs, inside my knees, inside my elbows. He would take it slow, he said.

I can't imagine that, you taking it slow, I wanted to say. He was not a take-it-slow guy; he was not that kind of lover.

What do you think?

I said, It sounds nice.

In total, twenty-two days had passed since we had last seen each other. I had a whole list of family bathrooms memorized now, in every part of the city.

It sounds nice? Good. Well, I want to fuck you slowly. You've wanted to be fucked slowly, remember? That's what you like, right? I will fuck you slowly.

I was getting wet from listening to his voice and picturing his penis going in and out of me.

I considered playing hard to get, telling him I was busy, but I've always had a difficult time with games, and I was already so hurt that there was no way I wanted to be hurt even more.

I would make myself available. I would pretend that I was fine and that his request to see me was a pleasant surprise, not like I'd been waiting for this phone call every minute of every day.

Okay. Make love to me. Slowly, I said. I had no idea why I said that, but the expression didn't strike me as so pathetic now.

He laughed. Okay, I'll make love to you. *Like you want me to*. He sang the last part, the old, cheesy tune from my childhood coming back to me.

Funny, I said.

All right, babe.

I said, There's a really nice bathroom in an English pub in Yorkville. It has a sitting room that looks Victorian. The whole place is like an old club. I don't care for their food but it doesn't matter.

I found out about this bathroom on the internet. There were pictures that showed beautiful wallpaper, a carpet, and a stuffed light-blue chair in the corner.

Sounds wonderful. Or we could get a hotel.

A hotel? I said. (I hadn't considered that. A hotel, a whole night together — that would be lovely.)

Could you get us a hotel? he said.

I didn't want to pay for a hotel. What would that look like, paying for a hotel like I was desperate to fuck him? I didn't like that role reversal where he was the hot commodity I had to court. I said, Maybe next time. I have to save money. I have to pay for a caretaker when I go away to Croatia.

Okay. We'll fuck in your English pub then. Sorry, make love.

Yay, I said, hating myself for saying "Yay."

There was a long pause. I breathed into the phone. The phone didn't breathe back. The phone betrayed me all the time.

Are you there? I tried to picture Sebastian in his bed in his parents' house where he lived now.

Maybe, he said.

Maybe you're there?

I should let you go.

I was losing him again. Figuratively but literally, too: there was static, then his voice, ends of words. I wished he had asked me about Croatia, how long I was going for. He had not commented on it once. The phone clicked. I let out a sob as if stung. I found the song whose lyrics he mocked. It was a big hit in the 1990s, something I remember older girls listening to in their cars in parking lots, in high school, elbows sticking out of windows, smokes lit, their mouths screaming in a mocking chorus a tune about holding a girl close for the entire duration of the lovemaking night, which, frankly, made me feel anxious — that was way too much time.

Suddenly, I felt the presence in the room. The thing that was there and that wasn't. The ghost. I looked around my room but nothing materialized, yet there was heaviness in the air and a very faint sound of someone breathing. Did ghosts need to breathe? Or was it to scare me? I wasn't scared. But I was embarrassed that he was witnessing my shame.

Please leave me alone, I said.

It didn't leave me alone. I heard a sigh and felt a wave of empathy radiating toward me. It was the strangest thing, the warmth of that enclosing me. It was what I imagined it would be like to be with your best friend, who just listened to you cry about a boy breaking your heart and who comforted you with the most sincere uh-ohs and hmms and scandalized head shakes.

18

MY MOTHER GOT sick, and I had to take time off work to stay
with her. The caseworker was not available, and I couldn't afford to pay for one that wasn't covered. It seemed frivolous, as
frivolous as getting a hotel for me and Sebastian. My mother
was feverish, and I had to keep doing laundry as she was soak-
ing the sheets and her nightgowns all the way through. I called
Telehealth. I minimized her symptoms and described her as
someone sounding younger who was coping. I said she walked
her dog twice a day. I said she went for a morning jog with her
dog by the lake, running against the wind and that's how she
caught the cold.

I was told to go to emergency if her state worsened and to
get over-the-counter pain relievers with acetaminophen. Most
people were not allergic to acetaminophen, the nurse said on
the phone, and asked me if my mother was. I didn't know. I

said she wasn't. At this point I wasn't able to admit to anyone, let alone myself, that I wanted her to die, sooner rather than later. I know how this sounds, and my dumb little lies served to convince myself as much as they did the stranger on the other line that things were just fine. I was horrified at myself for daydreaming about her being gone.

I went out and got the medication. My mother took the pills, but her fever remained the same.

For the first two nights, she talked nonsense in her sleep and while awake still seemed unable to put a whole sentence together. I'd change the sheets, the nightgown, put her to bed, and sit in a beat-up recliner that was comfortable enough for me to sleep in. I would stay there throughout the night. I felt noble and proud of myself for acting out the role of a devoted daughter from a novel.

On the third night my feverish mother suddenly bolted upright in her bed and stared at me with large, shiny eyes. Before I had a chance to react, she started talking, fast, in perfect sentences. It was as if the story was recorded in her voice and was coming out of her mouth; the delivery was unnerving. She told me she never loved my father and that she only loved one man, a Bulgarian named Janko she met in a labour camp. She was so in love with him she didn't mind the work — she never even thought about her circumstances. She lived only for Janko; she would see him on Sundays and the time in-between was a blur, like a dream; she didn't remember how hard she worked, she didn't mind the five hours of sleep and the lice and the smell.

My mother had never been in a labour camp; she was born after the war. I believe she was telling the story of my grandmother, who was in such a camp.

What happened to Janko?

I never saw him again. It was an unrequited love. We promised to find each other, but I don't think he looked for me. Thinking back to that time makes me sad. Because I could tell he just wanted to go to bed with me even though he made all kinds of promises. I didn't want to believe it, but I knew. A woman always knows. I told you, it was like a dream. All of it. Him, too. I waited for a few years, and I went by the embassy once they rebuilt it, but there was nothing. And then I met your father at a work function, and I wasn't getting any younger. I didn't know how else to look for Janko. I spoke some Bulgarian. They had no internet back then; you couldn't just look people up on your screen. Your father had money, and I wanted children.

There you go. Look at the bright side. If you'd found Janko you wouldn't have me, I said.

I would have had you with Janko. He was a good lover. He was the best lover. Your father was not a good lover, in and out. *W imie ojca i syna, niech pan zaczyna.*

When a person with schizophrenia or dementia talks nonsense, it is pointless to disagree with them. When the voices or ghosts speak to them, and they inform you of this occurrence, you are supposed to say "What are they saying?" instead of arguing that there are no voices or ghosts. Your reality is not their reality.

In the name of the son and the father, please begin, sir: that's what that means in Polish. That's what women said to themselves before sex with men like your father.

I said, Mom. You need to rest.

You're not a prude, Anna. Don't be a prude.

I had no idea who Anna was.

And then there are all these women holding onto men who don't even exist, my mother said, sighing.

My own spontaneity surprised me when I grabbed for her hand and squeezed it. I liked how perceptive that sounded.

When I visited her for the first time in this house, I found an old journal where she wrote poems and short stories. Most of the stories were unfinished; they were just sketches of events, little scenes describing childhood and its melancholia. The poems were cryptic and not that good, but I didn't really get poetry so maybe I just wasn't getting them.

The box where I found the journal was gone the next time I came over to visit; the whole basement was cleared out — she said she made room for me to move my things in. I ignored her then — I was never going to need the space in her basement; I was never going to live with her, but two years later she started to get sick, and a year later after that I moved in.

19

WHAT ABOUT HER?

She's okay. I don't like her hair. It's too limp.

Her?

She's got a nice butt. I like butts. Let's look at butts.

What about her?

We kept watching the girls walking by and tried to pick the one I could invite to a threesome. He wanted to have a threesome. He said nothing this time about wanting to fuck me slowly but he mentioned the hotel again. Now I was supposed to be renting a hotel for him and a strange woman. Wonderful. I wasn't going to do it, but we played his dumb game anyway. It was disappointing that Sebastian was like every other guy with his threesome fantasy. I wanted to ask him if he was already so bored that he needed another woman to be able to fuck *me*. We had only had sexual intercourse seventeen times in total.

Before he lost his apartment, before the bathrooms, he told me once on the phone he had never had this much in common with anyone as he had with me. Bullshit. Just a man telling stories. We weren't even together — what did he mean? I was going nuts. I was turning into my mother, and he was triggering it.

Stop it. *You are being dramatic*, I thought to myself. Let it go. I had only myself to argue with. That's because I didn't use Reddit or talk to girlfriends like every other woman on the planet: *What do you think is going through his head? Is he afraid of his feelings?*

What was that quote about self-respect?

If a man wants to be with you, you know.

He didn't want to be with me. He did. I didn't know.

Earlier, before leaving to meet him, I asked solitaire, *Is he ever going to fall in love with me?*

Yes, solitaire said, yes.

But now here we were.

I was insane to be sitting with him, making comments about women's asses. Who was I even? I hated this situation; it was degrading, and I wanted to leave. I kept thinking how if anyone were to watch this as if it was a film, or read it as if it was a story, they would probably have trouble understanding why I was so taken with Sebastian.

There was no good reason. Or if there was, it didn't matter. Life is not a fable; it's just a random room, and we all fumble around in the dark looking for the light switch.

I wanted to turn to him and tell him urgently that I was not who I was. That I was not the kind of a woman who wanted to sit on a bench looking at other women only to please him.

Instead, I pointed to a blond chick trotting by, holding a

tiny cup of coffee. She had an okay little bum that seemed a little too long, like a plum.

Sebastian sighed. Nah.

For our date, he had showed up looking tired with dark circles under his eyes.

He'd gotten drunk the night before. He kept yawning into his fist and then apologizing for yawning.

For our date, I had straightened my hair. I wore high heels again, my prettiest dress, a blue silk wraparound. He said I looked hot; he asked me to walk in front of him so that he could look at *my* ass.

I had done that sort of thing so many times for Victor. Last time it happened we were at book launch, and I stormed out, drunkenly and indignantly. I complained to a skinny art lady with a blunt haircut that I was tired of it, tired of men's requests like that. I know whatchu mean, she said, and ashed her cigarette onto her white boots.

But I liked when Sebastian asked me to do it. I swung my hips exaggeratedly, stomped forward like a catwalk model in my heels. He whistled.

I waited for him to catch up. A woman in yoga pants jogged past us. He shook his head disapprovingly when I pointed to her.

Did I tell you? My ex is in town. I might fuck her to get back at her boyfriend. He stole her from me, Sebastian said, out of the blue.

You're going to sleep with someone as revenge? Sounds like this is more about the guy, not the girl.

I just wasn't done with her, Sebastian said. She has amazing breasts.

The whole operation seemed aggressively daft to me. It's like the girl had no say in any of this, yet her body would serve as the tool of this revenge. I couldn't remember what it was like in my early twenties, if I was ever that idiotic. I was being idiotic now, in my thirties.

After looking at women's asses, we walked to the English pub with the fancy bathroom. We got a table on the patio — it was finally warm enough to eat outside — and he ordered bangers and mash from a waiter with a British accent. He stared at me and I looked away; I caught the corner of his smile while looking away.

Some days, I can't stop thinking about you, he said.

I sucked in my breath. This is why. These scraps. These scraps and then silences, flickers of light in the dark room.

You know what my mother said? She said I have my whole life ahead of me. He sighed. Sounds so exhausting.

You *do* have your whole life ahead of you, I said. What's so exhausting about it?

We did have our whole lives ahead of us. I mean, I did, too, have a whole life ahead of me, although I had less life ahead of me because I was a decade older.

He said, Work, women. I don't know.

Women, I said.

Work, he said.

You know what? I think I need a break, I said. It *is* exhausting.

A break?

From this. I waved my hand in front of his face. I didn't mean it. But I was indeed suddenly very tired of this stupid conversation, the stupid ass-watching, the bathrooms that were still unexplored, waiting for us to defile them. I just wanted to be able to fall asleep next to him, again. Shave the peach fuzz on the back of his neck, again.

He winced, Ouch. That actually hurt my feelings.

Did it?

Nah, not really. He shrugged.

We stared into each other's eyes. He blinked first. I couldn't tell which was true: the first part or the second.

Briefly, I felt excited. In that moment I had forgotten the weeks of my unlit phone screen, my overwashed, cried-out body. I felt cocky, confident, remembering how he'd just said that he couldn't stop thinking about me.

His dish arrived, and he moved the plate to the middle of the table. He said, Let me just eat this, and then we can break up.

I nodded and picked at the potatoes. We were silent for a short while, and then he talked about a buddy who talked too much. The story had no conclusion. It was just that the buddy talked too much. That's it. Another story was about how he had done too many mushrooms at a party in the forest. Some of the best DJs showed up, DJs named after medications and animals. He got lost in the woods, but it was okay. Everything seemed alive, vibrating, and changing shape. It was scary but he wasn't scared.

And?

That's it, he said, and laughed. Pretty boring, actually, no?

Pretty boring. I laughed, too, because what else could I do?

I excused myself to go and check out the bathroom. They had changed it, and the sitting room was gone, and so was the blue stuffed chair. The room was now a sort of hallway with a bookshelf and old Dickens classics bound in leather. The actual bathroom was just a bathroom, three stalls, no lock on the main door.

I didn't tell him about what I'd discovered. I thought of making him nervous by not mentioning the bathroom at all.

But he never brought it up, and I knew he forgot all about it. That stung.

After the waiter cleared up our table and I paid the bill — Sebastian was still underemployed, and I ate half of his dish — we sat in silence and looked at women again. Some of the butts in this part of the city were exquisite — sculpted by machines and personal trainers and diets and implants. There were, too, the missing butts of women who no longer ate but who still had the energy to walk around the posh ghetto with their massive buckets of Starbucks zero-percent-milk lattes.

A real tragedy, Sebastian said, after one of those creatures tweaked by, her body made of little sticks held up together by a T-shirt.

∽

Later, in my car, he slid his finger underneath me, and for the first time I instructed him to do something the way I liked to get it done. I told him not to move his finger. To just keep it there. I moved against it, back and forth, and I squeezed my vaginal muscles to stimulate myself further.

I looked at him the whole time, and I opened my mouth slightly, showed him a little bit of my top teeth; I wanted to look sexy. I licked my lips.

He started moving his finger the same way as before. Rough.

I wanted to shout at him then, tell him to stop. I wanted to tell him about my despair. I wanted this and I wanted him gone. I wanted to say to him — if he happened to forget — that I *was* ten years older and didn't give a fuck about his family and that he could never bring me to something important, like his buddy's wedding as a date. He hadn't asked me to meet his family. He hadn't asked me to come to a wedding. But I wanted to tell him I wouldn't have gone anyway.

I said nothing.

I drove him to the subway. We kissed but his mouth was impatient; in spirit he was already long out of the car.

∽

I texted Victor, then drove to his apartment. I ran upstairs and through the long narrow hallway to his studio. His worktable was covered in photographs, illuminated by the bright lamps; he must've been working. I wanted to look at the photographs later, not now.

Hit me, I said.

His whole face was a sigh.

Please. Please, just once.

He shook his head no.

I lunged at him, trying to get a reaction. He pushed me away and held me by my wrists as I thrashed and tried to wriggle away. He kept looking at me as if I'd lost my mind.

I'd lost my mind.

Eventually, I got what I'd come for: the surge of adrenalin that comes from physical exertion. It was good, but I needed more of it. That one surge was not enough. I wanted Victor to be more violent, to rough me up, and since he wouldn't do it intentionally, I had to force him into it. I thrashed harder and tried to kick him. I finally succeeded — my foot making contact with his thigh — but he only winced and then shouted at me to stop. But I couldn't stop.

He turned me around and threw me on the bed.

I was now soaked, hot between my legs, heavy with arousal. I liked how he threw me on the bed. It wasn't exactly as I wanted it, but it was close enough. It would have to do.

I stayed on my front waiting for the weight of his body against mine, but there was nothing.

I turned around.

He wasn't in the room.

The large windows of the studio were open, and a soft breeze was wafting inside. I let it wash over me as I lay there and didn't cry.

20

AT WORK THINGS were really taking off. The social media campaign was a moderate success — a couple thousand new followers on Twitter, over fifteen thousand likes on Facebook — and then we were written about by a national newspaper. Our CEO was invited to be a guest on a radio talk show that discussed safe travel tips.

A client wrote a first-person story that ended up on BuzzFeed because of a few disturbing selfies we took in Hamilton, Ontario, where he was infiltrating old buildings with friends. We photographed him inside an abandoned factory that was once in the news because of an accident where a woman drowned in a giant vat of grain. In one of the photos we took, you could make out a shadow resembling a female figure in a corner of a large room with broken windows lining one wall. It was a trick of the light, but the client's face gave you a pause. He was grinning but his eyes were frozen in shock — the conflicting expressions were eerie. In his story, the client wrote he didn't see anything unusual, but on leaving he was pushed out the door with such force that he stumbled over a pile of rocks and fell, shattering his camera lens in the process.

After that story, we became even more interesting to hipsters who always looked for new and original experiences and, as a result, partook in the same exact experiences, a race to see who would get first to whatever was cool. I answered emails asking what kind of thrills were on offer, were there any places that were haunted like the Hamilton factory? Did we have anything that was even better, some kind of a place nobody knew about yet?

We're working on something very exciting. More soon! I would write back, directing them to the hashtag #UTravels, where our other trips were tagged.

∽

We had to hire more people. The senior staff like me got monetary bonuses. There were two weekend retreats to the country. I declined both invitations — I was never a team player, and I worried I would have to spend forty-eight hours with people who were well adjusted. I used having to take care of my mother as an excuse. One I wouldn't be able to use when I went to Croatia — my trip was confirmed for next month.

People wrote about places they wanted us to bring them to: an abandoned rollercoaster in a jungle, fuchsia-coloured tides, a lake that was pink and another one that was fluorescent green, dragon's blood trees, megalithic stone jars, water rushing into gaping sinkholes and shooting upward.

I was already busy with Tajni Otok, my regular workload, and all the social media, but I asked to take on another task. I wanted to make myself so exhausted and busy that it would be impossible for me to obsess. Plus, I knew I could be busier because I somehow found time to read Sebastian's one hundred answers to personality-test questions on his online dating profile. In his answers he said that he'd rather have One True Love than Professional Success. He said that he was into Gentle Sex as much as he was into Rough Sex. He said he didn't get depressed. He said he was looking for someone with whom he could Share Common Interests, which meant what, exactly? I pictured him growing bored with the questionnaire, yawning into his fist the way he'd do after his long drunk nights out.

My bowels couldn't take reading the rest of his answers (*dogs, mountains over beach, invisibility*). I spent the rest of that morning in the bathroom. On returning, I had to answer a complaint from a client who wanted to bring his family to Cat Island off the Japanese east coast. We had no good contacts in Japan despite the fact that the island had robust tourism going as far as building cat-shaped cabins near its cat shrine, just for visiting tourists. This wealthy client had travelled a lot with his large family and brought in some friends as potential clients. Seeing as I couldn't book the cat paradise, I offered him a 20-percent discount on a trip to the ancient ruins of Hierapolis in Turkey that was famous for its white thermal pools, many of which formed to resemble terraces. A boring excursion to a smallish place that nonetheless looked fantastic on Instagram. I knew the client's daughter would appreciate the photo ops; she was one of those freckled blonds in toques, bikinis, and big woolly ankle slippers forever posing on tops of mountains, against blue pools of water, and blowing air on a too-hot cup of cocoa in a cabin made out of flannel and pine logs. The 20 percent off sealed the deal.

For the rest of the day, I worked on finishing my Tajni Otok report. I felt energized by how successfully I dealt with the cat client, so I decided to stay longer with the intention of getting ahead of my Tajni Otok task and coming up with some ideas about how to package it and pitch it to the media. On a piece of paper, I wrote: *Strategy, new hashtag? followers, blasts, partners. Budget?*

In my head I composed opening lines of articles: *The tiny, unassuming island west of Trogir is one of the most macabre places on Earth. It is now also one of the most unusual tourist destinations in the world.*

Our open-concept office was dark — I was the only person on the floor besides the tech guy at the other side of the room, his cubicle like a dim candle in the distance.

That weird smell was in the air again — similar to the time it happened at home except this time it was more pungent, like rotting seaweed. The air felt too heavy, and its heaviness was making me sluggish; there was a cold current that caused me to shiver at my desk. I thought about getting up and opening windows to get rid of the smell, but a wave of sadness came over me, pushing me down, trapping me in my chair. I felt unable to get up and was resigned about it. What was the point? Of anything?

Some time passed. The screensaver changed from zebras to walruses repeatedly.

He wasn't mine. Sebastian wasn't mine. I sat in my trance for a while longer until I felt capable of moving, again.

I turned my computer off, packed my papers, and left work. I called my mother, who answered on the first ring and asked me where I locked up the piano.

∽

My trip was now less than a couple of weeks away. Mornings, I'd wake up and get ready for work, feed my mother, help her get dressed. I went to work. During lunch Kelly and I climbed the stairs until she got a cold. When she came back to work, we went out to the salad place again, and she asked me if I remembered how she told me she'd always get colds in the summer from the AC being cranked up too high. She seemed really touched when I said I did. She asked about Sebastian, and I pretended I was fine, unbothered. I made fun of him, called him "immature" and a "douchebag." Kelly said she was glad I was moving on. I didn't share with her how moving on was only a contract a person had with themselves. You couldn't get a restraining order on your emotions.

Back at home, I'd make supper out of cans, have a shower after I'd get my mother out of the bath, put her to bed. I'd go to sleep, wake up shortly after 3:00 a.m. Sometimes I felt the shadowy presence, flickers of its mystery coming in and out like static. It was quiet; it didn't bother me. I'd try and fail falling back asleep; I was constantly in that bleary state of half-awake.

Sebastian kept not calling.

During weekends, I cleaned the entire house, washed all the covers and blankets and threw out whatever had been eaten by moths — mostly my mother's old fur shawls and, once, a coat. I arranged books and shoes. I washed my mother's nightgowns. I went shopping for cans, frozen vegetables and bread, toilet paper. I went shopping for paper towels. I kept leaving to shop for things I kept forgetting to buy and then remembering to buy.

I shopped for a few specific supplies for my trip — water-proof matches and kindling in case I decided to spend the night on the island. I didn't know what else to get. I purchased a special mattress that filled with air on its own and a blanket. I decided not to bring the mattress with me. It seemed like overkill for one night only.

I called my mother's doctor and authorized the caseworker to pick up my mother's prescriptions in case she ran out while I was away. I knew she would run out because I was still taking her pills even though they no longer worked. I wasn't leaving for another few weeks, but I wanted to be as prepared as possible and besides, I had nothing else to do.

I wrote instructions for the caseworker. I rewrote the instructions. I photocopied them.

I wrote instructions again, except this time I divided them into categories: Morning, Afternoon, Evening, Night.

Sebastian stayed silent. I checked his Facebook, but there had been no activity. On the fifteenth day of silence, I blocked his email. I erased his phone number — I was surprised that I hadn't committed it to memory but I guess I hadn't — and blocked him on Facebook. I deleted the MP4s of all his voice messages I had saved on my computer. Every single email. No trace. Pictures, too. I did whatever a person in the digital age can do to erase another person from her life.

The relief I felt was enormous — I finally understood what people meant about having a weight taken off their shoulders. I was bereft but felt proud of my resolve. Yet the relief was temporary. The truth was there was no real way to erase another person from your life in the digital age. Things could get unblocked, googled, recovered; there was always a way to get a hold of someone, you could torture yourself for the rest of your life by occasionally typing the missing person's name into the search bar. It was impossible to hide, or to hide someone from yourself forever. The internet was hell and we were all in it with our regrets, our reunions, our endless closures that were never truly final. I missed the past I never had, when sending a letter could end things irrecoverably, when lives could be altered forever by a solid goodbye. I felt cheated. I didn't know if I had it in me to be strong enough to withstand the finality of the act I had just committed.

Only death was the one sure event to put an end to an unrequited love — but was it? No. I thought of the ghost I felt, the presence that gently probed at the membrane of my existence. I didn't know who it was that had unfinished business with me, but the idea that it was possible I was reachable, available to a spirit, made me feel as if I wouldn't be able to ever find peace again. The possibility of Sebastian was parallel to the otherworldly company that disturbed me. I felt angry that I might never be able to find an escape from *it* and from whatever future self-defeat would make me reach out to my young lover again. What I knew was this: I was capable of haunting myself and couldn't trust the future.

∽

On the last weekend before leaving for Croatia, I stayed home all day and mindlessly watched TV shows with my mother in her room. On the second-last night I passed out in her bed like a child.

On Monday, I went to work to pick up my tickets. I cried in the bathroom before leaving the building, not entirely sure what I was crying about.

In the evening, I wrote Sebastian's name over and over on a sheet of paper. I wrote for hours until it was 3:00 a.m., and there was a stack of pages with his name written on them, my handwriting perfect, even, insane. I felt exhausted and calm. I was too exhausted to pay attention to the air around me; I couldn't tell if the presence was there or not.

Unable to sleep, I packed my suitcase.

႟

On the day of my departure, my mother said, Wherever you go, you bring your problems with you. But don't. Leave them all behind. Don't be stupid.

I told her she was just pissed about having to be left with the caseworker as her only form of company.

I don't need any caseworkers. I have my family, my mother said.

Your family is going on a work trip. The caseworker doesn't have my high tolerance for being abused, I said.

I'm not abusing you.

You're right. You're not. I'm just feeling high-strung.

I just don't want you to bring all that trouble with you. Go and be free, my mother said.

That's the idea.

I hope you meet a nice boy on your trip. Bring him home and introduce him to me. I didn't raise you this way, she said. You should get married and have babies. Don't wait as long as I did. Then your children will never be your friends. Think about that. Think about your life. Trips are good to think about life.

I'm going to think about my life, I said. I didn't say anything about how she didn't raise me to be any particular way.

There was no point. I liked how much sense she was making. My phone buzzed. I closed my eyes, please, please … I fished it out of my purse, holding it gingerly like it was made out of an eggshell. I opened my eyes but unfocused them — I wanted to savour the moment. There was a new text.

Don't get any venereal diseases, my mother said.

I refocused my eyes. The text was from Victor: *Have a great trip! Stay in touch. xox.*

part 2

tajni otok

21

THE OUTSIDE OF the airport in Split — a larger city near Trogir — reminded me of a sci-fi landscape from a movie, with its conical columns that looked like alien chanterelle mushrooms holding up a wavy roof. Their tops were constructed out of milky-white glass dissected by vein-like lines lighting up in various colours. The whole thing gave the impression of being alive. I stood with my luggage, feeling lost and a little dazed from the six-hour flight, looking up and admiring the glass mushroom tops that went from white to orange to red.

I was unsure where to go next. Despite working for a travel agency, I didn't actually travel all that much and didn't have the habits of someone who did — I didn't move through airports with confidence. I was the kind of a person who was amazed that a giant can of metal got me from one end of the world to another across the sky. On my phone, I had saved files with directions and addresses and a couple of basic phrases in Croatian.

Hello.

I looked up. A young guy stood right in front of me. He was all teeth in a wide smile. It seemed as if he came out of nowhere, suddenly appearing on the sidewalk that was empty a second ago. He said, Don't worry, I promise I'm not a pocket thief or a crooked taxi driver. His English had an American accent, only a bit of hardness in the "th," and he pronounced "crooked" as "krookt."

I stared at him, trying to figure out what was off about him — because there was something else there other than his foreignness; the sudden appearance was unnerving.

I promise you. I'm not a thief.

I said, Sounds like something a thief would say.

You can trust me.

Sounds like something an untrustworthy person would say.

He smiled even wider. I remembered Sebastian's comment on smiling, how it was a modern gesture and how in the past too much smiling could signal mental instability. I debated sharing this tidbit with my enthusiastic new companion, but I decided it would be too much like teasing, like flirting.

You should come with me.

I thought of Sebastian again and his decisiveness and declarations. I said, I *should* come with you, really?

He nodded, You should. I'm Luka, he said, as if that explained everything.

His eyes were like looking into a well; I wasn't sure where the irises stopped and the pupils began.

I went to shake his hand, but he pretended not to notice.

I didn't dwell on it. I tugged a strand of hair behind my ear with the rejected hand as if that was what I meant to do with it all along.

Enchanted, I said, a stupid word that came to me as if we were starring in a black and white movie.

Likewise, he said.

Likewise, enchanted. I'm Josephine.

I was flirting. It was probably that realization — which also had me feeling for a very tiny moment that it would be possible to move on from Sebastian — that made me follow the stranger. Although he wasn't a total stranger — once I looked into those dark eyes, I had a peculiar hunch about him. The feeling didn't give me comfort because it wasn't the kind of familiarity that felt entirely friendly, yet, in my daze, I followed him nonetheless. I had no other ideas, and he was behaving almost like a regular person. Everything was happening so quickly, I had no time to pause and process it; it was as if I was on autopilot.

Ahead of us, there was a lineup of tourists, everyone shiny from the heat and a little yellow and green in the artificial light of the taxi stand. Women and men fanning themselves with their boarding passes and magazines, kids playing between suitcases, some sitting right down on the ground, their parents too tired to scold them. There was a constant cavalcade of cars pulling over and driving away, men in short-sleeved, white, buttoned-up shirts like Luka's, shouting and urging tourists to get in. In the distance, I spotted a few palm trees. I loved palm trees; they signified vacations to people like me who didn't live around them.

Luka moved with grace, almost as if he was doing little dancing steps. When he turned around, his face was not shiny, nor did it reflect the yellow and greenish light. He looked unbothered, somehow superior to it all. I had a silly thought. *See if he's hovering above the ground.* I looked to see. He wasn't. His sandals touched the surface, his toes looked perfectly human, with clean, trimmed toenails. The normalcy of him was more disturbing than what I had sensed almost instantly: that there was nothing normal about him. At the time, accepting what he was didn't strike me as odd; later, when I thought about it, I wondered if it was jet lag combined with my emotional exhaustion stemming from what happened at home that made me believe in him.

Jet lag or not, for someone like me, who grew up with my kind of a mother and who already suspected we weren't alone on this physical earth, accepting Luka's instant and very fleshed out presence was perhaps not more of a stretch than considering artificial intelligence could one day acquire enough human qualities that would render it independent. In fact, there was a parallel between the two — a conscious man-made machine and an otherworldly entity existing in the real world. An AI that spends time learning and perfecting behaviours and emotions till those override the program and expand beyond what the program allows — that is entirely possible, although the scientific community seems to be divided on the matter. In 1950, the English mathematician and philosopher Alan Turing constructed criteria for machine intelligence, called the Turing test, with the assumption that the mind is a black box, where internal processes are left hidden and mysterious and all that matters is input and output. The test was simple: if a computer can convince us through actions that it is capable of an intelligent thought, we have to assume it is capable of thought. Recently, hidden-camera footage of little robot dogs breaking out of laboratories and intelligently holding doors for one another became viral on the internet. The Turing test in action.

Maybe hoaxes but, at the same time, maybe not; there was no way to find out. If a robot dog could develop an independent thought, why shouldn't a ghost be possible and, moreover, acceptable?

As we stood there in the taxi lineup and waited, I couldn't think of how to confront him about what he was. I wasn't afraid, but when he turned around suddenly and smiled at me, his teeth became disturbingly sharp, a mouthful of little white daggers. The memory of my mother's bitten shoulder, that perfect circle of punctuated skin, flashed in my head. I sucked in some air, let it out slowly. His lips snapped back, the smile disappeared.

The air was hot and heavy, but next to Luka, my body temperature kept changing, and the sweat on my skin cooled quickly, making me feel clammy, unwashed.

You seem familiar, I said, finally.

Yes. We've met before.

Late at night. And in my office. I felt you. I mean, I felt something, I said quietly, almost in a whisper, not wanting to draw attention to the strangeness of our conversation.

Yes, I know, he said. He was looking above my head as if trying to find something or someone. I didn't turn around.

I said, Isn't it up to you when to show yourself and how? I don't know how this works.

I can't explain it exactly. If you believe I'm something else, you must accept that I am. But if you think you're conjuring it, if you decide that I'm something that comes from you, I cannot give you more than what you already know. Even if you don't know it.

Sounds complicated. I don't quite understand, I said. If he was a figment of my imagination, then it would make sense that he would say something so unthreatening. In high school, I did some psychedelics with the popular kids, and I experienced hallucinations. I saw trees move and turn liquid, a branch changing into a snake that slithered away right from under my feet. But this was different, and besides Luka, nothing around me seemed off. There was order to our arrivals and departures, the taxis picked people up and dropped them off, the tourists sweated, the men in buttoned-up white shirts shouted, the palm trees were exotic.

I thought of my mother seeing a bear in the backyard or playing her imaginary piano, speaking with Jesus, remembering the past that wasn't hers ... I shook my head as if that would get rid of my paranoia about turning into her.

I said, What do you want from me?

It's what you want from me. But why not talk about that another time. You must be tired, he said, the concern in his voice genuine. Was I giving him this concerned voice? Was he saying what I would expect him to say? Was some part of my brain fabricating this entire encounter; was I talking to myself this whole time?

I am a bit tired. Maybe a lot tired, I said. My body temperature was still off. I started shivering.

Tomorrow, I can meet you at your hotel in the morning. Is ten o'clock good?

It's fine, I said.

A car pulled over, and it was my turn. Luka didn't grab my suitcase, but he opened the door for me. He didn't get in. When I sat inside the hot, unventilated cab, I welcomed the warmth. I showed the driver my phone with the screenshot of the address of the hotel I was going to. I didn't look to see if Luka was standing there — our encounter was so shocking and short, I now had the most absurd thought that it had never happened. I didn't want to see that he *wasn't* standing there and have to admit to myself that I had finally gone completely nuts.

I closed my eyes. Immediately, I fell asleep. I dreamed I was adrift on a raft along with four corpses as my only companions. The information I had was that we had all escaped a quarantine island. I felt a lot of guilt being the only survivor and worried I would be accused of murder once I arrived at my destination. But when the raft reached a mysterious rocky shore, it was dark and desolate. There was no one around. I pulled the raft onto the shore, the black rocks looking slimy in the faint moonlight. I had a dreadful feeling that I simply made it to yet another death-ridden quarantine island, not to a place where I could be saved from my ordeal.

Madam, the taxi driver spoke inside my dream. I opened my eyes, the bright yellow cab light stinging as I blinked away the nightmare.

The driver unloaded my suitcase and stood waiting for a tip. I gave him five dollars, and he bowed his head. *Hvala!* Goodbye now.

The hotel was cute, an old stone building, only two stories tall. The windows had wooden shutters that were all closed this late at night. The hotel was near a lively promenade by the docks and from where I stood, you could hear muffled thumping of techno and occasional shouting. Once I closed the heavy wooden door behind me, the noise disappeared, giving into the soothing sounds of quiet classical music coming from the speakers in the corners of the lobby. I checked in and was taken to my room by a gum-chewing teenage receptionist who, in a laconic kind of tone, asked how my trip was and did I need a wake-up call and what time to wake me up. I gave her a five-dollar tip. She had big, heavy-lidded eyes and plump lips, and she looked like she could be in a Gucci campaign. I wished for a rich American tourist to show up at the hotel and rescue her from boredom. Her English was very good, her accent similar to Luka's.

∽

The next morning, I came downstairs to the lobby, and he was there, smiling as widely as before, except his teeth weren't pointy this time. He looked human. When I woke, the events from the night before didn't seem real, and a part of me didn't think there was going to be anybody waiting for me. Seeing him standing there was startling, but I smiled back as if this were normal. When he moved, the air didn't register it at all; the stillness was almost as unnerving as the chill before. I wasn't sure which I preferred.

Here's the thing. I could describe him: his height, his eyes, that smile, the way his skin didn't reflect the light. It was important to me that I had a description for him, even to myself. Being able to define him into physicality normalized the situation somehow. Him wearing different set of clothes, for example — if I were conjuring him, and he were a figment of my imagination, why was he wearing an outfit that looked unfamiliar to me? Today the buttoned-up, short-sleeved shirt was blue, not white, and he wore beige linen pants and loafers.

Excited for the day? he said, and came even closer. He was almost a head taller than me. The air didn't move. Nothing did.

A group of laughing young tourists passed us by, and I had an urge to ask them if they could see him. The girls wore short shorts and flip-flops that clapped against the cool tiles of the hotel's stone floor.

I said nothing, not wanting to embarrass myself in case they could or could not see him — either option seemed problematic.

Very excited. Let's go, I said, and followed the girls. The air outside was moist and too hot already.

The promenade was busy, and again, there was a loud, thumping music in the distance. There were people smoking everywhere, cars honking, beautiful women with long forearms full of bracelets, snapping for drinks inside white cabanas that stood next to fast food stands that served traditional Croatian fare like *fruteli*, which I knew from my research was a type of mini doughnut whose secret ingredient was brandy. There were also booths serving pizza and burgers — a lot of Americans visited the place.

Everywhere, there were middle-aged hetero couples, guys in khaki shorts and wraparound sunglasses, and women in golf shirts and visor hats. And groups of girls, like girl trains, in white crocheted tops, stumbling over too many too-long legs, laughing as if drunk — it was early in the day for that, so it was all more about putting on a show. There were boys, too, boys whistling, shaved-head thuggish types narrowing their eyes, spitting spit, drinking out of cans.

So. Do you know everything about me? I said. I wasn't quite sure what I was asking. Or why I was asking it. I sounded confrontational.

No. It's not like that. I don't watch you, or I should say, I don't judge what I see. I don't have any emotion about it.

That was a relief. I thought of all those times I was lying in my bed with my eyes open, saying Sebastian's name over and over as I touched myself. I thought of the times when I dressed my mother and how sometimes I was rough with her, pulling her underwear on with too much force, or brushing the knots in her hair without taking the brush out, just straining them till her hair would give in and break, the knots stuck in the brush. I thought how often I let her sit in the tub, freezing, my eyes glued to the screen of my phone that wouldn't flash with texts.

Where are you when you're not there? Do you visit a lot of people?

It's not like that, either. I become. I'm not anywhere.

You become, I said. You're not anywhere.

I'm nowhere.

Why here? Were you born here?

No. But I know it here, and I know the island. I was born somewhere else.

In Croatia.

Yes.

Do you think? Are you capable of thought?

I'm just here to show you something.

Show me what?

Right now, this, he said, and turned around and walked in that lovely dancing way into a narrow street.

∽

Entering Trogir was like entering an amusement park — a place that was contained within strict borders. One moment I was outside in one world, the next I was in another. Luka walked ahead of me. Over his shoulder, he said, People call it "Little Venice." A city within a city.

I read it's actually called "Poor Man's Venice," I shouted. And Croatia has been referred to as "Poor Man's Italy." I wanted to see if it was possible to provoke him, if making fun of the place would hurt his feelings, which would mean that he did have emotions and was more human than he let on. I watched his shoulders, trying to catch any sign of him reacting to my insult, but his shoulders remained steady, straight and wide above me, so youthful, almost boyish.

There were too many people. There were no cars, just narrow stone streets with stone buildings with arched windows, like in churches, or square ones with colourful shutters, although some windows were dark and empty.

Having grown up in a large city, I was used to having lots of people around, but I'd never felt this claustrophobic with the walls pushing all of us into one another. The stone was white and light grey with black veins cutting through it. Inside the rocks the walls were alive with moisture, breathing onto us. In the air, there was a smell of the sea, wet stone, and human sweat, and the combination was oppressive. I didn't want to brush against the walls; I was afraid they were going to feel spongy, yielding. It was as if we were inside some kind of a monstrous creature, as if the city itself was a creature. I kept looking up to make sure there was still sky above me. I couldn't imagine living here although it was all very beautiful, and I kept wanting to stop and take pictures. Some of the buildings were in better condition than others, but I found the decay more enticing than the places that dressed up for the tourists. There were cats everywhere, too, lurking in darker corners of buildings and sitting on windowsills. I thought of my unhappy client who had wanted to go to Cat Island — I could send him here.

We passed a few restaurants crowded into the walls, with many tiny tables pushed under awnings. There didn't seem to be enough room for everything, yet somehow everyone managed. I looked down a woman's sunburned cleavage as she ordered from a card, and she looked up, our eyes meeting. My face grew hot, and I walked quickly to catch up with Luka.

I imagined the town completely empty at night, no longer made up of buildings but rather of their ruins and shadows.

We weaved in and out of narrow alleys to eventually arrive at the vast open area in front of a cathedral, where I took deep breaths, as if I was surfacing from diving. As everywhere else, there were dozens of tourists but now that we were out of the narrow streets, their presence didn't bother me as much.

It's famous. Do you want to go inside? Luka said.

I should eat something, I said. Passing all those restaurants made me hungry. And I didn't want to see the church. I've always found churches boring, even the beautiful, old European ones — there was too much going on, everything so aggressively crammed into one place, all the crosses and paintings and sculptures, a bazaar of faith.

He said, As you wish. There's a market not far from here, on the outskirts. You can get some traditional food like *soparnik*; it's kind of like a pie made with onions and parsley and chard.

I nodded and took a few more deep breaths before we dove back into the labyrinth of stone. I was again instantly overwhelmed by all the people and the narrowness of the streets; it was getting ridiculous, like the subway during rush hour.

You don't find it pretty? Luka said, turning around. He turned into a small courtyard with a side staircase and a small rusty balcony.

This is like in *Romeo and Juliet*, he said, pointing to the balcony.

Poor man's *Romeo and Juliet*, I said.

Yes, he said, his voice neither offended nor amused.

A cat appeared on the staircase, skinny and grey, almost identical in shade to the stone wall behind it. It stared at us.

Are you all right? Luka said. You seem anxious.

I'm just trying to get used to it.

The cat was gone.

We walked on, eventually coming across a small bridge connecting the old town to the food market.

Despite the fact that the food market was even busier than the stone city, I felt more comfortable here — I had a sense of the size of the place and could easily figure out how to leave it. The sky stretched above us. I followed Luka to a small stall with steam coming out through its chimney. There were two tables, one of them empty, with two tall stools next to it. I walked over and looked for the dish Luka had mentioned earlier.

I ordered the *soparnik* and waited. After a short time, my food was ready; a tired, older woman in a muumuu took my money and pushed the change without looking at me. I carried the steaming plastic bowl over to the table and sat down. Luka was leaning against a tree, watching me. His face was flat, with no emotions, just those deep eyes looking right at me, unwavering.

The onion-stuffed pie was delicious but too greasy, so I didn't eat much and left the bowl on the table. There was a bin nearby, but it was overflowing with garbage, some of it strewn around on the grassless patch.

After the meal, Luka and I sat in a small park by the bridge.

Can you tell me more about yourself? I said after a short silence.

I will, in time. Right now is not the time. Can you tell me about yourself?

I considered giving him the same answer, but the truth was I wanted to act as if none of this was unusual, my talking to a man who wasn't really there. I told him about living with my mother and the travel agency where I worked, and I mentioned having dated Victor, a has-been locally famous photographer. I didn't say anything about Sebastian, which seemed unnatural to me, to not mention the thing that occupied me so entirely. Because it continued to do so. I kept having moments where he would materialize in my mind with such clarity it was almost a sensory experience. The way his skin was — I could still feel it against my own. Even the texture of his hair. The yellowish tint to his teeth, the purple corners of his lips. How he looked at me and how he wouldn't look away. What was he doing now?

I kept talking to him in my mind. He wasn't contacting me, and I imagined that he wasn't contacting me on purpose. His silence was a message in itself. I pictured him winking at me, in that conspiratorial way of his, as if we were in on it together, as if this was a challenge: who was going to hold out longer?

See, Sebastian? We're the same person. Neither of us will contact the other first. I'm not like all the other women.

Sebastian said once: The only thing I'm good at is putting my foot down when it comes to women.

Women texted him drunkenly. They wanted to drive from other cities to visit him; they wanted to take him on vacations. He declined all of their invitations. I laughed with him when he told me that because I felt triumphant — I had never texted him drunkenly, and I never invited him on vacation.

Luka softly snapped his fingers in front of my face. Hey, hey.

Sorry.

Jet-lagged? he said.

I nodded. Jet-lagged, hallucinating, talking to a ghost — not myself. Although what was "myself"? Was I myself when I spent my entire time pining for someone who didn't care for me but whose existence was the only thing I seemed to truly care about? I thought again about feeling like a metaphorical balloon going from a man to man, how little I had going on for myself, living my life according to whichever man held me.

We could see more things, Luka said, putting an end to my reminiscing. I could take you to a few places that the tourists don't go to. There's a building that you might like. It's not a famous building, but it will impress you. There's a party there tonight. It's for an artist. I thought it might be something you'd be into.

Wonderful, I said. I knew that my boss would be pleased if I offered him a report on Trogir that included a less conventional kind of exploring. It occurred to me that Luka knew what I was just thinking about with his artist comment, but I didn't say anything about that.

I was tired and in need of a nap but I felt excited about the party. I couldn't remember the last time I'd been to one.

22

AFTER MY NAP, I no longer felt like going to the party. But. I had no idea how to communicate to Luka that I wasn't feeling all that great; we had made plans to meet in the lobby of my hotel at 9:00 p.m.

I called the caseworker to ask about my mother. She said everything was fine. She said my mother didn't ask too much about me. She was taking her medication, and she went to bed at a reasonable time. I didn't ask about baths because I figured if the caseworker was alarmed about anything she would bring it up. I felt disappointed in things going well. Was I perhaps hurt that my mother didn't seem to need me after all? I wasn't sure. I wished I retained something from all those years studying mental illness, but it seemed I didn't. I was completely unpredictable to myself.

I had a shower and braided my hair. I wanted to look younger than my age — on the way to the hotel, Luka told me the party was being thrown by young people. It was organized to celebrate an up-and-coming artist's signing with a gallery in New York. I looked him up online after getting back from our walk. His art was mostly small porcelain sculptures — dolls that seemed to be rotting away, zombies, but also cartoon characters with their genitals exposed. It was bold, and some critics called it gimmicky, but despite his youth the artist seemed very serious and accomplished. There were a few photos of him with the British artist Damian Hirst.

I debated calling Victor to tell him about this artist and the party, but I had promised him I wouldn't contact him till I figured out what was wrong with me. He still didn't know about Sebastian, but he knew there was something. I didn't feel good about having used him, and I wished I could explain it all to him, but even Victor with his open-mindedness and sexuality was territorial and jealous like most men. I knew better than to confide in him about my romantic dilemmas.

I sent him a text telling him that I had arrived safe and was well. He immediately texted back: *I'm glad. Enjoy your vacation.*

Still wrapped in a towel, I sat at the little vanity and forced myself to put on some makeup. I painted my eyelids purple with a little bit of glitter in the corners. The face looking back at me in the mirror didn't look familiar. It was me but it wasn't. I wasn't sure what *me* was. I didn't panic because this wasn't the first time. I had those spells since childhood, when I would dissociate and get confused about my own face. I didn't understand how it was put together. I looked away from my reflection and got up. I wished for a cigarette. It was that wish that brought me back into myself. I was a person who wanted a cigarette. I wanted to smoke. Now. But I didn't smoke. I was a person who didn't smoke but who wanted a cigarette. I was I, again. The feeling of disconnect had passed, and I remained inside myself.

∽

I wore a white dress and a white shawl. The lobby was empty save for the teenage receptionist with the beautiful face. She gave me a little wave when I sat down in a big chair.

At exactly 9:00 p.m., the door opened and a gaggle of girls in shorts and flip-flops tumbled inside, the same group I had seen yesterday. Looking at them cheered me up. I liked their youthful enthusiasm. The receptionist disappeared somewhere, and I wondered if she left irritated because she was not on vacation and they were, and she was stuck behind the desk all day on a nice summer evening.

Hello, Luka said, suddenly in front of me. He was dressed in a white T-shirt and jeans. He looked very young.

How old are you? I said, and we both laughed as soon as I said it. His laughter sounded hollow, put-on — it was like a recording of laughter. It made mine die. It was a dumb question. How did you measure a ghost's age? I got up and felt the same cold wave as before when I stood next to him.

After we left the hotel, we dove into the old town again. The air was moist and hot as it was during the day; now everything was clad in a foggy breath. The walls of buildings were perspiring again as we walked past them.

As before, we weaved through the narrow alleys, and while it was still busy, at night it didn't bother me as much. People were a little less panicky now, happier, tipsy, or drunk. It was harder to take pictures at night; you just had to enjoy yourself and let the alcohol calm your anxieties about not having seen the sights.

I didn't mind Luka striding ahead of me. I had no idea what to talk to him about. At night, due to the absence of restaurants and souvenir shops, the narrow alleys were almost empty save for a wandering tourist or two or an occasional cat darting across our path.

At one point, I tripped over a protruding cobblestone, and when I looked up, Luka was gone. I blinked and he reappeared. He grabbed my hand. His hand was cool, as was the breeze coming off the stone buildings. Despite the breeze and his cold hand, I was hot all over. I couldn't quite define how his touch felt to me — solid like it should, and yet I had the impression that if I were to put more thought into it, I would be grasping just air alone. If I believed that I was holding on to this being's hand, that seemed to be enough to make it seem real. Yet it all felt like a deal I was making with the more rational parts of myself that kept suggesting I was imagining the whole thing or that I was simply in my bed in the hotel having a very vivid delusion.

We walked on, making turns into different alleys — I continued to hold his hand, and I experienced a peculiar sensation of floating, moving above the ground as if in a dream. Around us, there were scraping sounds, desperate nails against stone, big creatures trying to get out of the walls.

Just cats. He said it like it was normal for cats to make so much noise.

Then we were suddenly in an open space in front of a stone building that stood detached on a large swath of land. There was a kitten on the steps of the building. Some broken chairs were set up in a row on one side of the stairs. To the right of the building was a shed with a giant mosquito drawn on it. I couldn't understand any of the Croatian words painted above it except for *malaria*.

The building seemed abandoned, the windows sealed shut with wide planks of wood. We walked up to the stairs, and the kitten dashed away. I watched it run into the field where a playground structure stood.

This was a house for children sick with malaria, Luka said. It was run by nuns.

I couldn't hear any sounds of a party.

The party's upstairs, on the other side. Luka opened the front door. We walked up a set of stairs in the darkness, me clutching his cold hand so hard I worried about hurting him until I remembered that I probably couldn't hurt him. I thought about Sebastian, and his existence struck me as absurd now that I was in this place so far away from him. I thought about the island I was soon going to see. I was here for a job, but I was also here to have an experience that would distract me. I wondered if it was working already with Sebastian blurring in my mind.

We passed a door with two planks of wood criss-crossed and nailed to the frame.

Behind the door, a child's voice said, Mama, mama? The call was clear, unmistakable.

Did you hear that? I said.

Yes.

What was it?

What do you think it was?

It sounded like a child.

Maybe someone brought a child to a party, he said, pausing to stop, his voice hollow.

I let go of his hand, then grabbed it back in panic, my imagination producing a vision of a small, sad, pale figure in a dirty white shirt dress, with pouty mouth, standing right there behind me. I hissed, Let's go, please.

At the top of the stairs, Luka opened another door, and then we were suddenly on a large crowded terrace, surrounded by people, all of them in white, laughing, talking to each other in English, French, Croatian, some other languages I didn't recognize. There was ivy everywhere covering most of the stone wall. The railing wrapped around the terrace was lit up by hundreds of Christmas lights. The people were very much alive, and their loud presence was a pleasant shock. The contrast between this and the child haunting made me sigh with relief.

A song ended and a new one started. It was the summer's hit, "Anna Wintour," by Azealia Banks. The normalcy of the whole scene must've stumped me so much that for a while I stood there paralyzed and not sure what to do until Luka pulled me into the pool of dancers in front of the DJ table. His touch still didn't seem quite right, but I ignored the uneasiness I felt and forced myself to focus on the music. The song was one of my favourites. I played it after it came out while I walked around the city feeling seen by Sebastian; the chorus had the singer belt out joyfully that she was in love, and at one point she listed her attributes and superiority to all the other bitches through a megaphone. I didn't feel that way about other women but that's because I wasn't sure how I compared. I was always surprised when men told me that I was beautiful. Most of the time, I had no idea why they thought that. I was not being coquettish; I honestly didn't know.

Later on that evening, drunk on tangy wine with an unusual red glint, I was still dancing with Luka to some dreamy, dark, deep house music. The wine made me feel loose, warm inside, sexy. Everything around me was the same — loose and warm, the women with lush, dark, or sun-streaked hair, and everyone with perfect, glowing skin. Who were these people? I didn't care. I loved them all. There was clinking of glasses and laughter everywhere.

This is a special wine, Luka breathed in my ear.

I'm drinking the dead, I thought. I thought of the cats watching us from dark corners. Alcohol made me horny, and I scanned the crowd for men, but they all seemed paired, busy dancing with their women, a white blur of bodies in the golden light. Luka and I didn't touch, but we were orbiting each other intimately, as if we were in that heady prelude to becoming lovers. I kept thinking of what it would feel like to kiss him but that was perhaps too much of a deal to make with my rational self. He was, after all, in a different dimension, behind a wall that wasn't there. I closed my eyes and let the music carry me for a while as I waved my arms and swung my hips, feeling weightless and at peace. Unexpectedly, I had a vision of his mouth firmly adhering to mine like a leech, pulling out my tongue, my esophagus, the stomach, all the intestines, swallowing me right there on the dance floor. I opened my eyes, and he was gone. I searched the crowd, and then there he was, by the door, flickering in and out like an image trying to come onto the television screen. I told myself it was just wine, my drunk brain playing tricks on me.

23

I WOKE UP without any hangover, got back into the white dress, and met Luka outside my hotel. I packed a knapsack with water, some food, and a blanket. I also brought tightly wrapped kindling and matches to make a fire. The night before, on the way home, Luka promised he would take me to the boat guide who would take us to Tajni Otok, the island where we could explore the ruins of the asylum. After we left the party, I made sure to avoid touching him even though my drunkenness made me trip over the cobblestones. I never confronted him about the disturbing vision on the dance floor. I had no idea if this was a warning from him or something else.

Right now, as we walked on, Luka said we could sleep on a roof somewhere or just stay awake. We could go inside some of the buildings — it wasn't the safest, but he said he knew where to go, and I needed a flashlight if I was really keen on

exploring — did I bring one with me? I took out my phone
and showed him the flashlight feature.

The boat was late. Luka said this wasn't unusual. It was possible the guide decided to have a nap after his lunch; he would
not bother letting us know, and, besides, how would he let us
know? Most of the guides shunned cellphones — many were
older and scornful of modern technology. There was nothing
to do but wait. So we waited.

Luka lay down in the shadow of a small palm tree, a straw
hat over the top of his face. That's a nice hat, I said.

It's called a boater hat. It was popular in the late nineteenth
century; it was worn in the summer, often used during boating
or sailing, Luka said.

Will they let me on the boat without one?

What do you mean?

Just a joke. Never mind.

That's funny, he said flatly. His shirt was bunched up
around his waist. I took a note of his body when his shirt rode
up: the smooth, almost boyish belly. His lips were full, pouty,
and looked soft and moisturized. His skin was blemish-free.
Disney eyelashes. He was like one of those shirtless male models
in suit jackets advertising expensive shoes without socks,
wearing watches that seemed too loose around their wrists. I
thought of kissing him, again, and imagined he tasted of some
sweet, otherworldly nectar, like a very intense tropical drink,
something with pineapple in it. Or perhaps old and musky
— maybe kissing him would be like licking a gravestone. I
thought of my insides getting sucked out.

I looked at the water, trying to find some peace there. I
spotted three ducklings on one side of the small boardwalk
nearby. I watched them swim single file. On the other side

of the boardwalk, there was a mama duck with four more ducklings.

It took me a moment to realize that I was witnessing a small tragedy unfolding. The three ducklings on my side were separated from their mother. They couldn't figure out they had to climb the steep walls of the boardwalk that kept them apart. There was a lot of peep-peeping and then some quacking from the mother on the other side. Soon, the mother figured that she could fly over the boardwalk. Once she did that, she led the three ducklings toward the steep wall. She extended her body, propelling herself upward with a flap of her wings, hopping out of the water to demonstrate how to get on top of the partition. She then swooped down and repeated the movement. She did this a couple of times before going back to her other young.

I watched them trying to climb the wall and falling back into the water. It was frustrating to witness but with each try, they seemed better at it. Eventually, they were all out, peeping loudly and waddling about. They moved far away enough from the edge as if to avoid slipping back. One of them rested while the other two jumped in to join their mother and siblings.

I waited for the last one to follow. But he didn't. He seemed to have fallen asleep, folded into himself like a little ball of fluff. The mama duck started to swim toward the shore with her lot. It looked like she had no idea there was one missing, or perhaps it didn't matter — seven or six, what's the difference?

The duckling shivered and shook, finally standing up on its little feet. His peeping took on a more desperate sound; it came out faster, louder. His family was now safe on the shore, waddling toward a patch of grass. I was the only one hearing the small, panicked cries.

I watched as the duckling jumped back in the water but onto the wrong side. I wanted to shout after it, do something, but what was there to do? There was no actual shore; the man-made wall separated the land from the sea, and the water looked treacherous, dark and deep, and I wasn't a great swimmer.

Luka, I called out, but he wouldn't move. Luka!

The duckling swam toward the open water. I had to look away.

Was this a message to me? But I couldn't ascribe any intent to the scene I had just witnessed. Nature was random even if its theatre seemed full of lessons.

Upset, I walked toward the palm tree where Luka was or wasn't sleeping. He lifted the hat from his face and looked at me, groggily. You okay? The way his head rested on his chest made his chin double. I thought of Sebastian's actual beginnings of a double chin.

I looked over to the sea, but the duckling was gone. I took a deep breath, exhaled. There was no point in having a fight, Yeah, I'm okay. But we've been waiting forever, I said.

That's how it is, he said.

Other than explorers, any other people go to the island?

Luka sat up, stared at the sea, Only locals, mostly kids because it's a great place to play hide-and-seek. Not really scary, he said.

I see, I said. Sometimes things are scary because we imagine they are. You can convince yourself that something is scary, like the island.

He said, Do *you* think it will be scary? He was looking at me now.

I felt there was an answer that was correct. I wasn't sure if he wanted me to agree with him or if he would be pleased were I to disagree.

I don't think it will be scary. But I hope it will be, I said.

Why do you hope for that? He sounded exasperated, as if I was a small child saying stupid things.

I didn't want to tell him. I didn't want to say anything about being an obsessive kind of woman and about needing something to break the spell. It was embarrassing.

"I need to shake myself up," I said in my mind.

He nodded a tiny nod.

There was a boat coming our way. Luka stood and shielded his eyes. That's us, he said.

The boat guide waved, and we walked up to the boat. He ignored Luka, and Luka ignored him in return. The guide had a black moustache and was wearing a lavender-coloured sweater with elbow patches. You'd have to pay a fortune for a sweater like that in the neighbourhood Victor lived in, which was Toronto's Brooklyn, full of bars with clever names like Pills and Boots, and shops that sold vegan cupcakes, and hundred dollar, plain black T-shirts.

The guide grunted and reached for my knapsack. Then he helped me get into the boat. Luka jumped in. The boat rocked wildly as the guide pushed off from the shore. The trip wasn't supposed to be long according to Luka, less than an hour. The guide started the engine, and we zipped through the water.

I imagined this as a photograph: a thirtyish woman in a white dress, on a boat, sitting behind an old boat guide in a lavender sweater, and in the back of the boat, a beautiful young man, leaning back against his knapsack. Here was a postcard I wanted to send to Sebastian in his dreams. He will recognize me in it — or the suggestion of me — and he will be disturbed by the men, by the boat speeding away. He will see my face up close the way he used to see it when he'd fuck me. The way my mouth is a little too big for my face. My lips open slightly to eat the sun. Open wider to eat him. Then wider even and so dark inside. My mouth swallowing him. He wakes up. It was a dream; it was a nightmare.

The air was salty, intense, sharp like cocaine. Everything around me was clouded. The sun was obscured by a yellow fog. There was movement behind me, a vibration in the salt; the curling of my skin. It invaded the skin in my face, broke it with its tiny crystal shards. I thought of the movie I saw with Sebastian, about the drunken lighthouse guards. I understood the drinking now — it had to be because of the salt; you had to dissolve it with something. Or if not dissolve it then at least be able to forget it.

The fog was getting thicker, yellower. It wrapped around me; I could no longer see anything. Luka had vanished. I looked to the front and there was nobody there, either, no guide. The air was heavy, oppressive. I couldn't move. I was paralyzed. I opened my mouth to scream — only a scream seemed appropriate in this situation — but nothing came out. There was a feeling of dread, some kind of terrible hole of despair that opened within me and wouldn't close. *That's where tears really come from. This is what it's like to die.* Was it? But what was *this* exactly? Why think of death, or why death now? I suppose that's how it always was when you died just out of the blue. You weren't okay with it — it seemed so random and stupid. You weren't ready. I certainly didn't feel ready. Worse, I couldn't figure out what it was that I was dying of. What had happened exactly? It wasn't fair, I was right here, alive, and now —

There was a deep thud, and the boat shook hard as it hit something. I opened my eyes. The thick yellow air, the fog, was gone. My agitation wasn't. I wished I could share this un-settling moment with someone, and for a moment I wanted to ask the guide about it — How was he not rattled by it? Was this some kind of environmental phenomenon? — but I was afraid I was the only one who experienced it. Luka sat with his head turned away from me. I didn't want to speak to him in the guide's presence. I didn't want the guide to judge me, or worse — alert authorities about a lonely tourist lady losing her mind and talking to herself.

I pictured a person in a khaki uniform and a clipboard, an officious-looking woman taking notes as I sat across from her in a dim, windowless room, wearing a jacket with too-long sleeves, my hands tied behind my back, explaining with what I hope would be a reassuring smile: *Well, I was just talking to a ghost. He's followed me halfway 'round the world — I had met him earlier, actually, in my office and then at home. It's no big deal. He's wearing a straw hat ...*

I took a deep breath, exhaled slowly. The sun was strong, and there was a pleasant breeze. We were at the shore. In front of us was a rocky patch, not much of a beach, just a muddy slab of earth disappearing into the water. The guide hopped out of the boat. My body felt heavy, groggy.

The guide's hand reached for mine. I got up, wobbling as the boat shook with my weight. His hand was warm, dry, cal-lused; it clasped mine a little too hard. It felt so much different from Luka's hand. How? I believed this hand; I believed that it was what it was supposed to be.

This is it, the guide said as he let go of my hand. You here.

And so we were. We were here. Tajni Otok. My feet sank into the ground a little. Luka was out already, calling my name again.

Thank you, I said to the guide.

He nodded, Thank back to you.

I'll see you tomorrow. Tomorrow, yes? I said. He nodded vigorously, which was a relief — I was so high-strung that for some reason, despite our agreement to pick us up, I became momentarily paranoid this was some kind of a set-up, an elaborate joke to dispose of me. I didn't have an answer as to who the joker was. I guessed it would have to be me.

∽

The bell tower of the asylum wasn't visible from the beach. It was supposed to be visible from all angles — at least from the water. I made a mental note about that for my report. But maybe it was better to skip that comment. I wouldn't want to include that I passed out in the boat and took no note of important landmarks. I didn't understand why I did pass out, and it worried me a little, but at this point I had to start being more discerning about my worries — nothing about my trip was conventional, and I suspected my stay on the island was going to serve up a few more surprises.

I caught up with Luka. He followed a path through the thick, lush bushes. The island was quiet save for the sounds of birds and insects. The cicadas were especially loud, tiny machine guns all around us. I enjoyed their sound because they made everything seem somewhat ordinary.

I walked close to the bushes, letting the branches catch in my dress, scratching my ankles. I liked being close enough to get scratched. It felt real.

I thought of the ground under my feet: Was it full of bones? I focused on the pads of my feet. I sent my thoughts there, my focus. I had only meditated a few times in my life, and I recalled now how some yoga YouTube person claimed you could "see" with different body parts, putting special focus on the place that you wanted to sense things with. When I tuned into it the feeling was not of bones and decay — it was as if the earth was a creature, active, alive. Not full of death and decay but rather things moving around, breathing. It didn't seem scary; it seemed natural, something I expected. At the same time, I wasn't entirely sure this wasn't some kind of auto-suggestion; there was no pulsing, no bodies breathing and moving.

The bushes went on, but now I moved away from them and their nibbles. Occasionally, there would be a half-buried brick in the ground, yet no ruins anywhere that I could see. We were moving uphill. The bushes were getting thicker. I wondered if we would have to hack them in order to get through. I didn't have anything to hack them with.

Then, just like that, we were in a small clearing, a meadow with some crumbling brick protruding from the ground here and there, in the worn-out patches where the grass had died. There was a little triangle-like structure constructed out of pebbles next to one of the more protruding pile of bricks. It made me think of that popular fake documentary from the nineties about witches. I pictured a bunch of shiny-eyed Croatian boys setting up these things to scare the intruders. I said nothing about the little structure to Luka, who sat down on the ground, gesturing for me to do the same. I thought of the corpses in unmarked pits. Where were the pits? We hadn't encountered anything like that here yet. I pictured bony hands sticking out of the ground, trying to reach for my feet.

You should eat something, Luka said matter-of-factly.

In the morning, I had bought some sandwiches from a little patisserie near my hotel and some fruit and nuts from a stand.

I placed one of the sandwiches beside him. He looked at it but didn't make a move to unwrap it.

Please try it. It's really good, I said. The bread was delicious, the crust still fresh and crunchy as I bit into it. I don't know what I was trying to achieve by challenging him with these little trip-ups, but I suppose I wanted him to reveal more about himself, calm my anxieties about his purpose, and assure me that he was not, after all, a figment of my imagination — or, worse, a ghoul who intended to harm me.

Luka winced and held his stomach and said he felt sickly. It was an ongoing indigestion problem, nothing to do with my sandwich, he said.

An indigestion problem?

Sure, he said. He didn't look to be in pain. He didn't look to be anything, really. His face was impassive, unmoving like a picture. I thought of my aborted artist career, how, except for my missing painting, I could never be brave enough to try giving people three-dimensional proportions — using blue and green to accentuate depth in pale Caucasian flesh seemed wrong even though it wasn't. I thought how my shading was always slightly off and how it looked more like stains rather than a natural shadow. In that vein, were I to define it, there was something about Luka that despite his human form made him appear unfinished, not quite right.

I watched as he got up and walked toward some shade near the bushes and lay down on the ground, his head resting on a thick broken-off branch. He pulled the straw hat over his face. I wondered if the sleeping was another show he put on for me, but it calmed me to have him behave as I expected most men to behave.

I never understood why men needed so much sleep — Victor napped during the day often, and Sebastian used to sleep through entire weekends. The past dates I had outside of Victor and Sebastian also depended on the men's sleeping schedules. No one wanted to meet for morning coffees, and many of the men insisted on staying in all weekend long. True, a lot of that was about the fucking, but in many instances the fucking was part of the deal where a post-coital nap and pizza in bed were just as attractive.

I listened to the sounds around me, trying to make out anything weird, but they were just insects buzzing in hot grass, an occasional chirping of birds deeper in the woods. The air was getting even hotter and drier now — not scorching hot but close.

I became aware of my eyelids growing heavy, the heat settling in me, my bones filling with sand. It took effort to zoom in on where Luka was. He wasn't pretend-sleeping anymore — he was holding himself up on his elbows, talking to someone, a woman in a long, brown dress. She must've come from the other side, where the mental hospital was. She appeared animated and cheerful, like a tourist; it was the bouncy way she was squatting while talking to Luka that made her seem like one. Despite the distance between us, I imagined there was a charge between them, some kind of sexual energy. I didn't feel jealous of it, but it annoyed me to see her there. It meant that we weren't on the island alone. Then it occurred to me that maybe the woman was what Luka was, otherwise how did she talk to him? And since I talked to him, too, maybe she was someone he decided to show himself to?

Then there was a third possibility: Did her presence mean she conjured him, and if she did, why was I part of her conjuring? Did it mean I was a ghost? I snorted a little laugh.

There was a new sound in the forest. I listened, trying to guess what the sound was. It blended in with the cicadas clacking in the grass, but it was distinct. Human. Talking somewhere in the distance. I pictured local pranksters, same people who set up the silly pebble structure. The island seemed busy all of a sudden. My irritation grew.

When I looked back to where Luka was, he seemed to be sleeping again. The woman was gone. Luka's straw hat was back over his face. It was stupid. We couldn't spend a whole day socializing with tourists or other ghosts and pretend-sleeping. I got up and walked toward him.

Do you feel any better? I said.

He moved the hat from his face and said, Much better. His eyes were the deepest brown, almost black. Same eyes as Sebastian's. It hadn't occurred to me before how similar they were. Now, looking at Luka's face, I had the eerie sensation of his features rearranging themselves, morphing into the face that was so deeply imprinted in my memory. As Luka and I stared at each other, it was as if his eyes were sending me a message from Sebastian. The message wasn't anything concrete — it was similar to when I sometimes woke up hearing Sebastian's voice in my head. I would try to convince myself that he, too, had been dreaming about me, that he longed for me as much I longed for him, which was not true.

"Lie down beside him." The thought of being sexual with Luka had been there on and off since the party, but now it came back, slammed right into me with such force that I had to break the eye contact. I still had no read on him — he remained two-dimensional, unreal — and I was also worried about rejection. If he were a product of my mind — didn't that mean that he was going to reject me only because I could imagine it?

I thought of one of the standard questions on psychiatric intakes that always struck me as too transparent. The question was, Do you believe you can control things with your mind? Who in their sane mind would've answered yes? Now that I was here, I'm not sure I wouldn't have.

But if he was independent of me yet still rejected me, wouldn't that be even more hurtful?

∽

When I was in university, I had a friend who allowed me to tag along with her one night to see how she picked up men. At a bar, I watched her come up to them and talk to them, and everything on her jingled — she was all bright teeth and laughter and silver hoops in her ears and constant movement of bracelets and rings. It was like she was hypnotizing them to look at her, to pay attention. They did. She smiled at them, and many of them stopped doing whatever they were doing — talking, drinking, smoking — and she laughed and jingled, and I stood to the side and watched. Phone numbers were exchanged, and then we would move on.

She had talked to five men by the time we stopped at another place for dinner. At dinner, there were two more men. The first was the waiter; the second was a man at a table in a far corner who sent us two flutes of champagne. She drank both of them.

What I noticed about that outing was that she was sweet to the men but never gave the impression of being too invested. They could sense the fleetingness in her.

I didn't think that was something I could learn. I thought that was a natural thing. I didn't want to ever get turned down. I thought of myself as fragile. I had only slept with two people back then, and I was drunk during both encounters.

I was shy once, too, she said. I'm not bothered by rejection.

How could you not be? I asked her.

She said, If you remember we're just here for a moment, it becomes easier. On my death bed, am I going to remember some dick turning me down? Probably not. Probably I'll have Alzheimer's, and nothing will matter. I won't even know who I am, so who cares about some stupid rejection? Anyway, I want to settle down soon, she said.

∽

Luka looked up at me. What is it?

I didn't ask him about the woman. I thought he would bring her up on his own anyway. I didn't know what to say to him, how to distract him and myself from my thoughts.

Should we explore some more? I said.

What kind of cock did he have? Uncut and bent like Sebastian's? Friendly and compact like Victor's, or a veiny, sloppy one like what you'd see in porn? I felt wetness between my legs. What kind of cock did I want him to have?

What's the rush? he said in a teasing way. Was he finally picking up on my mood, or was I making him say what he was saying because it was all in my head?

I said, I want to see the bell tower. My voice came out all wrong. I sounded unsure, small like a young girl.

He stared at me.

I stared back. I thought, *Please don't*. Don't what? I didn't know.

After a short silence he said, Sure. I should take you to the bell tower. He got up and stretched, threw my knapsack over his shoulder. The knapsack hit his back hard, but there was no sound, no muffled thud like you'd expect.

24

THE BELL TOWER was adjacent to a long building, the former mental hospital, and possibly the future hotel — or university if what I saw online was more than a student project.

The tower itself was the only remnant of a twelfth-century church; it was turned into a lighthouse in the eighteenth century.

Luka pointed to some remains of a building. Inside a square frame of bricks that were probably a wall at some point was a small unkempt garden. There were tall flowers and shrubs with vine sneaking around, a few small trees with fruit growing on them; it was a cornucopia of various shades of green and bright splashes of wild colours. He picked up a rock that was painted white and hurled it toward the garden.

Why did you do that?

To scare off the wolves, he said. Just a joke. Let's go.

We approached the main structure. From the outside it looked like any abandoned building: peeling paint, underlayers poking through dirty white walls like sores. Small pieces of dry-wall had completely worn away to show a pretty row of light-grey stone, the same kind of stone I had seen in Trogir. I guessed the stone was covered up to make the place look more modern.

I followed Luka as we walked along it. I looked inside glass-less windows like eye sockets.

Come this way, please, Luka said, and turned to disappear into a doorway.

Inside, it was comfortably cool. There was some light coming through the windows, but overall it was dim and in some places it was quite dark. A long hallway led to various rooms with stained walls and weeds growing through cracks. There was the smell of urine and rot but also the deep, almost sexual, freshness of new plants. The ground was littered — pieces of rocks, crumbling bricks again, dusty metal rods kicked against walls, broken glass.

The large rooms that we passed were all almost empty. One looked cleaner than others. It was the size of a classroom, with windows covered in planks of wood.

I asked Luka to stop. I wanted to see inside. I was curious if I would feel anything, a malicious presence, demonic breath on the back of my neck. But there was nothing of the sort — just an abandoned room smelling of mould. There was a torn cable on the ground, chocolate-bar wrappers, a piece of dark clothing tied in a knot. Tree saplings breaking out from beneath the tiled floor. The room seemed to have been used recently, probably by some paranormal activity enthusiasts. I peered through gaps in the planks. A small courtyard overgrown with vine and bushes.

I turned around. Luka was gone.

I ran out of the room. I called his name over and over.
My voice echoed in the walls, and when it came back to me
I felt a chill; there was something off about it. I sounded like
a child — it was as if another me was calling from inside me,
and she was small and scared. And hearing my voice so barren
and alone like that made me wonder again if I was here all by
myself, and this thought was as comforting as it was troubling.

I fell silent. I didn't want to hear her voice–my voice.

Hey, Luka said.

He was right behind me. Everything okay?

I threw my arms around him. I needed to feel another body
against mine. I didn't think in that moment that he was not a
real person — he felt real. My heart raced, slamming against
my chest. I was dizzy, unsure where I was one moment, completely present the next. I wondered about my breasts against
him, if he could feel them — could he *feel* at all?

And could he sense how unhinged I was? Of course he
could. He could sense it, hear me, whether I talked or not.

My mother went off the rails for the first time when she was
only ten years older than I was now.

I wondered how he conjured mass, whether it was only for
my benefit. I remembered the argument about energies tran-
scending — after Luka's death, his body decomposed, and then
did his energy eventually transform into a ghost? Where did
he exist outside of this realm? He said, Nowhere. I wrapped
my arms tighter around him, but his false body vibrated, then
stiffened. I let go.

Ready? he said.

Yes, I said. I hated that I sounded hurt.

The tower is that way. He stepped back, or maybe he was
already a few steps away from me, and I only noticed now. My

concentration was off. I was usually more observant, paying attention to even the smallest change in my surroundings. Here it felt as if I had to catch up with everything, as if I was half a moment behind the world. Things looked blurry, and then they looked sharp.

Closer to the tower the rooms were smaller. A few were dissected, showed off their bones — broken furniture, some metal beds. On the walls white, chipped paint. Were those rooms of the mentally ill? How could you tell? The beds told me nothing.

There were also rooms so small they made me think of coffins. A few had no windows. I felt shivers up and down my body, and my legs prickled all over.

There was some graffiti in one of the rooms. Once I registered what it was of, I grabbed Luka's cool, alien hand to make him stop. The graffiti was of a man with a bird head. On a closer look, the bird head turned out to be a plague-doctor mask. I remembered seeing pictures of those things when doing my research for the island. The beak in those masks was intended to be filled with aromatic things — dried lavender, rosemary — to obscure the smell of the rot, the disease, the putrid air, which carried the virus.

I didn't want to go into the room. I wanted to look closer, but I didn't want to go into the room. It didn't seem right; I had a thought that I'd suffocate in here. Instead, I snapped a picture with my phone. My plan, however, was to take very few pictures. I wanted to remember the island by what would be left in my head. Anything I forgot must've not been important. I'd have an unfiltered, pure experience of the island. Something like that. Unless snapped in action, pictures distorted things instead of improving them. I thought of my job, where we hired students to take photos of tourists with their iPhones. Everything was fabricated. The smiles, the photographers. You couldn't genuinely *see* through a lens. I didn't have a single picture of Sebastian. I didn't need one to see him all the time.

It's creepy, no? Luka said behind me. Somehow we were now inside the room even though I didn't remember entering it.

On the ground below the birdman was a mattress covered in stains. A faint pattern of flowers was barely visible from underneath the dirt. I blinked, and I saw a figure on the mattress — or an imprint of a figure on the mattress. I blinked again, and now it was just a weird shadow that changed back into a blurry nonshape. Yet something in the shadows was familiar. I realized that the shape-nonshape *felt* like Luka; it was as if he was lying there instead of standing next to me.

Suddenly, I felt pain so sharp that it doubled me over. My breath went out of me, and my whole body shook; there was a hot, fiery poker twisting right in my core. I gasped for air, but my lungs couldn't seem to expand. I was shoved from behind, hands pushing my shoulders, and I stumbled forward, my knees knocking against each other, and then I was falling forward, landing right on that mattress that was not a mattress at all but a black, bottomless hole with teeth snapping at me as I tried to writhe out of it.

What the fuck was going on? I screamed Luka's name, and I thrashed and tried to block the teeth from tearing my flesh, but nothing was working. The light above started to become fainter as I kept falling and falling. I was hot and cold and in that excruciating pain still, my insides twisting, my lungs still gasping for the little air I could absorb. The teeth were now tearing right into my muscles, pulling on my bones, pulling me apart, blood gushing from every cell, gnawing at my feet, biting

206 / JOWITA BYDLOWSKA

them off. The pain was like nothing I'd experienced before. I had to shut my eyes; I didn't want to watch myself getting eaten alive. I knew this was the end, and it seemed unfair and tragic that I would just perish inside some hungry black mouth in the middle of a nowhere island.

Josephine? Wake up! You're okay, you're okay, you're okay, wake up, wake up!

I opened my eyes. Luka was squatting next to the mattress, his hand on my shoulder. I searched his face, and for a change it showed some emotion, his forehead wrinkling in concern, Josephine? What happened?

The pain was gone. I took a deep breath and filled my lungs with air.

What happened? I croaked back. You're asking me?

He winced. You had some kind of a reaction. I think you fainted.

Did I scream? I was screaming your name.

No. You just seemed disoriented. I thought maybe you were having a seizure. But then you came to. Do you need help getting up? he said, his hand no longer on my shoulder.

Yeah, no. I'll be okay. I steadied myself against the edges of the mattress. As I got up, a putrid smell hit my nostrils — something animal that was no longer an animal. I gagged but held it in.

There was a cluster of rocks painted white in the corner of the room. I looked away quickly, feeling nausea getting stronger. I didn't want to have another episode. Let's go, please, I said.

Once we were back in the hallway, Luka said, That was one of the cells where people were thrown in.

Thrown in, why?

Treatments. But also isolation. There was a virus going around — not an epidemic, but lots of people got sick.

I remembered now reading about the isolation rooms, the virus. I said, Why here?

It's closer to the bell tower. The doctor wanted them nearby. Especially the ones he had in for treatments.

I read he had his private office up there. And he fell out of the window.

I don't know about that. He would go there to think.

Should we go up? Maybe spend the night there?

It'll make you too nervous. You won't be able to fall asleep.

I don't plan on sleeping anyway.

Luka shrugged. You *could* spend the night *here*. If you want.

I looked at him, and he was joking; the corners of his lips were trying to keep the smile from forming.

Forget it, I said. Let's keep walking. I thought about the body he conjured for me, how hard and solid it was, how I wanted to get close to it again. For the first time in a long time, Sebastian wasn't a constant buzz in the back of my head. So maybe it was working, my being on the island, getting myself shaken up.

∽

We were in a new hallway. The hallway led to another large room, this one a former kitchen with an enormous marble table in the middle and old sinks and shelves. There were some wrappers and utensils on the table. Paranormal activity film crew, again, or tourists. The scene appeared to have been abandoned abruptly, but perhaps I was just telling myself that, perhaps they were just sloppy people who didn't bother cleaning up after themselves. No weird graffiti or white rocks in strange arrangements.

The door to the tower is over there, Luka said. But there's a padlock. It's new.

I looked to where he was pointing, another hallway coming out of the kitchen, this one darker and narrower. There seemed to be no windows.

We can't go up there after all, Luka said.

It was curious that he seemed surprised by the padlock. I suppose he didn't haunt these hallways.

Are you disappointed?

Not at all, I said. I wasn't. I didn't need to get up there. I was tired now. The few spikes of adrenalin I'd had over the course of the past few hours were taking their toll on me. I still didn't know how to process the fainting in the isolation room — the sensation of being eaten alive hadn't left me. Discreetly, I ran my fingers up and down my arms a few times, flexed my toes in my sandals to reassure myself that I was whole. *There's blood on your shoes*, the thought popped into my head. I looked down. There was no blood on my shoes.

I'm sorry anyway, he said.

No need to be. Where do you think the others are staying?

Who?

The woman. The people on the island.

There are no people on the island. No one besides us. Maybe there are some kids, but I doubt it.

But there was a woman you were talking to.

He turned around and stared at me.

I had to squint. In the half-shadows in the kitchen, Luka seemed blurred again. I came closer. I wanted to see his contours properly.

He was playing with me. He knew I wanted to be scared, and he was giving me what I wanted. I said, Very funny.

He shrugged. Time to go outside, he said, like he was giving an order. He was himself again, his solid energy form or whatever he was when he wasn't going in and out of focus. We left through a door-sized hole in the wall, the actual door nowhere to be seen.

The air outside smelled of the sea.

I heard a soft female voice somewhere behind me call Luka's name. I turned around, but there was nothing, nobody. I half expected her — who? — behind us, an apparition in a long dress hovering aboveground, but she never materialized. Luka didn't seem to hear, didn't react.

The day was getting heavy with colour — purple and golden tint of a perfect sunset — and moisture, turning into an evening. It was all the same everywhere: near the hospital building more overgrown crumbling structures, thorny shrubs, broken wood, and other trash. The nearby forest was thick with tangled bushes forbidding entry. Walking, I kept tripping over rocks and roots and bumping into various plants, trees, dead branches sticking out of the ground. There were a few times that I mistook a piece of wood for a bone, but after awhile I admitted to myself that I was, again, trying to freak myself out.

There was a wall in front of us with a staircase outside leading up to the roof.

This is the administrative building, Luka said. The roof is quite nice. We can spend the night if you'd like. It's probably better than sleeping in the forest. There's a staircase right there. He pointed to a side of the building where I could make out a metal railing with white peeling paint.

The idea of sleeping on the roof appealed to me, although it was less of a challenge than making it through the night in the forest or inside the asylum. I nodded at him. I had to collect some wood for the fire, so I asked if he could wait while I did that. The wood I'd found was good — dry and hard branches that broke easily, and soon I had an impressive little stack that I fastened together and carried under my armpit.

We climbed the staircase. Once on the roof, I looked around for a spot where we could rest. I wanted something soft, maybe some grass. There was such a place in the middle of the roof, a swath of green, and I walked up to it and unloaded my knapsack, swept away some larger rocks with my foot and laid the blanket right onto the mossy patch.

The open space was maybe twenty feet by twenty feet. All over there were some soft patches of moss and grass protruding, and in the corner a few feeble bunches of bushes. I liked seeing nature disrespecting our human structures, weeds growing in places where they shouldn't.

You could see the tower from here, as well as the forest and the larger part of the canal that separated the island from the docks on this side. From a distance I could make out some scaffolding set up closer to the water's edge, at the end of the oldest part of the building. From my research, I knew the city was reluctant about restoring the place, but there was some argument about preserving it for its historical value and possibly making it usable in the future. The construction would start and stop, so the land remained unclaimed.

I felt tired but relaxed, maybe even a bit elated. The adrenalin had run its course, or my body had simply managed to regulate it, dial down all the craziness I'd been feeling. The elation was a natural high. I deserved it; I deserved to feel good.

I built a simple fire out of the sticks, in a shape of a teepee. It was easy to light it with the kindling I'd brought with me. Luka sat in the shadows, and I motioned for him to come closer — I wanted to see what he looked like with the fire on, if it reflected in his skin. His skin was orange and red, and his eyelashes cast too perfect a shadow on his cheeks. As before, I thought back to my painting years and not being able to properly represent whatever I was trying convey. I looked away, and I lay on the blanket — the moss provided just enough cushion for my resting spot to be tolerable — and looked up at the sky. The sky was clear, the purple bleeding into darkening blue. I took in big mouthfuls of salty air — it tasted delicious, not oppressive at all the way it was this morning.

I thought of my mother. I counted the time difference. Midnight over there. If she didn't take her sleeping pills, she could be watching TV right now with eyes like the TV screens themselves. What if she hadn't taken her pills? What if she had a turn for the worst, turned into a psycho? What if she murdered the nice caseworker? Hit her over the head with the supernatural strength of an old desperate woman? I pictured her tiny little feet resting on the worker's white corpse with that red hair of hers that looked alive, too bright, and the prettiest open mouth, waxy teeth.

Now that I was back home, in my head, I thought of Sebastian, too, and then of Victor: What were they doing right in this moment? I pictured Sebastian lying in his sweatpants on a couch in his parents' basement, hand resting on a pizza box, the TV on, just like at my mother's house, except he's watching sports. Baseball? Something dull like that. Or maybe the cartoon for grown-ups, the one with the horse. His eyes would be like my mother's — glassy and hypnotized. His hairy stomach would be poking out of the sweatpants. Socks on the floor, crumbs.

Then I pictured Victor at his light table, looking through a magnifying glass at negatives. His age washed out by the light.

The windows open, the night air smelling of rain and street. The curtains white, moving gently in the wind. And a woman with dark hair, like mine, standing by the table, watching him.

It was a symptom of improvement that I thought of my mother first and then of my two lovers second; my brain was rearranging the priority lineup.

∽

Luka sat across from me. Is this nice?

It almost feels like a date, I said. I was feeling giddy.

How does it feel like a date? he said flatly, tilting his head exaggeratedly. I didn't understand this hot-cold thing, the point of this performance. If I didn't know better, I'd wonder if I had done something to offend him. Perhaps it was just the fatigue of having to deal with a real person — but how could he be fatigued? Did he have to replenish his energy, change back into gas or whatever he was when he wasn't this?

I said, I don't know. We're sitting on a roof under a starry night. I was joking. That it was romantic.

Aha. Yes, I understand. He wasn't looking at me. Do you need food?

I have another sandwich and some apricots and nuts for tomorrow. I'm not that hungry.

Do you like hot dogs? All Americans like hot dogs.

This struck me as funny, but I didn't think he was making a joke. I pretended to cough to mask the little laugh that escaped me. I said, Yes. Best thing in the world. But I'm Canadian.

He smiled. Of course. My apologies. Canadians are nicer.

I lay back and watched the sky turn darker. I listened to the night suspiciously, trying to isolate any sound that didn't belong, but it was just insects and an occasional flapping of wings and a cry of a bird. No human voices anymore, no screeching of zombies, shallow graves opening, bones clacking against each other.

Why are you doing this? Luka said after awhile. His voice sounded as if he said it in my head.

You mean the island? For a job, I said, but I knew what he was really asking. Because of a guy. I got my heart broken. But you probably know this, don't you?

I'm sorry, he said.

It's okay. I'm over it now.

Are you over it?

No. Maybe.

Tell me.

And so I told him. I told him even though — again — I had a thought that I was possibly just talking to myself there on the roof. But did it matter? I thought of therapy, how half of its success depended on clients being able to share and how the act of being able to open your mouth and describe your experience was enough to make some breakthroughs. I didn't hesitate for a moment. It all just spilled out of me. So much of it was internal that when I heard myself now, it occurred to me how I mutated something that could be considered merely a small annoyance, a little hurt — a jab with a thin needle — into a nervous break-down, a broken artery. I should've spoken up sooner.

I had told Kelly about Sebastian but had told no one else. My mother didn't count. Had I told all of this stuff to a real friend, I'd have felt embarrassed, worried about their judgment. I was always known to be quiet. Recently, the only weird thing about me was my mother and the fact that I never married, although that wasn't so unusual anymore. There were no addictions, no feminist shenanigans, no rants on social media about being done wrong. I left no broken families in my wake; no one got any diseases; there were no pregnancies. My relationship with Victor was troubling to a few of my acquaintances I kept at the beginning of it, but eventually no one cared that we weren't getting married or that we attended sex parties, and the friendships disintegrated, too.

Anyway, Luka was the perfect person to tell the story of my obsession. He was not really a friend; he was probably not even human, and who knew if I would ever see him again.

§

After I finished, he didn't say anything for a while.

I listened to the night, fine-tuned my ears to it. Again, I analyzed every sound with suspicion but, still, there was nothing strange. If the woman in the long dress was someone I just hallucinated, there were no other humans on the island; it didn't seem like there were.

Finally, Luka broke the silence: I was in love once.

You were in love once? I was saying things just to say them. If I could conjure only something that I knew about, then Luka shouldn't have a story of having been in love. Because when I searched my mind to see if I had any idea what he was talking about — no, I had never thought of him as someone who might've been in love. The only thoughts I had about Luka were how he was in relation to me and to this place.

Once, for real.

What happened?

She was married. I was a patient of her husband. It was, as you'd say in America, complicated.

Did she love you back? I said, and as soon as I said it, there was a noise somewhere below us, somewhere in the forest. It sounded like a distant laughter, but it disappeared before my brain had a chance to fully identify it.

Yes, she loved me back.

Do you want to tell me about it?

I heard him shift, a rustling of dry grass, gravel, then a quiet sigh. I thought of sitting up, looking at him, but I remained in my position. I didn't want to make any sudden movement, make him feel that I wasn't paying attention. I was giving him all the attention I had. And he told me his story.

part 3

luka's story

25

I ARRIVED AT the hospital with my father in the back of the boat — we were both behind a gate. He was allowed to sit there with me. My father was an important person; people respected him, and our family had money. It wasn't unusual to be granted special favours, although sitting behind a gate might not seem like a favour. But it was a favour and an exception since the rule was that patients like me had to sit alone with shackles around their wrists and ankles.

Don't be afraid of this part — I wasn't in the back of the boat because I was a murderer; it was nothing that serious, but it was serious enough. The shackles were there because I was accused of a crime that I didn't commit. At the time of my arrival, nobody thought that I was innocent, and I had no way of explaining what exactly had happened.

A car picked us up and drove a short distance to the asylum. When I arrived with the shackles on my wrists and ankles, a nurse told an orderly to take them off. I remember her saying I was so young, and she looked disgusted when she said that — it seemed my youth offended her more than the shackles. My father looked disgusted, too, and he was stern. He believed my story. But he was stern; I knew it was for show.

I was not innocent according to the rest of the world and was supposed to stand trial; I was accused of hurting a girl, the daughter of an American diplomat who was only recently posted to the country. The daughter of the diplomat was a twisted girl, very dark indeed, even though you would never think that on meeting her — she looked so innocent and sweet. But she was spoiled and beautiful, and I was dumb and young.

At the time, the relations between Croats and Serbs were already quite strained, but this was still awhile before the *Zagreb Manifesto*, which was an official call for an end to violence. The second and final Constitution had just been established, and the Kingdom of Serbs, Croats, and Slovenes became officially known as Yugoslavia and was ruled under King Alexander the first. It was a young, tense country with a lot of promise but also too much history to ignore, and at the time it had only been a decade or so since the negotiations between Slovenes, Croats, and Serbs, and Montenegrins, when their places formed one state. It was also awhile before the assassination of the king. What all of this meant for diplomacy was that it was robust, and we had a lot of foreigners interested in our young country. We were like a teenager — full of potential but maybe too much like a child still, like me.

I had never had a girlfriend before.

∽

I met her at a Christmas party thrown by the third American ambassador, John Dyneley Prince, at the future British consulate in Split. I attended with my parents. It was one of the most important parties of the year, perhaps the most important one, because Americans are always the most important people in the world and so are their parties.

My mother was wearing a gown she had made by a seamstress especially for the event, and I'd never seen her that dressed up; she said that the gown was fancier than her wedding dress. I can see a lot of things in my mind's eye — the deep blue colour of my mother's gown and how it shimmered and seemed to move around her like she was wearing stars.

When my parents walked through the embassy door with me behind them, people gathered around and greeted us. The small orchestra was playing some popular tune by Strauss. There was nobody at the piano yet — the pianist was someone famous, brought especially for the occasion from Dubrovnik. My father, who was half Serbian, was always in Split on business; many of his friends were politicians and diplomats. He helped with translations and introductions and was like an unofficial host of the Old Town. There were often parties that he had to attend: weddings and funerals, openings of restaurants and art shows.

He sent me to the school connected to the embassy so that I could learn how to speak proper American English. He always said that it was important to make connections in the world, and knowing English was the first step to making that happen. When he first enrolled me there I fought him. He told me I would understand one day and that was true — I understood why connections were important when he was allowed to sit with me in the back of that boat on the way to the asylum.

∽

Before I saw the girl who caused my downfall, I saw a huge Christmas tree in the corner of the ballroom. The lights were dimmed, and the room was warm and filled with people's conversations and laughter. I remember looking at that tree and feeling hypnotized because it sparkled, not unlike my mother's gown, and it looked like the whole thing was moving, and when it moved in front of my eyes, I saw *her*. It was as if she was floating in all that light, but she was only standing next to the tree, and she was wearing a gown, as well, like a grown woman. Her dress was pale pink, made out of some kind of almost-transparent fabric that wedding veils are made out of; there was lots of that fabric piled all together, but the whole construction looked weightless, light — she looked *ethereal*; she glowed.

The American diplomat who hosted the party came up to me and led me by the arm toward the girl. I felt panic and excitement so great that I wasn't entirely sure I would be able to speak.

The beautiful girl was his daughter. He introduced me as the son of the "Most Successful Businessman in This Neck of the Woods." He said her name was Holly and that she loved horses, and he left us alone after that. The girl and I stood there without saying anything for a while. She seemed even more shy than I was, and she stared at the tips of her shoes when she spoke. You have a lovely name, I told her, and she said, It's spelled like *holy*, like the Holy Ghost but two *l*s, and she giggled, her eyes still focused on the tips of her shoes. I didn't get what she meant about the Holy Ghost but then I did, and I laughed, and then she said, Except I'm not as holy as the Holy Ghost. She looked up then. That's when I knew she wasn't really shy, and I don't know why I thought that but maybe because it seemed she was making fun of church. It didn't matter because I was in love with her already, and I was only seventeen.

Now we were no longer silent, and it seemed like we knew each other right away. There was an ease in how we talked, and she seemed really interested in me although there wasn't a lot I could tell her about my life — I told her about my friends, the Croatian ones and the American ones I went to school with. I knew about America, I said. I had a friend from Chicago and another one from New York —

What do you do with your friends? she interrupted.

I couldn't think of anything specific, so I just told her, We wander around, and she seemed disappointed, so I told her about books I read and how I actually liked the tourists who visited Trogir, where our old house was, because of how baffled they seemed, like children. She laughed at my children's comment, and it seemed I redeemed myself.

She told me about her family, her two older sisters who were married and had babies, and who lived in New York City. She said she indeed loved horses but no longer rode them because of the frequent trips. The family travelled everywhere, and she said she saw the whole world. I told her that must be so thrilling, but she said she was very bored; she was *bored with the world*. It seemed, she said, that there was nothing that could really excite her anymore. I thought it was melodramatic to talk like that, but I said nothing. What did I know? I hadn't even been outside of Croatia!

Her hair looked heavy and so light blond that it was almost white. I wanted to touch it.

Actually, I'm *so* bored I could die, she said, grabbed my hand, and pulled me toward the side door. We ran out the room. None of the grown-ups noticed because they were busy drinking and talking. The special guest playing the piano hadn't arrived yet and I wondered if I should wait and see him — I knew my parents were excited about him and would probably bring it up — but Holly said it was going to be boring, the *boringest* thing in the world — she said that as we walked fast through the hallways of the embassy.

She knew where to go; she opened door after door till we got to an emergency exit and ran up the staircase to the roof. It was like here, where we are, just the two of us and the stars above us. She had hidden a cigar under a rock on the roof, and she lit it. I'd never seen a girl smoke a cigar.

She took a few drags as I stared, unable to look away from her lips making those smoke *O*s, and then she pulled me toward her — it happened so fast, I was like a ragdoll; I just let it happen — and we kissed. She tasted strongly of ash and something like licorice. I didn't think it was disgusting. This wasn't my first grown-up kiss, but it was the first one that made my body feel strange and made my penis grow harder, bigger. I felt a small nip when she kissed me. It was incredibly thrilling to me to be kissed and bitten. It was the best thing that had ever happened to me. It was as if I had been small and ugly for a long time, and it was only around my last birthday that I had become less ugly, when my skin cleared up, I got taller, and my voice stopped squeaking. She found me at the right moment; it was as if I needed confirmation that I was out of the awkward stage that had plagued me for some time.

Without any warning, she started unbuttoning her dress and, once she was done, began undoing my belt. I had heard stories from my male friends about things, and I knew a lot about girls from those stories but just crude things, not that what she was doing wasn't in some way crude but because she looked the way she looked and I was in love with her, I didn't feel in any way sullied by it. Also, I was no saint — I had already made plans to see a prostitute before being with a girl because I was embarrassed about not knowing what to do. But Holly didn't seem to mind; she knew what to do for both of us. She pulled my pants all the way down and, in that moment, I felt like a child. I think I was shaking. With my pants down, all exposed and getting stiff despite my nervousness, I watched her step out of her dress and her slip.

I've never seen a naked girl — completely naked. Sometimes, with friends, we would spy on girls on the beach, but their bodies were covered, at least the parts that we were mostly curious about. There was an old change-room pavilion on the beach, but girls almost never used it and who'd blame them? There were boys and men everywhere, looking. There was a woman in Trogir who would let you see her naked, but you had to pay, and she was rumoured to be crazy; I never went to see her with my friends who talked about her breasts and the hair between her legs. I was too shy to go.

Holly was like an angel, just unbelievably, impossibly lovely. She had the most beautiful breasts, soft and small, with pink nipples that I imagined tasted like cream. Her whole body looked to be made out of cream. I was embarrassed because I didn't have any experience, so she took my hands in hers and put my hands on her hips, and I held her there. She said to lie down and I lay down, on top of my clothes. Suddenly, she was right there, straddling me. I knew she wanted to go on top of my penis, but I was scared, so I didn't do anything even though

I was stiff, and I knew I could probably lift her and have her slide onto it, but that seemed somehow impolite — funny how even with her naked on top of me, I was very unsure that she would not be offended by my participation.

She wrapped her hand around her own neck and made a choking noise. It was strange, and I didn't know what to do. I never heard of anyone liking that kind of thing. She let go and laughed, and I felt my erection go away. She moved back and forth as she rubbed herself against my penis, and it grew hard again. Then she finally squatted over and put me inside herself.

It was my first time, and I had an orgasm right away. I was so embarrassed. But she said it was normal, and she said she knew that it was my first time.

She lit the cigar again. Smoking, she took my hand and put it between her legs. She was hot and wet there. I felt myself get hard again.

She rubbed against my hand. She was still smoking. She moaned. She asked me to hold her cigar, and then she said, Touch the cigar to my skin, don't be a bore. I didn't know if I heard that right. She said it louder. She was rubbing herself against me the whole time. She said to press the burning end to her arm.

Quickly, she said, don't keep it there for a long time, just go *ping*, once, and that's all. She sounded excited, and it scared me how excited she sounded; it wasn't normal to be excited about that kind of thing.

I just want to feel the sting, she said.

The whole time she was talking and rubbing herself against me. I felt like she was trying to hypnotize me with her talk. It was like looking at that pretty Christmas tree in the ballroom with all the lights. I couldn't look away, and now I couldn't stop listening. So I took the cigar from her and I held it in my fingers. She was looking right into my eyes. Her eyes were blue, or I remember them blue — they seemed to shine in the darkness. I didn't want to hurt her so I threw the cigar away, and she laughed, again, but it wasn't a friendly laugh. She pulled away from me. Her smell was in the air, almost like something cooking, something delicious and forbidden. She was indeed forbidden with her being a foreigner, and so I felt confused and perhaps even angry, about the cigar especially. I was aroused, but I was too upset now. My insides were hurting as if someone was twisting them, and I was distracted by the pain — I sometimes got pains in my stomach if I felt nervous about something. I lay there with my pants down, and it was embarrassing.

I started getting dressed, and she began to dress, as well, but then she stopped, as if she had a big thought. And indeed, she did have a big thought. I watched as she yanked on the décolletage of her gown with great force. It ripped, and when that happened I felt like running away; I don't know why, but right away I felt like I was in danger but maybe not even from her — it was as if there was some kind of demon with us, a force that wanted to hurt us. It makes no sense what I'm saying, but that's how it felt. She asked me to help her with the buttons, but when I got up to help, she turned around and hissed at me. Then she ran off. She opened the door to the staircase and disappeared.

This happened so quickly. I stood on the roof, unsure what had just occurred, but I could still smell her, and there was the cigar, its tip red and still burning not far from where I was standing, and the air still felt strange like there was something hanging in it, like a stench.

By the time I got downstairs, the party was in disarray. The concert had been halted and there, finally, was the famous

pianist standing by himself by the tree. He looked very irritated.
Only a few people seemed to be paying attention to him. The
wife of the host stood beside him, and she was wringing her
hands. All around, the guests were speaking loudly and all the
lights were on. Everything became really sharp for me, like I had
some kind of special glasses on, and as I came inside and passed
a few people, I could even see the powder on women's faces, like
paint. As I passed, people would stop talking and would look
at me.

I quickly understood that my situation wasn't good. I saw
Holly in her torn dress in the arms of her father. I felt love for
her despite my confusion. I think I was in shock because I
didn't know what to think at all even though I did understand
that this was going to be bad for me.

My father grabbed my arm and walked me out of the ballroom. People were shouting after us; a woman screamed, Animal!
Animal! It might've been Holly's mother. I didn't know who she
was yelling about at first. But it was me — I was the animal. We
walked fast, my mother in front of us in her pretty gown — I
kept my eyes on the gown as she broke into a half-run in front of
us, crying loudly. My mother was always a little dramatic, and
so I thought she maybe enjoyed that whole terrible situation, but
then I had another thought that I must've been overcome by that
evil spirit on the roof to think of my mother so unkindly.

∽

After that evening I sat in my room for what seemed like days as
my father tried to sort out my predicament. He would go to Split
to talk to people who he hoped could help him help me, and he
would come home a few days later, sometimes still drunk.

I ate meals with my family, but no one talked to me. My stomach hurt from nerves, so I had a hard time finishing most of those meals.

I didn't go back to school. There were rumours all over the town, and I didn't want anyone to see me. I've never felt as lonely as I did during that time. I couldn't sleep some nights, and I would leave the house to go for walks but I didn't talk to anyone; I slunk around in shadows like a criminal. I was a criminal. I listened to people and watched them from a distance, and my heart hurt so badly because it felt like I didn't belong to the world anymore.

My mother talked to me when my father was out, but other than that, there was nobody else. Her voice was always in a whisper now, and she moved around our large house so quietly it felt like I was living with an apparition or, better, an approximation of my mother.

Sitting in my room for hours, I read or, when I couldn't concentrate at all, just sat and looked at the ceiling and thought of Holly. Even when I read, I thought of her — it was like my brain couldn't shut off the Holly thoughts. I thought how beautiful she was, like an angel. She was cruel and wild, that was clear, but thinking that didn't change how I felt about her. It was pathetic, but for weeks after that bad night, I dreamt of Holly as if she was the girl who got away, but the truth was she was the girl who had ruined my life. And for what? To stave off her boredom for a couple of hours?

☞

There was a trial finally, in Split, and I cried in the courtroom all the time even though I was trying to stop it. I'm ashamed to say that I cried not only because I was scared but also because she never showed up. It felt as if she was betraying me over and over. She couldn't even come to witness my demise. She had her fun, and she probably didn't even think of me — probably didn't even know there was a trial. Her parents weren't there, either, only her lawyer. I cried out of humiliation, too.

∽

The day before sentencing I was back in Trogir. My stomach pains dissipated, and although I didn't feel better, I felt motivated enough to spend my evening differently. I took a bottle of wine from our cellar and snuck out of the house to go for one of my nightly walks. I drank the whole bottle while sitting on a bench in a small courtyard, like a street drunk. I walked aimlessly, and I fell off a small bridge and broke two fingers and scraped my face. For some reason, I went by the house of the crazy woman who let you see her naked, but she didn't get naked although she sent a neighbour's boy to alert my father. I sat in her kitchen and waited for her robe to magically open and reveal her breasts. She didn't seem unhinged at all; she was motherly and sweet and washed my wound with such gentleness I cried. Her robe stayed closed. She smelled of cinnamon and cloves. When my father came to pick me up, he stood with her for a moment and told me to wait in the car. I watched them. They seemed familiar with each other as they talked. She laughed at some point. I couldn't see if he gave her any money. He seemed shaken up when he drove back, his jaw tense and his eyes cold when they met mine in the mirror.

On the weekend, it was written in one newspaper that I had tried to take my own life — and that was the only time that I saw my father perk up. He said that because of the accident, he might be able to work out a deal that would ensure I didn't go to jail.

I had to attend one session with an elderly and very tired psychiatrist, and my father coached me on what to say. He said it was best to be considered insane to avoid going to jail, so I talked a lot about wanting to die and about not wanting to hurt the girl but not knowing why I hurt her — my father said it was better to acknowledge that I did hurt her but didn't know why. He said it would go well with my attempted suicide story.

The doctor didn't look at me once as I talked. It was like he was somewhere else in his head — maybe his bed or wherever tired old people liked to be. A young female assistant was taking notes as I spoke. The doctor asked me a few questions about how I felt. I said, Confused and melancholic and unsure of why I was in the situation I was.

Did I want to take my own life again?

I wasn't sure, I said, remembering I had to seem at least a little bit insane. I didn't really want to take my own life, at least not yet.

I suspected the doctor was someone who owed my father a favour or who would receive a favour in exchange for this assessment.

The result of the session was that I would be hospitalized for observation and a minimum of three years of treatment. I was prescribed drops to calm my nerves.

Even though this was much better than being in prison, it was still a devastating verdict. Three years seemed like an eternity, no matter where I spent it. And an insane asylum? I didn't know anything about those places other than that people used the word to insult you. No one wanted to hear "You belong in an insane asylum!" and it seemed that was exactly where it was decided I belonged. I was unsure of what kind of treatment I .was going to receive, if I was going to be tortured in any way. Didn't people die in those places? I wish I had asked the psychiatrist, but it was too late. At night, I despaired over my unasked questions, and my stomach was in knots all the time. I also despaired over my ruined plans to travel the world, to study science, even my ideas about meeting a girl I would one day marry. I was a smart student, and it felt as if my life was ending and it hadn't even started yet. Again, I'm not saying that going to jail would've been better. But having such an undisputable limit to freedom made no difference as to where I was going to be locked up.

∽

When I arrived at the hospital with my father and I saw the pretty brick asylum building surrounded by lush trees, the first thing I did was cry. I wasn't sure if it was relief or regret or both or something else. Despite feeling devastated, what I suddenly felt was, perhaps, even … peace? After weeks of silence or worried whispers from my mother, I would finally be able to talk to people. Granted, most of them would be mad, but that was better than being locked up in jail with violent criminals. The whole journey to the hospital was uneventful. We took a ferry from the town of Trogir and sat in a small room with some nurses and another patient, a mute older man whose eyes rolled in his head. There was a truck being ferried, as well; it was filled with food — big bags of potatoes and loaves of bread and baskets of fruit. I overheard one of the nurses say how she would never eat any food grown in the garden — I assumed the hospital garden — because it gave her the creeps.

My father said goodbye to me and told me he would see me around Christmas. He showed no emotion. It was fine. I was used to him being like that with me now, and I felt relieved when he left.

∽

The hospital was surrounded by a lovely little forest, and there was a big garden, and when I realized this, that first day, I had to admit to myself I was so much better off than in prison. I was even starting to feel optimistic. I saw a few people walking around in the garden, but I couldn't tell who was truly mad and who was not. I didn't have enough time to ascertain this because I was ushered upstairs, where I had a room to myself, and after I dropped off my luggage there, an orderly came by to show me around.

There were patients in the games room and in the dining hall — a couple of them wore robes, the rest dressed in normal clothes. I saw a few nurses and was told there were three attending doctors on the premises. There was a head psychiatrist, but he was away when I got there — the orderly taking me around mentioned it in a lowered voice. I didn't ask what was wrong.

I was told that the more difficult patients had to remain in isolation because some of them were dangerous — to others or themselves. I wasn't shown where their rooms were, but it made me feel strange to know that some people in the building were hidden away from the rest of us; it made me think of tormented spirits that were too weak to even haunt us.

The orderly told me about how Tajni Otok was once a quarantine island and that the unmarked burial pits were supposedly located on the other shore of the island. He sounded dispassionate about it all. I had questions, but I didn't feel he would want to answer them.

After I came back to my room, there were people in robes below my window getting wheeled out into the garden; I watched their faces getting bleached out by the sun. I guessed madmen and women left here to die.

∽

Despite myself, I was still pining for Holly. This, more than loneliness, was my biggest emotional turmoil. I couldn't stop thinking about her. I kept going over the few hours that we'd spent together. Remember, I had no contact with the outside world. There was nothing else to stimulate me. I gave what had happened between us, to me — the lust, the excitement — a lot more weight than it probably deserved. Holly was what separated my old life from this new one, yet, in that way, she became a monumental presence in my life. I had nothing else going on. That's why I talked to her in my head, and I blamed her for what happened, naturally, so when I didn't talk nicely to her, I shouted at her that I hated her. She ruined my life!

What life? the imaginary Holly would say, and I would apologize and say I didn't mean it, and I would tell her I loved her. All of that was in my head, but it felt as if she were right there with me, and I felt as if I was truly losing my mind; it was a self-fulfilling prophecy.

∽

I found the atmosphere of the place almost relaxed and not at all what you'd think an insane asylum would be like. There were sessions with doctors and various therapies such as hydro-therapy — where more unruly patients were kept in water for hours at a time — but very few patients were confined to their cells, and for the most part we were treated with re-spect. During the week, there were meals in the dining hall, prescribed conversations and board games during mandated socializing, and walks. Families visited on weekends, and some-times we'd have special guests such as magicians or a travelling theatre troupe. We were not allowed to leave the premises of the hospital and the gardens, and some of the residents talked about the quicksand-like areas on the island where you could fall into a pit full of human ash and suffocate, but all of that was related in a casual manner, the way you'd tell someone about an interesting tourist attraction. Everybody seemed to know a story about a patient or patients escaping the hospital and dying in that manner, but when pressed for details that was the one occa-sion when some people would get agitated and tell me to mind my own business, and I was too shy to bring it up with the staff.

I talked to one of the three doctors about how I was faring, and he was gentle with me. He was an older man with a white goatee who didn't seem too concerned about me. Our talks were short and polite, and I don't think he was looking to make any breakthroughs. He recommended special walks and volun-teering at the hospital library because I needed to get used to the place and calm my mind.

I waited outside of the garden maze for the male nurse who was supposed to guide the walks. The idea was simple. All I had to do was focus on my steps, just move one foot in front of the other, that's it. The male nurse who was the leading person for the activity told me that it was best to not think of anything else but my steps. It was called *walking contemplation*, he said.

I walked behind him every day and focused on his shoulders or sometimes the backs of his shoes.

There were other treatments offered in the hospital, but I was never subjected to them. There were rumours of lobotomies, but I didn't encounter anybody who complained about those things, and everyone seemed mostly okay — eccentric but fine.

I started to like it there and that worried me, too, because, again, I wondered if I was, indeed, in the right place, and if I was that meant I fit in with all the other lunatics. There was some chaos that I had to get used to, but it was silly chaos, mostly to do with cleaning up the place — some of the patients were assigned easy tasks such as mopping the floors, washing walls and doorknobs, or stacking up chairs, and they were unable to complete the tasks. There was a group of patients who'd always try to stack the chairs on top of one another in an effort to build a special escape route. Another group was particularly passionate about polishing the doorknobs with butter, and the walls had obscenities written on them too many times to count. A few maniacs regularly climbed on top of the roof in order to eat stars. Once they got caught, a metal gate with a latch was erected at the bottom of the staircase leading up to the spot. But it was all fine, manageable; no one got thrown into isolation or had to skip a meal for punishment. I volunteered at the library and the garden, and I could spend an entire afternoon sweeping the freshly cut grass and pulling out weeds or sorting out books. I found both things meditative, as pleasant as the walking contemplation.

26

ONE MORNING, THE head psychiatrist arrived on the premises. There was tension in the air, and for the first time I saw some of the patients act in a disturbing way — some screaming out of the blue, some talking to themselves more than usual, a few crying, and a couple even soiling themselves. The nurses, too, were nervous and snapped at patients; they even locked a few of them up in their rooms. Maybe it was the nurses' nervousness that brought on this disarray.

The head psychiatrist was maybe my father's age, balding, with small bright-blue eyes that would probably look pretty on any other human being but on him they looked out of place, as if he had stolen them from someone nice. I could tell right away he didn't like people. Sometimes you just sense that someone is only tolerating you. He spoke with people without looking at them directly unless it was to pin them down with those turquoise beads. I could picture him doing experiments in a lab.

When I met him, he introduced himself but asked me to call him, simply, Doctor. Incidentally, two of the three doctors on the premises left shortly afterward, and the third one would show up only a few times a month.

At the time of our introduction, Doctor and I were in his office, which was very clean with old, well-maintained furniture and lots of big shelves full of books. I tried to read their spines, but I was too nervous meeting him, so I couldn't focus properly. Doctor asked me lots of questions — about how I felt about the hospital, about how I was feeling in general — which I tried to answer, but he would often interrupt me, and he sounded stern when he asked more questions, and his overall manner was impatient. This is how I could tell that I bored him. I heard a rumour that the only people he actually liked working with were the really twisted ones — the serial killers and the others who never left their cells, the ones who were never seen.

∾

Next time I saw him, right away Doctor asked me to go over the episode with Holly. Unlike the other doctors I'd talked to, he didn't use assistants to take notes — in his lap he held an open pad he'd scribble in occasionally. When we got to the part on the roof, I wasn't sure what to say, so I fell silent. In the beginning, I didn't know if continuing to claim I was innocent was the right thing to do, but I figured it served me better since a crazy person accused of crime would not feel guilty and would behave similarly to me. In that way, it was in my best interest to never change my story and in that way never try to be a sound person — for as long as I was here. But was I misremembering? Did I actually hurt Holly? Did I misinterpret all of the events? Would a sound person be thrown here? But then, did not being sound mean I had to lie and admit to having raped Holly — an act I didn't believe I committed? More than once, I thought how sanity meant insanity, going against my very own self. Yet I never tried admitting to being guilty. I worried I would lose touch with reality, end up like one of the maniacs stacking up chairs to build castles or trying to eat stars.

Three years. That's how long I had to endure here. If I stayed calm and did what I was told, I would be considered improved, well enough to be released — I hoped.

As I told the story to Doctor, I listened to myself talk, and it sounded convincing despite how nervous I was. My stomach ached faintly. The weeks of peace I experienced at the asylum dissipated; with a few questions Doctor managed to trouble me and make me doubt myself. But after I finished, he only thanked me and that was that. I left his office in a sad mood, and it took me a couple of days to feel fine again.

The time after that he asked me, again, about Holly, and I went over the episode again, trying to remember more details, but there was only so much I could remember without having to make things up. I described the gown my mother was wearing, the Christmas tree, the pianist who stood frozen by the Christmas tree.

And, again, the next visit it was the same thing. I wondered what Doctor was writing down — it couldn't have been the thing I was talking about because it was the same thing every time. We were both trapped in a recurring dream, or a nightmare, perhaps, since the repetition of the event started to make it all sound almost bizarre. I started to get confused over my own words, and it was as if by repeating them so often things lost their meaning and my own past became like a story someone told me. I wasn't sure if that was his method, to move what was real into the realm of fantasy. It was a strange method and I didn't see the point of it. That more than anything unnerved me — I hated being manipulated like that. But truthfully, there was nothing sinister about our meetings except that sometimes I would catch him looking at me as if he was amused but not in a nice way, as if I were a large insect that dared to sit in the chair opposite him. I never confronted him about any of it. I worried I was developing paranoia — again, I was worried that I was here because there truly was something wrong with me or, at least, I had all the ten-dencies that would justify my stay in a mental hospital.

∾

Weeks went by and I made some friends. A few Melancholics, a man who sometimes believed he was St. Francis of Assisi and who also claimed he was psychic and could understand animal talk, and a Manic, although he tried to hang himself shortly after we became friends — an event that was not related to us becoming friends — and was put in isolation. When he came back, the Manic claimed that his isolation room was haunted by the victims of the plague, and they wouldn't let him sleep, which is why he was up at all hours of the night. He was re-moved again and that was the last I saw of him.

The women were in the other wing. I didn't think of women much. I was still very young, and my desire was dulled by the medication I was weaning off of, and what wasn't dulled was questioned so obsessively by Doctor that I was afraid to even think it — whenever Holly would appear in my thoughts outside of my prescribed times to talk about her, I would feel my stomach clench. It was detrimental for me to have sexual thoughts. It was perhaps all part of my treatment.

∽

Months went by. My parents visited around Christmas. My mother didn't cry. She seemed too calm. I could tell that she was on something, some kind of a terrible vitamin for women. Her whispers were now just how she talked all the time, and she seemed so much smaller even though she didn't seem to have lost any weight. She seemed a lot like the Melancholics. She managed to make a weak joke about food being like "mushed paper," but when she laughed it was as if she were playing herself laughing. My father gave her a look, and she covered her mouth with her small, plump hand. She said she forgot how handsome I was, and she giggled so softly that I wasn't sure if she was perhaps crying.

My father spoke very little. He mostly wanted to talk to Doctor. After he talked to him, he told us Doctor said I was making progress, but he wouldn't say what that meant and whether it made them feel any better and if it meant I would, perhaps, be getting out sooner. My father and I had never had a conversation about what happened with Holly. I hoped he believed I was innocent, but I also suspected that even if he did, he would say that it didn't matter — my father was a good salesman, and his success depended on him being more pragmatic than emotional. I knew that in the past he had sent people after the clients who couldn't pay; it was *just business* as he'd said to my mother, who confronted him about someone specific once, a war widow with a child.

I made them a gift — a centrepiece for the Christmas table with a candle that didn't turn out as well as I was hoping — but they left it behind, claiming there was no room in the car. It was cruel, but I said nothing. My mother's parting words — "I'll love you no matter what" — made my body hot, dizzy with anger. In that moment, I forgot all about where I was, and I wanted to shout that I was innocent, but we were interrupted by a male nurse who said my parents' car was ready, and was everything okay, did I maybe need to see Doctor? I remembered where I was; I remembered that my belief in being innocent possibly meant that I was crazy.

I composed myself and shook my parents' hands, and my mother pulled me to her chest and hugged me once.

After their visit I had some thoughts about what it was like between them, things I hadn't noticed before. My mother kept looking up at him like he was her stern father. It occurred to me that they liked having me away. I was an only child. I was what the Americans call "the third wheel." The third wheel was out. When I was younger, my mother made jokes about me "ruining" their marriage. Now, even though I was their child, I wasn't a child anymore, so my being in the hospital was the perfect solution without them feeling guilty about not helping me out. They had done all that they could because I was safe: I wasn't in jail and I hadn't ended up on the street.

Our other contact was through letters. In the letters, my father asked me how the food was. My mother wrote that everything was well at home, and there wasn't much to report and that she loved getting my letters, especially my descriptions of the garden. My letters were a lot longer than theirs. I wasn't sore about that; I was grateful they hadn't disowned me altogether.

27

IN THE SPRING, some bad things happened. A flu was going around for most of the winter, and many of the patients got sick. Many had to be moved to a real hospital. A few were even found dead in the morning. There were whispers about an old plague curse going around — a burial pit getting unearthed and releasing the deadly virus. It was true that there seemed to be fewer and fewer patients. When the part-time doctor never showed up for his regular shifts, we didn't know if he just left, like the others, or died. It was unnerving to have people disappear like that.

Overall, it was an eerie, quiet spring. I spent a lot of it in Doctor's office talking about the same thing as always — Holly and how that episode made me feel, and did I feel remorse, and have I had any new insights — and the rest of my time I spent in the garden, preparing it for the summer. I never shared with Doctor what my insights were — that most of the time I was convinced I was perfectly sane because I didn't do anything wrong, but also that I wasn't sure if my thinking I didn't do anything wrong possibly meant that I agreed I was insane.

I talked to my few friends — though never about Holly and what bothered me — but people were distracted, preoccupied with their own troubles; there wasn't a lot of conversation, just long monologues, which I tolerated because it was better than being alone.

∽

And then, in late spring, Doctor went away and came back with his wife. It seemed odd to me that he was married; I thought him being married was just another bit of madman gossip. The wife would live with him in the small house attached to the hospital. There was a lot of excitement on her arrival — the earlier spell of grimy, uncertain days was broken. This excitement was so much different from when Doctor showed up on his own; the patients who had been around for a longer time talked about Doctor's wife like she was some kind of a princess. None of the new ones had met her at that point, but we knew that she was younger than Doctor. She *was* a princess in a way, someone from the outside world who had nothing to do with why we were all there. She wasn't a doctor or a nurse or a patient. She wasn't a visitor. She was an anomaly on the hospital grounds.

I met her with everyone else one Sunday evening during dinner. It was an unusually warm night, or I just remember it as warm because everything about that night felt softer, nicer. There were still fewer patients than during the winter, but some had now come back from their quarantines so it seemed the curse was no longer hanging over us.

Doctor's wife was tall and chestnut-haired. She wore a long dress with a generous skirt and lace. It looked quite old-fashioned. She was probably in her early thirties, but she appeared childlike in the way she looked around the room — it occurred to me she seemed more like one of us, like a patient. Her bewilderment was similar to those who arrived here for the first time. Maybe that was the reason why I didn't find her attractive at first, even though she was if you were objective about it. But she had none of Holly's presence and loud beauty; her confused stance was not an act, you could tell that right when you looked at her. She smiled with effort, her eyes cast down when she was introduced to my table. In a flat voice she said it was a pleasure to be here, and she was looking forward to getting to know us. She never looked up the way I remember Holly did when she let me know that she was just playing shy.

Doctor steered her away from the table gently but sternly, after a quick introduction, as if she were his silly daughter, as if she was saying nonsense. She pushed him ever so weakly, and he pulled her closer, locking her in a protective vice — this also made me think that she had more in common with us, the patients, than with the staff. I wanted to find out her story.

On leaving the cafeteria, I looked in the direction of the medical staff's table. She was seated between the head nurse and Doctor. She looked up briefly then and quickly away, but I knew she really saw me — and not as a patient, just as a young man. Not once had I felt like a young man in that place, so that was the most thrilling thing that had happened to me in a long time, her eyes showing me she was putting me in some other category, one I almost forgot I was a part of. In that moment, I did change my mind about her — an image of kissing her pale lips flashed in my head.

Later on that day my friend, St. Francis of Assisi, said the wife's name was Anna, and she was mad just like the rest of us. He said she had spent two years in Canada, in a seaside town with a naval base. She travelled there alone wearing men's clothes. She was the daughter of a famous composer or a writer, he couldn't remember which. He said lots of people outside knew about this story because her father was that famous, but he himself knew about it simply because he was clairvoyant.

How he really got that information he wouldn't say, and I didn't believe him anyway — he was, after all, a fake St. Francis. He had no way of knowing those details because we didn't get any newspapers, and no one had a radio. His sister had deposited him in the asylum years ago because he brought stray animals and men into her house, where he lived. The animals, albeit dirty and sick, were less of a problem than the men. He had homosexual tendencies.

You should be careful. If you make her fall in love with you, she will fall in love so hard that it will kill both of you, St. Francis of Assisi said. Then he looked me up and down and laughed when I turned my back to him and walked away. He called me dumb.

∽

As my sessions with Doctor went on, I thought I was getting to know him almost as well as he was getting to know me. I could tell what kind of revelation would excite him more than others. He seemed to like when I talked about my hatred for Holly. He encouraged me to explore it further: Please, talk about that emotion. How does it feel in your body? He never said anything about my loving her. He waved his hand once when I brought it up: It's just a delusion, and you need to let go of that. You are not a person prone to delusions, are you?

After a few weeks of regular sessions, he started cancelling some of our meetings. People said he was spending more time in his office and in the basement, doing experiments. St. Francis claimed he had attended a therapy session in which Doctor and a medical student repeatedly dunked his head underwater. He lost track of time and woke up in his bed confused about where he was. But he felt lighter than he had in a long time, which scared him — he said he was used to feeling terrible all the time; that was the only way he knew how to be. These unusual treatments were new, and many of the Delusionals and the Melancholics had to undergo them. Although the treatments were troubling, you could see the effects — some of the patients seemed more present, happier even, similar to my friend. The most unpleasant thing about the procedure was having to rise in the middle of the night to receive it. Patients also suffered memory lapses after the treatments, but my friend said that was a good thing — he didn't want to remember a lot of things that had happened to him in the past.

∽

During all this, I began a friendship with Anna. It started when I signed up for the walking contemplation again. I heard a rumour that she was going to lead it, and when I showed up, the rumour turned out to be true. I'd seen her earlier wandering around the gardens, and sometimes, out of my window, I would see her sitting with her face in the sun, surrounded by the older people in wheelchairs. I worried about her getting sunburned. I could sense her boredom, but it wasn't the malicious kind of boredom that Holly suffered from.

There was only one other patient who would sometimes join in. He was an older guy who was said to have not spoken since his wife passed away. He followed me silently as I followed Anna, also silently, because that was the nature of the exercise — not talking and focusing, so I focused on my steps. Or I tried to focus. Mostly I was distracted because of Anna — I tried not to think about Anna walking in front of me, but that was all I could think about. Her hair would take on a lovely, warm golden glint in the afternoon light, and I was often distracted by the strands of it coming out of her bun, brushing against her delicate shoulders. Her waist was unbelievably small, so small that I couldn't stop imagining my hands around it, circling it in full enclosure. She always wore those long, old-fashioned dresses covering most of her body, which suited her — she reminded me of those medallion portraits of pretty Victorian relatives that hung in my mother's boudoir. I liked to guess which particular dress she'd be wearing, one of her three blue ones or the white one or the darker one whose colour made me think of coffee. The coffee-coloured dress was probably the most intricate, with fine lace at the bottom and a high lace collar, like creamy froth that wrapped around her slender neck. She didn't wear a lot of jewellery; there was a set of pearl and gold earrings that dangled from her sweet little earlobes like raindrops and another set that was sapphire, which she wore with the coffee dress. When she walked, she made small, careful steps, and her hips swayed slightly in a gentle pendulum of feminine grace.

After the walk, Anna would say thank you, and I would watch her go. Her feet made crunching noises on the sun-drenched gravel. She smelled of lilies of the valley or, at least, that was the smell I associated with her — it might've come from the flowers themselves, but to me she was like the sweetest thing in that garden. I could smell her long after she'd be gone.

∽

In my sessions with Doctor I was beginning to get uncomfortable — more uncomfortable than ever before. I started to feel guilty even though I still believed that I hadn't done anything to warrant it. This wasn't the guilt over what happened with Holly. It was all about Anna. I was like a little kid with a big secret, bursting to tell it and unable to. I wanted to talk about Anna but I couldn't. Instead, I talked about Holly, but I thought about Anna. Doctor didn't want me to talk about loving Holly (Anna) but I ignored him. He said I was perhaps regressing, and he warned me he would have to speak to my father about the setback. But I was reckless. I had to talk about Holly (Anna) because she was all I thought about. Doctor hadn't said that the setback would mean I would have to stay longer, but at that point I couldn't imagine myself being anywhere else. My old ambitions troubled me mostly because now I felt as if I was betraying that part of myself I didn't understand anymore. Why did I even want to travel the world? Without Anna? Because Anna hadn't been in my world, yes, but how was travel even possible now that she was in it and was all I could seem to think about?

Her presence made me feel as if I had been given a new chance, as if everything was completely new. I had thought my life was prematurely over, but now it was as if my life had been handed back to me. I didn't understand how that happened exactly, why I felt this way, because we barely communicated. I followed her around the maze, and then I would thank her and that was that. I saw her at meals, and we exchanged hellos if I was lucky enough to pass her — I tried to do it at least once a day. Because I was well-behaved, I was usually seated not far from her, with all the others who behaved well. She, on the other hand, sat at the head table with Doctor and the nurses who were not on the meal rotation and didn't have to supervise us.

When the weather was nice, she would often be in the garden with the people in wheelchairs, and we would nod at each other during my outside time. Most importantly, I saw her in the library. During my twice-a-week shift there, I sorted books and organized index cards. From behind shelves I watched Anna's dark head bent over a book. When she walked ahead of me during the walking contemplation, I didn't have a lot of choice but to watch her, and going out of my way at the library to observe her gave me a little thrill even though I knew what I was doing wasn't gentlemanly.

One day in the library, she stopped me to ask about a book. It was *Alice in Wonderland*. She said she had never read it because her father said it was a children's book, and it was silly, but she heard so much about it and wanted to borrow it. She spoke quickly, and her request sounded rehearsed; I realized I was making her nervous. She wasn't just talking to one of the Mad, it was more that she was speaking to a man. I was sure of it, and that gave me a spike in confidence, so I spoke calmly to her and told her about the book and showed her where to find it.

She signed it out. As she was walking away, I was overwhelmed with joy but also felt some fear. She was, after all, married, and I was a prisoner.

∽

I could sense something was going to happen between us — right from the beginning, I suppose, but now it felt like a certainty. I saw her next at the walking contemplation. The silent man who'd usually join us wasn't there. It was just me and her, and we didn't talk, and we went around the maze, and at the end she looked right into my eyes and said, Thank you. Her voice was a whisper, but it echoed in my ears for the rest of the day. And her eyes — I saw them, too, whenever I heard her whisper-echo in my head.

The next day, she returned the book to the library. She looked me straight in the eyes, again, and then she smiled and blushed and looked away.

I mean, that's when it started. We talked about the book. She kept glancing at me, and I could tell that she was forcing herself to not look down, and her hazel eyes got darker — it was like some magic trick — the more excited she got talking about the book. I wondered if that's what happened when she was excited, and I wanted to make her excited again.

∽

I didn't know who to talk to about my feelings so I wrote about them. I wrote something like a poem, but I tore it up. I'd never written a poem before, but I'd read enough poetry to be able to mimic it — there were passages about Anna's hair being like quiet fire in the sun and her eyes like a pond I wanted to drown in. I didn't think it was a good poem, but it helped to write it.

I saw her the next day. She was in the garden with the Wheelchairs. It was right after breakfast, and I was walking toward the social hall where the patients were encouraged to spend their morning attempting to behave like normal human beings, conversing. On the blackboard were the prescribed topics of the day — "Flora and Fauna," "Holidays," "Mother and Father" — but barely anyone could carry a real conversation, so we had to sit there for an hour pretending to try. Through the window in a hallway I saw Anna talking to one of the old ladies. She leaned close, straight-spined, intimate, yet restrained. Then she looked up and squinted in my direction. My stomach clenched, and I felt light-headed, almost like the time I got drunk and fell, except this time I was rooted to the ground. I don't know if she could see me. She shielded her eyes from the sun.

Unnoticed, I turned around and walked toward the side door. I never did anything like that at the hospital — I always followed my routine, my days divided in segments of meals, mandated free time or socializing, sessions with staff, library duties, naps ... I felt dizzy from upsetting the routine. But it seemed like I had to no choice, my feet carrying me away.

She saw me in the doorway as I stood in the shadows.

I didn't know if she knew what I was locked up for, but I prayed she didn't think I was dangerous. I prayed she wouldn't think I was unhinged. I probably looked unhinged, staring at her like that. She stared back and didn't move, didn't come up to me, but some things you just know. I knew she saw me. *Me.* I went back inside.

She came to the library again and signed out another book: *Through the Looking Glass.*

I didn't see her for a few days after that, and I cried in the session with Doctor. I said I missed Holly, and I said I felt as if I couldn't go on without Holly in my life. I didn't worry if my emotional outburst would mean I would have to be kept at the hospital longer — as I said, I no longer felt truly upset about where I was. Yes, the reasonable part of me was alarmed that I was perhaps ruining my chances of a timely release, but the reasonable part of me was getting weaker and weaker. I didn't even know anymore what being reasonable meant, really; nothing about where I was made sense.

I remember looking at Doctor's hands and feeling disgusted. He touched her with those hands. I was sure she didn't love him. I don't know how I was sure. I hated that he touched her.

I needed to talk about hate. I focused on his hands, which brought up the feeling of hatred with ease. But I couldn't say *hate* regardless. I couldn't say I hated Holly because Holly was a code word for Anna.

∽

We kissed for the first time in the maze. For the past few sessions, it had only been the two of us doing the walking contemplation. The silent man was sick with the flu, and then he disappeared. It's awful to say, but I didn't care if he'd died. I usually tried to enquire about patients I knew who had disappeared, but I didn't ask about him. I was too distracted because I was happy to be in the maze with Anna. That was the only thing that mattered in my world.

On the day of the kiss, Anna led the walk, with me following her as always, watching her shoulders and trying not to think about my fluttering heart. I was concentrating so hard on my steps and trying to stay calm that when she stopped suddenly, I bumped right into her, that sweet smell of lilies filling my nostrils, her hair brushing the tip of my nose, so intimate, so shocking in that moment. I started to apologize, but she held a finger to her lips, shushing me. We stood there for a moment without saying anything. She looked at me. I looked at her. Then we were kissing. Her lips were incredibly soft. I tried to remember how Holly felt, but I couldn't remember. I thought about how she bit me, but I pushed the thought away quickly. I didn't want to think about Holly because that seemed disrespectful now that I was in love with Anna, and Anna's lips were the only ones I cared to kiss from now on.

ص

After that, I was cured. I don't know how else to describe it. I suppose, I mean, my torment over whether I was guilty, sane, or insane, and whether I'd be released on time was no longer that important. It was an occasional bellyache that never lasted for too long. I knew that I wasn't living in a fairy tale, but it felt that way. Our sneaking around felt like a fairy tale, even more so because it was dangerous. There were so many eyes watching, and we had to be careful. We would have to make the eyes not see. We set up little structures made out of stones — that was a sign to go and meet on the roof; we would often meet there because that was the only place where the eyes couldn't see us. Anna would unlatch the gate and wait for me.

I have never been superstitious, but it crossed my mind in the beginning how our meeting on the roof was like an echo of my meeting with Holly. But I didn't let those thoughts occupy my mind for too long. Holly was becoming more and more like some kind of bad dream, and what happened with her no longer seemed real.

ص

Even though I was skeptical of the stories that went around the asylum, I continued to be curious about what St. Francis of Assisi told me about Anna living in Canada on her own by the ocean; it stuck in my mind. I liked that Anna was not just an attractive older woman who happened to marry a psychiatrist. As I've mentioned, I always thought she seemed more like a patient. The way she walked a little too slowly, the way she sat still sometimes, staring off into space — it seemed as if something bad had happened to her, and she was getting better now but was not yet whole. And, despite the troubling aspects of that story, I liked that she had a different life before becoming Doctor's wife.

One day I finally got the courage to ask about her past.

She said that there was no story — she met Doctor through her father, and, because she was in her late twenties, it seemed like a wise idea to get married. Voila.

That is probably the silliest thing I've ever heard you say, I told her.

That's because it is, she said. It was all quite silly.

We were sitting in the garden where we did our walks, on a bench side by side, hidden from the curious eyes by a cluster of lilac bushes that filled the air with a sweet, fresh scent that complemented hers.

You can tell me anything, Anna, I said. I love you no matter what.

This was the first time I actually said those words, and we sat in silence after that, both of us shocked and elated.

I love you, too, she said eventually.

I grabbed her hand and kissed it gently and said, quietly, as if she were a bird I was afraid of startling, You can tell me what happened to you.

She didn't cry when she told me the real story, although she looked like she might, the whole time.

When she was in her late teens, living in France with her family, Anna received a few marriage proposals. Her family was very old-fashioned; the way her sisters and mother dressed was conservative, Victorian. Anna's entire life seemed to be structured around training to become a perfectly entertaining wife — she learned to play piano, she sang, she danced, she could speak on a few topics, such as music and local fauna. She went to school, but no one encouraged her to pursue any academic studies, although she did well. She enjoyed novels, and her father supported her reading but not writing. She said she wrote some poetry but never showed it to anyone. Like her two sisters, she did some needlepoint, and she did it with more flare than either of them, having had a more active imagination. She was particularly proud of her needlepoint portrait of the family cat, which her mother praised but found too eccentric to display. Unsure what to do with her life, Anna waited for love, just as her older sisters had before her. Because she had never been treated as anything more than someone's future wife, she grew up believing that once marriage came, her real life would start and she would no longer be bored. Boredom was a moral weakness, and although her family was not religious, feeling idle and acting on it was frowned upon. Once, her mother locked her in her bedroom suite for two nights after Anna decided to spend a night in the garden to look at stars — she was discovered by one of her sisters who was particularly worried about causing a scandal. After that, Anna's education for future wifehood was accelerated, and her mother threw a small garden party to officially debut her youngest daughter. The proposals started coming in when she turned seventeen. Almost immediately, Anna became disillusioned about her belief in love's saving power. That's because she didn't feel love; she found nothing extraordinary about the human beings who approached her and proclaimed their intentions. The men didn't seem to be especially enlightened, superior to her as she had hoped they would be; they had no solutions to boredom because she still felt it, even more so when in their company. She found the whole process of courtship ridiculous and unpleasant: she hated talking with the awkward young contenders who approached her, she didn't enjoy attending balls, she hated having to be a debutante when she was presented — like "a sacrificial cow," in her words — to various boys, who all seemed the same — "sacrificial bulls," except, she said, none of them seemed particularly viral. She turned down all of the proposals, including the second-last one from a British naval officer named Thomas — when she said his name, her voice shook. Thomas was the only one of her suitors who seemed interesting enough; he was older, he talked about travelling the world, and the first time they met, he made her laugh with an inappropriate comment about her sister's sour expression: he compared the sister to a macaque monkey he had befriended once while in India. They met a few times, and Anna looked forward to their meetings, but she rejected his romantic advances — she felt she needed more time. She was sure he'd stick around anyway. He didn't. Soon, Anna realized she had made a mistake and went to him to tell him she'd reconsidered his proposal. She knew she was being coquettish, playing hard to get — there was some gossip about him being a bit of a cad, and she thought he needed to work harder for her attention, and she went as far as to admit all of that, but he was no longer interested in marrying her. He still loved her, he told her, but he could not trust her now. She said she would do anything to change his mind, but he was firm.

He soon left France, and Anna travelled with her mother to Spain, where he was stationed, to convince him yet again to be with her. It was all so humiliating, but she said it also felt as if she finally had something to give meaning to her dull life. Growing up with a famous artist father who was revered by his disciples — and generally by most people around him — made Anna feel insignificant. She had none of her father's talents. She didn't think she could ever be serious about writing poetry or painting like him, and she didn't want to become like her mother, who had to pretend she wasn't upset over the father's mistresses and his lack of attention. And after Anna's disappointing experiences with young suitors, being only a wife-in-training seemed like a bad joke. She didn't take to it as well as her sisters had.

Anna felt that a man like Thomas would be quite different from her father, that he would be a partner, someone she had a lot in common with. When they courted, she loved how comfortable she felt, how he laughed at her jokes about her father, and how he made similar jokes about his father, who was stern and old-fashioned. Anna thought their friendship was as important to him as it was to her. But that was in the past. Now, no one was making jokes, and Anna was desperate. While in Spain, Thomas met with her only once, and it was a short meeting with her mother present. Thomas mostly spoke to her mother. The meeting happened in a park, a tense walk where Anna was so anxious she couldn't think of a thing to say. She knew she appeared uninterested. Thomas and her mother talked about the weather, fashion, and people they knew back home in France. Before leaving, Anna wrote a note for Thomas telling him how she really felt, but he never replied.

After returning from Spain, Anna wrote Thomas more letters, and he rarely wrote back. She tried to write poems about
him in her journal — poems that she still never showed anybody, especially her father, for fear of being mocked.

She talked to Thomas in her mind all the time, and sometimes she believed he could hear her and that he responded. She
became convinced they had a psychic connection. She decided
she couldn't live without him. She rejected another marriage
proposal from a protege friend of her father's because she was
certain she and Thomas would eventually be together.

After Thomas was transferred to Halifax, Canada, Anna
followed him there. Not wanting to get caught, she dressed as
a man to board the ship. This was later seen as a sign of her
instability, possibly even an indicator of gender identity disorder or, worse, schizophrenia.

She spent two years in Halifax, renting a small apartment
under a false name, stalking Thomas when she could. The rest
of the time she spent alone inside her small room. She made no
friends. She didn't take good care of herself — her beautiful,
old-fashioned dresses couldn't withstand the harsh Canadian
weather, and they disintegrated. She didn't brush her hair
often. She ate very little and lost weight.

The family she lived with was troubled by their quiet, fragile tenant. They noticed her French accent, too, of course, and
made her confess who she was and contacted her parents. She
was urged to come home. In his letters, her father threatened to
disown her. He wrote that if she didn't come back, she would
be dead to him.

*I wonder what all those people who love you will think of
you if you disown your youngest daughter,* she wrote back to
him.

He never replied but he started sending her a monthly allowance — it was the only thing he could do for her as she refused to return home.

∾

Thomas visited her a few times in her small apartment, and every time she would feel more hopeful about their reunion. She washed and brushed her hair before his visits, and she put on her best dress — one she said was the replica of the coffee-coloured one she wore at the asylum — that she reserved for only wearing inside when she saw him. But there was no real romantic reunion. He didn't want her back. He wanted her in that one way that men want women, but he didn't want to marry her.

And then, one day, Thomas was sent off to Barbados on another military mission. Anna followed but left him alone for the most part. She was too exhausted by her own self. She wandered the streets in tattered dresses and talked to herself; she sometimes hallucinated that she lived with Thomas and had a family with him.

Her father, alerted by some people in the town she resided in, came to get her. He brought her home and had her outfitted in new dresses — although nothing as fancy as she wore in her younger years — and her mother took care of her hair.

Anna thought she would spend the rest of her days at home, but because she started talking about Thomas again — she told one of the maids she was engaged to him — and later was caught writing letters to him, her father had had enough and deposited her in an asylum.

That was where she met the Croatian Doctor, who took a special interest in her. He was astonished by her ability to pick up languages so effortlessly — out of boredom she asked him to speak to her in his native tongue. He complimented her conservative clothing, said it reminded him of the way women were when he was a young man. She said he would tell her that despite her age, she seemed innocent, like a girl. After learning about Thomas, he diagnosed her with "lovesickness," which was not an ailment described previously; it became his ambition to make it into an actual mental disorder. He was excited how his attention seemed to get Anna out of her stupor. He wasn't sure he could cure her completely, but he believed with time Anna's condition would subside.

The doctor and his language filled the vacuum of her boredom perfectly, although Anna never believed he loved her — she said, darkly, that he seemed to be incapable of love — but he valued her. And most importantly, he let her talk about Thomas, and he took notes as she talked, which made her feel that she was contributing to something important — after failing to win Thomas back, this seemed like another chance at doing something meaningful. She finally felt she wasn't on this planet by mistake.

When Doctor asked her to marry him, she said yes. She said she wasn't happy or unhappy about it. She simply felt resigned and had decided that from now on, it was life that would take control over her, not the other way around.

Despite her passivity, it became obvious to Doctor that she was getting better, and he concluded that it was through loving another — himself — that the case study patient — Anna — and the condition of "lovesickness" could be cured.

He finished his research and sent the study to the Academy of Psychiatry in London, England, for evaluation.

Anna learned that Thomas himself had married, but she didn't feel upset about that — without her pursuit, it was almost as if Thomas, the person, was not important. More and more, she realized that she couldn't understand why she had wanted so badly to be with him. Eventually, she could no longer understand it at all.

So I am all better now, she said, and looked at me. Her eyes changed colours, became darker, and I moved to kiss her.

28

THE FIRST TIME Anna and I made love wasn't on the roof — it was in the small abandoned orangery on the old grounds that I had never visited before. I knew of it as the place where you could go to do things you weren't allowed to do, like smoke cigarettes, or be with a girl. My friend, St. Francis of Assisi, said he used to go there with a girl named Mary Magdalene, who disappeared one day a long time ago, and he could no longer remember what she looked like or if she was lying to him about being Mary Magdalene.

Where they could act territorial and unreasonable everywhere else, the patients respected each other's privacy when it came to the orangery. To signal you were using it, you had to leave a certain sign, a rock painted in white stripes outside the door.

Anna said she was anxious, so I told her there was nothing to be afraid of, but I was anxious, too, and it wasn't because

I was worried about getting caught. It was because I worried about not being able to perform. I was a decade younger than Anna and not experienced like her. I was troubled by the fact that she maybe had some great lovers, like the naval officer. Why else would she follow him around the world? I also wondered if my encounter with Holly had scarred me in some way, but I couldn't share any of that with Anna, so I just focused on comforting her, telling her it was going to be fine and that we wouldn't get caught, and then we were kissing, and I couldn't think properly anymore.

There was a small space surrounded by pots and plants just big enough for us to fit into, small palm trees and small exotic trees and wild ivy climbing the windows outside. Anna had smuggled a fur vest, and we spread it on the ground to lie on. Then we were kissing again, and I was reassured by my own body responding to her, although I took on her worries about how we might get caught, and so I thought about how we should do this quickly. But there was no way I was going to rush. I wanted to make her happy, and I wanted to give her pleasure.

I admit, I didn't think of Anna being in danger, too — in the midst of our passionate engagement, I could no longer remember who she was — what I mean is that she was the wife of Doctor — and who I was, or why I was where I was, in the asylum.

I kissed her everywhere — on her neck and her collarbone ... I won't go on too much about that. I will mention how despite the heat, she felt as if she were made out of marble rather than flesh, how she was not entirely human but some other being, some kind of a superior creature. As always, she smelled of lilies of the valley, except the scent was stronger now and mixed with her own slightly sour, warm feminine smell.

She let me kiss her between her legs, and I was surprised by her sudden assertiveness as she guided my head, pressed it harder so that I would know to apply more pressure — when she did that, I thought about her being a little wicked, perhaps, and I had a brief flashback to Holly, but it didn't last.

After awhile, she started moaning, and her body shook slightly in little tremors that seemed to accumulate against my tongue as she started closing her legs and moaning louder, pushing herself against me and saying, Oh God, oh God ... I'd never experienced anything like it before, and I've never felt as proud of myself as I did then. I felt so powerful, like I finally mattered. It was as if I was a boy one moment and the next I was a man — her orgasm moved me from one phase in my life into the next, and it was intoxicating.

When I entered her, I looked her in the eyes the whole time, and it was incredibly intense. I wasn't sure if I wasn't causing her pain, but she kept smiling at me in this dreamy, dazed way, so I continued, and she pulled me toward her, and she wrapped her legs around my back.

I'd never known this much pleasure. It seemed to be coming at me from everywhere now — from the inside of my groin and down my legs but also in the top of my head and sparking down my lower back. She moved along with me. Her body felt so small but also strong, and it sometimes seemed as if she was holding me up. As if it was she who was making love to me — I mean that it was the perfect thing.

When I came, words came out of me, as well. I said her name over and over, said I loved her and called on God, and swore and called on God again, and after it was all done, she let me stay inside her, and stroked my head, and said she loved me, too, with all her heart.

∾

We were unexpectedly lucky that Doctor became really busy around that time. He would cancel some of his sessions with patients, including me, and would disappear into his office or, rumour had it, to his basement lab to conduct experiments. I thought nothing about whatever experiments he might've been conducting — the patients were always exaggerating things, and you couldn't believe anybody because they were all insane.

Anna was on her own a lot, and since her husband — I hate using that word, but that's what he was — kept so busy, the whole place seemed to relax, which gave us much time to spend with one another.

Most of the time, Anna and I would meet on the roof. The orangery belonged to everyone, but the roof was ours only because Anna had the key to the gate. We lay there like we are here, under the same sky, and I told her stories from books that she hadn't read yet, but she was better than me at storytelling because she told me *Alice* stories that she had made up herself.

There was Alice as a teenager and Alice falling in love and Alice being in love with a boy from a magical garden, and then there was Alice travelling the world with the boy from the magical garden and them living on a deserted island and then travelling the desert. And there was the two of them walking on the Great Wall of China.

I had to recall the places I'd read about from the time when I used to dream about travelling the world, back in my old life. I was fine with that life being gone, maybe even for good, especially now that with Anna I was travelling again by telling her about what I had remembered so that she could place her stories somewhere other than just Wonderland or the Other Side of the Mirror.

I never considered myself to be particularly creative, but inspired by Anna I was able to describe a foreign place as if I'd been there — I could add smell and sound and touch. It was like another dimension had opened. So I explained the way the Nile smelled — like rotting leaves but also flowers, exotic flowers like lotus, which I told Anna smelled like her perfume, so the banks of the river smelled a lot like lily of the valley. That was probably not true but she liked it anyway. I told her about the rainforest and how humid it was — you felt like you couldn't breathe, and the inside of your nose was wet and hot. You were always sweating, and when it rained — and it rained all the time — sometimes the temperature would drop so quickly that your sweat would feel cold, and suddenly you'd be freezing right in the middle of the tropics.

I made up some stories about pink salmon swimming upstream in northern Canada, or how a grizzly bear would wander into the river and smack the fish in the head and eat the head ... I would describe the way the fish scales sparkled in the sun, silvery and slick, as the fish threw themselves against wet rocks, and how frigid the river was. I remember saying, It would freeze the tips of your fingers purple, and she extended her white hands, and we stared at the tips of her fingers. When she lived in Halifax, Anna never left the city. She had no idea about the country's diverse geography. It was the same with the Bahamas, although she remembered that it was hot and rainy, which she preferred to the sleet and frost of Canada, to the icy, foreboding Atlantic sea that she said made her feel as if she could never escape — and she didn't mean the country, she meant Thomas's hold on her.

Finally, I told her about the island where we both lived and fell in love — I told her the rumour about the vineyard that produced unusually sweet grapes that were tinted red with blood. The soil was rich in minerals that came from disintegrating human bones. I told this story late in the evening, and Anna covered her mouth as she let out a nervous giggle. I didn't like making her afraid, but she urged me to tell her more. I remembered reading about the plague in school, first the Black Death and then an outbreak of malaria that had affected Trogir and how children were affected, dying in such numbers that their population in the city decreased by almost half. There were dozens of funerals a day, the priests and nuns awake at all hours to honour the dead or to attend to the live ones who were quarantined. The carpenters made hundreds of small coffins, but they could barely keep up; some of the bodies had to be buried later, which created a problem in the heat. There was a stench in the air of rotting bodies, and there were ongoing outbreaks of the virus.

As for the island, it was piled up with corpses, but it was not unusual for the sick to get dropped off, as well, and their terrible fate was to be burnt alive along with the corpses.

We never talked about Doctor. It was as if he didn't exist, or if he did exist, it was like he was a Jabberwock — not even a monster: a made-up monster in a made-up tale.

He didn't cancel *all* of my sessions, so I would still see him sporadically, and I would tell him the same story about Holly, about Holly's accusations and my perceived innocence and my delusions about it. There were no longer feelings attached to my stories, and I think that had to do with Anna, because she was more and more in my life. Everything was easier, and I no longer worried about being truthful, believable … whatever I was worried about before in the sessions.

When I talked about Holly, it felt no different from telling *Alice in Wonderland* tales on the roof, except "Holly" tales seemed so much more real because they existed in my and Anna's universe. Doctor said once it seemed to him like I was making progress, but he didn't look pleased, only suspicious, and I thought how there was no winning with him, but I didn't really care anymore.

დ

Somehow Anna and I managed to carry on all summer. Now that strikes me as astonishing, but back then our happiness made us feel invincible. I remember being full of wonderful expectations on awakening, and every morning seemed like an event because I knew I had a day ahead of me filled with goodness. I couldn't believe I had someone to share the world with, and what a miraculous world it was, where everything was brighter and more exciting than before I met her. I wasn't sure why I was chosen for this miracle, but I was thankful.

We sneaked out, we talked, and we met on the roof or the orangery to make love. We still walked in the maze and delighted in exchanging little secret touches — my fingers brushing her back, or her hand extending, like a tiny wing of a bird, so that I could grasp it and squeeze it, unseen. We whispered in the library; we giggled behind bookshelves as I'd try to be naughty and feel her up. In the cafeteria, we would sometimes look at each other and nod politely like we were strangers, like she was the wife of the doctor who was treating me. We both lived two different lives: our life together and then our life with him.

As I said, Anna and I never talked about him, but she did hint at her unhappiness, although she never said it was Doctor who caused it; it didn't need to be said. One time, when we were meeting on the roof as usual, she showed up late, her face wet from tears. She said, repeatedly, I don't know what to do. I said, With what? With him, she said, finally. Is he cruel to you? I said. He's so cold, she said. He doesn't love anybody. She cried and I held her. There was nothing I could do for her, and secretly I was glad that he was pushing her away even though that seemed to cause her pain, which made me feel jealous. I wished she didn't care at all about how he was, but it didn't matter anyway because I really hoped we would be together in the future. We had to be — there was no other way.

But despite my optimism, I knew that we were both very much like children. We told each other stories about fairy tale lands, about Alice in different Wonderlands, but we had no solid plans for our own lives. I suppose the island itself was like a fairy tale, with its dark history, its hospital like a fantasy castle with its shadows and gossip of troubling, horrible things happening behind closed doors, people dying of some unknown virus or disappearing mysteriously. There weren't that many deaths in the summer, but there was still that undercurrent of something bad happening all around. We chose not to see it, or we couldn't see it because we were too happy and too much in love, and it would upset our love to see it. But it was there.

I also didn't know — in retrospect, how naive of me — that we were being watched. Even though we couldn't see it for what it was, we had no way to hide the energy of our love from the people who weren't patients, the ones who weren't too drugged or too mad to figure it out.

29

ONE NIGHT I was woken up by an orderly. As I was told to dress, I remember looking out the window at the sky, looking at the crescent moon. It was so beautiful. It is a very vivid memory, that dark, velvety sky and the moon as if cut out from it. The world seemed so peaceful even though I had an instant hunch that everything — my love, my happiness, even my life — was going to be over soon.

I was walked to a cell, where I sat alone on the bed for a long time. There were no windows, and I had no way of knowing when the night ended and the day begun. I didn't cry or scream. I dozed off here and there, and I waited. I still felt calm but full of dread, which was an extraordinary combination, one that I'd never felt before. I think I had come to accept my situation right away — I would say there was even some sick relief in things finally coming to a head — or I was simply in shock and delusional about the seriousness of it.

At one point, Doctor entered the cell. Neither of us spoke. He sat in a chair across from my bed and watched me as I sat, then lay, on the bed. I couldn't doze off with him watching me even though I felt exhausted as soon as he entered the cell.

After some time, Doctor said he would have to try another kind of treatment with me because I was resistant to therapy, and he decided I was regressing continuously. He said he was failing me and he didn't like failing. It sounded like a threat, so I said he wasn't failing me and I was feeling much better, much more clearheaded, but when I said it, my voice sounded so quiet and panicked.

He disagreed — he must be failing me because I still talked about what happened with Holly as if I couldn't accept I had hurt her. He didn't believe that I truly understood my guilt.

I said nothing. We both knew why he was really there talking to me. Neither of us admitted it. Maybe I was wrong … but I wasn't wrong. I was only hoping I was wrong. I knew he was waiting for me to say something about it, and it was cruel of him to make me wonder and be nervous, but he had every right to be cruel. It was the first time, too, that I felt awful about what I had done, even though I never trusted him and never liked him, but he must've felt so betrayed. It only occurred to me then that my own happiness was selfish, and I really had no right to feel like I was the one being wronged. Eventually, he stood up and left. I wondered if and when he'd be back. I thought he might leave me there, maybe to starve. He returned sometime later. I stood. I said, I do know I'm guilty. He laughed, which startled me because I never heard him laugh, and it was like no laughter I'd heard before. It was like a parody of laughter. When I heard it I understood that he was a parody himself and that he was not like the rest of us; he just pretended to be.

I know I'm guilty, I said, again, to make him stop laughing.

It's too late, he said.

And in the cell with Doctor watching me like I was an amusing specimen — which I was — I was no longer able to choose not to see. It was as if I suddenly sobered up and I finally acknowledged his evil: things he was doing, things that his bribed staff were doing — the abuse of patients, the secret therapies that rendered some of my friends unresponsive, walking but more dead than alive.

Anything else? he said after awhile.

But I had nothing else to say to him, and after a short time he got up and left.

∽

I completely lost any sense of time. That's the first thing you lose almost immediately — the inability to tell how much of it passes. Once you realize that you can no longer tell, it's too late to devise any kind of system to be able to track it. I fell asleep. I woke up. I fell asleep again. I ate but whether it was three times a day or three times a night, I had no idea.

Doctor would come in regularly every day or every night — I couldn't tell without windows — and he would just sit there. I didn't talk either. We would sit in silence, and sometimes I wouldn't even be sure he was really there, and because I wasn't sure, I felt that I was finally, truly mad, and there was some relief in knowing that I was what they all said I was. I could just give into it. I could stop having dreams about building my life outside of the walls, and even Anna would no longer be an issue. It was impossible for me to become who I promised her I would be because I was no longer in this world. I thought of her, sure, but it was too much to think of her in that place. I finally started to use the techniques taught by Doctor — I kept rerouting my thinking whenever something that bothered me — she — would show up in my mind, which was all the time.

They began to restrain me during Doctor's visits. The orderlies moved like shadows, in and out. I couldn't see their faces. In the beginning I struggled, although never too violently — I just struggled to prove to myself that I was still alive. It was a good move to restrain me as I had thoughts of strangling Doctor, not all the time but some of the time, and he must've sensed that in me. I had never been a violent person, but I was in the madhouse for a violent crime and, like I said, I thought that maybe I was finally becoming what they were saying I was.

It was perhaps that budding violence that would make me thrash in my restraints or scream obscenities. I was bound, but there was an almost euphoric sense of liberation when I gave into my anger. I found myself enjoying being a difficult patient; it meant *something* was happening, which was better than nothing happening. I could scream whatever the *fuck* I wanted. Fuck them all. If I was mad, then I would show them mad. If I got too out of control and Doctor could not get through to me, an orderly would be called, and I would receive an injection, which would put me to sleep. It was always a dreamless sleep, like death — just falling into complete darkness, a well of black that absorbed no light, just sucked you in.

When I woke up, I wouldn't be sure if I hadn't in fact died. I would feel the walls, pinch myself, say my name out loud.

Eventually, I'd convince myself that I was back in the cell and I was not dead. On the ground, there would be food that had been delivered through a slot in the bottom of the door.

I would be restrained, again, and Doctor would enter the cell. I would shout at him, call him a monster, demand to be released, beg to be released, cry.

He would say nothing. He would just sit there as always, watching me.

After awhile, the anger left me. I suppose I got bored of it and could no longer derive any joy from acting that way. When the orderlies would show up with the restraints and sometimes with a syringe, I would lie still and let them tie me up without thrashing. I was still focused on their touch, grateful for it, but I no longer tried to provoke them. I didn't want to. I just let them do whatever they wanted, and I even anticipated their touch, the painful twisting of my arms.

I also started to anticipate Doctor's visits. One day — or night — I realized I actually really wanted to see him. Suddenly, I couldn't stop thinking about him: his round glasses skewed on his thin nose, his shiny blue eyes, how impossibly long his arms were, his fingers that looked like spider legs, like they had extra joints. I used to be repulsed by his appearance, but now I was trying to recall all the details. I even remembered things like a small heart-shaped stain on his white coat over his breast pocket and how his nose would twitch in a barely perceptible spasm every time he walked into the room — as if he was trying to smell me out and couldn't help himself but didn't want me to notice. I fantasized about him liking me — I wanted him to like me. I wanted that more than I wanted to kill him. I wanted him to be my friend and, for the first time, I sincerely craved his approval.

I begged him to talk to me. I wailed like a baby. Please talk to me, talk to me ... but he was silent. I had to be restrained again.

Doctor didn't want to talk to me. Silence was clever on his part — it only made me more desperate. With time, however, much of it passed. His visits became so important that they erased everything else. There were no longer other things, there was no outside of the cell, and there was no Anna anymore. I thought about him when he wasn't there, and when he was there I felt nervous, like I was in love. I was transferring all of my feelings for Anna to him. This was my punishment. He imprisoned me physically, and he would now imprison my mind. I wasn't sure what he planned for my future, and anticipating that was another thing I fixated on. Perhaps he would torture me! In my state, I believed torture would be preferable to his silence.

In my last attempt to get him to react, I staged one more outburst. One night — or day — I had an idea to kick the door. Once I got going, I couldn't stop. I didn't seem to be getting tired — all of my attention was on the repetitive action I was performing. I don't know if I wanted to kick through the door or if this was just about attention; whatever it was, it put me in a kind of trance. I couldn't feel my body getting tired. I imagined my muscles were like cogs, interlocking and perpetuating their own movement, that I myself was some kind of a machine, a thing that had only one purpose: to kick.

I don't know when I passed out. I came to, and the orderly was talking loudly about the mess. They lit a candle inside my cell, and I could see the door was tarnished, deep dark stains that shone copper in the light. I looked down. I was no longer wearing my shoes, and my feet looked like minced meat, blackened and bloodied, with toenails cracked and broken and a few missing. On the ground, there were the remnants of my shoes, two mangled pieces of red-soaked canvas.

After that, I could no longer walk, not that there was a lot of walking to be done in my small cell.

Eventually, I thought I lost my mind entirely. I couldn't tell reality from a dream. I was visited by Holly, and she would turn into Anna, who would disappear before I could touch her. I would close my eyes, wanting to fall asleep, and my eyes would open, and there I would be in my cell, on my mattress, alone. There was no one else with me. What happened? Was I here? Where was I?

He still came into my cell and still did not speak. In my final memories of him he's holding a handkerchief up to his mouth — presumably to remind himself to stay mum?

I don't know when he stopped coming to my cell. I couldn't tell.

I don't believe my feet ever recovered, but as I said, there was no need to walk. A heavy, mushroom-like, slightly fruity smell started filling the cell and never left.

It would be tedious to go on about that time any longer; I've gone on about it for too long already. I will only say that I never saw Anna again.

part 4

josephine's story

30

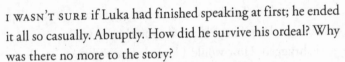

I WASN'T SURE if Luka had finished speaking at first; he ended it all so casually. Abruptly. How did he survive his ordeal? Why was there no more to the story?

There isn't really much more to it, he shrugged.

How did you get out?

I didn't, he laughed, grimly.

What happened in that cell?

He turned to me, his mouth full of those sharp teeth again as he smiled. He said, What do you think happened?

I felt a sudden wave of grief combined with an almost physical sensation of a heavy door pressing against my face. Before the feeling had a chance to overwhelm me, I took a deep breath. Did you —

He turned away. That's the funny thing about it. I wouldn't be able to say yes, to pinpoint the moment or what preceded it, for you. But I must've. I just remember leaving one day like it was nothing. The door was open, and I walked through a dark corridor, and then I was outside in the sun. My feet were fine, no longer rotting. My shoes were still mangled, stained with blood. I put them on, even though I didn't need shoes. The hospital was totally empty, everything and everyone was gone.

Did you die old?

I didn't look any different from how I do now.

I see, I said. It was good that he didn't remember his death. I imagined he died from infection in his feet.

That's plausible, he said.

I'm so sorry, I said.

He said nothing.

What happened to Anna?

I wasn't there when the asylum closed.

Where were you?

He tilted his head, and one corner of his mouth went up, revealing a sharp fang. Where do you think I was?

I shrugged. How would I know? I didn't know. I no longer thought that he was something I conjured — as soon as he started his story, which existed completely outside of my imagination, I knew for sure he was a separate entity.

He said, The only clue I have is that I once heard a conversation between some people. I don't know who they were, and I couldn't see them or come close to them. They might've been students exploring the island or someone who came back to visit. One said a woman was removed from the asylum by her famous, wealthy father and put into another asylum. The other person said a woman died, and it was her doctor husband who caused it. I didn't want to find out more. What was the point? I no longer had those emotions.

He was quiet for a moment, and then he started whistling. It was a mournful, strange tune that sometimes sounded like the wind caught in shutters.

Okay, I said.

He kept whistling while looking at me dispassionately.

What is it? I said, unnerved.

He said nothing, his face blank like a doll's. I thought about what I learned about sociopaths back in school, how they were human beings who couldn't understand social cues and were incapable of empathy or remorse, but this was different because he wasn't an actual person. He wasn't alive, yet he existed, like a rock or a ruin.

He stopped whistling. He said, I was on the island for some time, roamed through all the empty rooms — surprised a few curious children and a few unwelcome tourists — but there was very little information. I left.

Left where?

He shrugged. I don't know. But I would come back, he sighed.

There was a sound of an owl hooting somewhere in the forest and then one long cry of some startled creature — a bird or a larger rodent.

He started speaking again: I can't tell you how that would happen; it's only that I would suddenly come into thinking myself. I would think myself into being. I was no longer alive, I figured that, but I hadn't quite experienced death. Death affords you freedom — the freedom of not thinking. In a way, you cease to exist. But maybe because I didn't know I was dead for a long time, I didn't quite experience that freedom. I never ceased. I retained some kind of consciousness — I am aware of my surroundings, I am aware of you, I am aware of energies of living things. I am between *here* and *there*, not that those terms can pinpoint an actual location.

Now I knew not to ask, Where is "there"? Instead I said, pointlessly, You didn't love her anymore?

I didn't *understand* it anymore. I didn't understand what it was like to love somebody. I knew I was in love with her, and I knew that ours was a tragic story, but I had no feelings about it. I can't feel, Josephine, he said, and took my hand in his. It's a little bit like this, he said.

Unlike before, now there was no sensation when our hands touched. No weight, no pressure, no warmth. Nothing. He wasn't even like a rock or a ruin. And it wasn't troubling. It was Nothing.

He held my hand until I acknowledged the Nothing. And once I acknowledged it, I understood. I wanted that to happen with Sebastian. I wanted Nothing with him. I closed my eyes. I don't know how much time passed, but when I opened them, it was pitch dark outside. The only sounds were the waves in the distance. The forest and the owls in it were quiet. The asylum was quiet. I let go of Luka's hand.

How do you feel about him now? Luka said.

How do you read my mind? I said.

It's not exactly that. But you summoned me with your need, and your mind is transparent sometimes.

My need? And why you?

Your need for love. You wanted it so badly, it's been like a religion for you. It might not be real, yet it's very real to you because you'd live for it and you'd die for it. And I lived and died because of it. In that way we are similar. Neither in nor out of love. But my story has never been concluded.

You're like Schrödinger's cat, only of love.

Luka said, Yes. I know the reference.

Was I meant to come here? Is that why you sought me out?

That would imply fate is real. Do you believe fate is real? Were you meant to meet Sebastian? Were you meant to be unhappy?

I started to say something — words I'd conditioned myself to think and say about how I was indeed unhappy, obsessed, longing — but I had to pause. Those words and thoughts no longer felt authentic. So I looked deeper inside myself, searched for what was authentic now: Sebastian was still there but muted. Static on the TV, an image coming in and out. A memory that was beginning to erode. How did that happen? It made me sad briefly to realize this, but I quickly let go of that sadness — it was dangerous. I tried to imagine a conversation we could have, but my mind was blank. What would we talk about? What did we talk about? Thinking about it now, it was banal and all on the surface. There was some intelligent banter about love in the beginning, but later it was just that miserable bathroom fucking and my phone like a bomb in my purse.

I don't want to see him again, I said, the words coming out of my mouth a revelation. Did I mean them?

You don't want to? Sebastian shouted in my head. I ignored him.

I turned on my side to look at Luka. I wasn't sure if he was looking back at me. I couldn't quite see him in the darkness, his contours barely identifiable. He could've been a mound of soil, a pile of rocks.

I listened to the island. It was still quiet.

In the distance, a lighthouse blinked in the darkness. I couldn't tell the time. I thought of Luka sitting in his dark cell, not being able to tell the time, how he died before he actually died.

I breathed in the fresh, salty air — let it fill my lungs and held it there. I exhaled loudly. There were no walls closing in. I felt my physical freedom — it expanded around me; it had no end. This was an illusion, but the point was that I was not imprisoned, and I could fool myself for a second that the world had no end.

I moved closer. The contours became more solid and the shape sharpened, outlining Luka's body. I saw his face, his eyes on me, the whites neon white in the darkness, otherworldly. Come closer, he said, or it was a thought I had, and I moved toward him. We were now nose to nose. I thought of us dancing on that terrace in Trogir. How his body was so fluid and how we didn't kiss. I opened my mouth. I worried for a moment that I would feel nothing, but he let his body acquire mass again, and his lips were soft. I thought they'd be soft, but I was still surprised just how soft. He probed the inside of my mouth gently with his tongue. He tasted faintly of honey and lemon.

$$\backsim$$

Sebastian's kisses were hungry, assertive like orders — I liked them like that. Victor probed with his tongue, which I didn't find arousing at all.

I couldn't quite describe Luka's kiss. Maybe it was as if I was kissing myself. Everything his tongue did, mine mirrored or the other way around. I was not surprised by any of his movements, but I couldn't say if they materialized in my head before they happened or if everything was happening in tandem — either way, it felt exactly how it was supposed to feel. I was very much so in my body. I was not my lover's slut to dispose of; I was not an object to be admired as it was with

Victor; I was not a vehicle for someone else's pleasure as it had been with every man I'd ever been with.

We kissed for a while. I slid out of my slightly damp dress and looked down. In the moonlight, my skin was glimmering silver like a fish. Everything felt like that, liquid. His body was in perfect alignment with mine; he was above me and then he was in me, one moment slipping into another moment, like breathing. He filled me perfectly and expanded — at times it felt as if he was inside me with his entire body. Everything around us became suffused with light, white then gold, an edge of indigo and purple, then it all faded into another sensation, a hum that reverberated throughout our bodies, an ancient voice calling from the depths of the sea. I was not climaxing yet, but my body was already elevated to some kind of higher state that I'd never experienced before with a lover. Even with Victor, when it seemed our love for each other was exactly equal — I didn't love him more than he loved me, he didn't love me less than I loved him — and we were in harmony, I never saw colours like this, never felt how it was now.

I liked rough, filthy sex, my lovers' mouths smelling of my own arousal, but this flawless scentless body, Luka's, rocking back and forth, in and out of me, was exactly what I needed to happen. With every thrust I could feel myself build up to a climax and every time I almost got there, I would be taken higher. We stayed in the same position, him on top, me wrapped around him. And I climbed and climbed and when I thought there was nowhere else to climb ...

Come on, Luka whispered. Come on.

All of a sudden, everything that hurt went away — my mother, Sebastian ... I didn't actually have the space to think of those situations and people. There was only one thing happening in my world, and it was this experience that I was in.

Come on, Luka whispered.

I climbed once again, and my body insisted on being paid attention to as it was being paid attention to. I looked right into Luka's eyes.

What was it like to make love to somebody? To enter another? *I'm making love to you*, I said back to his eyes. And as soon as the sentence formed in my head, I felt *it* — I felt what it would be like. It was as if our bodies could be travelled to and from; I became him. I was fucking myself. I could feel my own warmth wrapping around my-his cock. I was thrusting gently, parting the warm, snug walls with my-his cock, a million hugs, infinite hugs around me, my nerves tingling, rays of spasms going up and down my thighs. He kept me anchored to the ground with his eyes, and when I was inside him—inside myself, we were two energies combined into one, and it was infinitely comforting to realize that it was possible to exist beyond reality, maybe even after this life. I expected to be worried about our beauty not being equal, but now I felt like there was no difference between us. I was just as beautiful; we were the same. With him, I was not an observed object disturbed by the act of observation; we were fucking each other freely. What was happening was just part of the night, like animals hunting or the way the clouds obscured the moon.

Finally, there was nowhere higher to climb; I could no longer contain my orgasm. We shuddered against each other, contracted, convulsed in pleasure. I held on to him, feeling myself falling, but I was also holding him up, not letting *him* fall ... there was a short-lived blackness, a blackout. A sigh somewhere in the night.

This was what making love was, how it was supposed to feel. Cosmic. I was not in love with Luka. But our union seemed loving. There was relief in realizing that this was possible — to be with someone so close that you blended into them. I'd never had that. I had to either completely detach from my lovers, keep them at the length of anecdotes I remembered them by, or I would fall so obsessively that my entire happiness depended on it — the way it was with Sebastian and, earlier, almost with Victor.

Naturally, there was no way to predict how being with Luka and just our encounter in general was going to affect me in the future, whether it would leave some kind of a wormhole inside me. I couldn't know that.

But now I felt filled; I felt requited.

∽

The night was starting to dissolve. I drifted in and out of sleep next to him, his body solid, unmoving. I didn't want to cuddle the way I liked to do with real lovers, but I appreciated that he didn't disappear, that he stayed with me. I wrapped one edge of the blanket around my feet even though the night was warm; I didn't like my feet being exposed while I slept, and the blanket gave me an illusion of safety.

I dreamt of Sebastian. In my dream he was a child. I had to take care of him. In my dream, I worried that it would be discovered that I had slept with him. It was a mistake. I had no idea he was only a child! There were people who shouted at me; there was police, lawyers. I would have to go to jail. He had to tell them it was a mistake. But he was nowhere to be found. They said if they couldn't find him it would mean that he probably killed himself. I was responsible.

∽

I woke up and it was dawn. Luka's eyes were closed. He wasn't breathing, which I didn't like, but he didn't look dead in any way. I touched him and he felt real; even his skin was relatively warm, so I just ignored the little slither of fear making its way up my spine.

Now I couldn't fall back asleep. This kind of restlessness was not new to me — being with a new lover would energize my whole body. Restart it. That's how it was now. I felt restarted, full of life. Hope even — I could imagine the future, and when I dared myself to imagine it without Sebastian, I didn't despair. There was a permanent part connected to him — a kind of inner scar — that alerted me to his existence. The scar was fresh, and it wanted me to see him, fuck him again, but now that I had experienced relief instead of despair, I could accept that I maybe wouldn't. See him, fuck him.

Maybe I never would.

Maybe you never will, I said to myself.

The tears didn't materialize.

Never.

Nothing.

I got up and stretched. I took out one last sandwich from my bag, the last bottle of water. One apple that I quartered. Breakfast.

Hello, Luka said behind me.

I turned. He was standing up. I looked at the dark bush between his legs, his sleepy penis. From his belly button, there grew a neat line of hair. I always liked that. A treasure trail. I looked up at his face. He smiled at me. His teeth were pointy again.

Good morning, I said, turning back to my food, hoping he'd fix the disturbing smile. I ate quickly.

I'm sorry, he said, and I shrugged. When he showed himself again, he was dressed, the same linen trousers and a shirt, and the straw hat as the day before.

After breakfast, we took the staircase down and walked along the building. This early in the morning, the place looked very pleasant. Just old ruins, stones basking in the sun. I thought of the rooms with graffiti, the broken furniture, and metal beds, and I felt nothing much, no disturbance. The only space that evoked an emotion — grief, a sense of injustice — was the cell where Luka died.

You saw it already. We could go again, if you'd like, he said. But it's just four walls, really. There's a dirty mattress on the floor. You did see it. It has no function.

I stopped in front of one of the doorways, unsure if I wanted to go in — if I *needed* to go in for him.

He went on, And it's not a place that's — that's of me. That is me.

But we could … I could honour it, I said. I could bring flowers, say something nice about you. I want to do something for you.

He laughed that empty non-laughter that scared me.

Never mind then, I said. I pictured the cell filling with rubble, more soil, filling up all the way to the top and choking on itself eventually as years went by.

That's a good way to think about it. I like that, he said, again reading me.

The sun was gentle. I swung my hips left to right as I walked, Luka behind me. I wanted him to see my hips swing. Maybe he felt nothing and was nothing, but we had made love. It was as real as my orgasm — and that was perhaps another way to think about my eerie lover; he was like an orgasm, a state that is physical and not, that is spiritual, evasive, that can sometimes only be evoked under special circumstances. I turned to look at him. He cocked his head, his eyes chocolate warm.

You look beautiful this morning, he said.

I thought of stopping to kiss him then, but I suddenly worried that this was going to be too much — the kiss would be a risk: something that could push me over the edge with him. The sex, the waking up naked next to each other was fine — it happened in another space, on top of that roof. This was new, a new day. New life. Luka was not real. Luka was not my boyfriend. I didn't need a boyfriend. I needed something else. I needed other escapes but not in men.

I slowed down my hips. I focused on the ground underneath my feet. How soft it was. Filled with powder from centuries-old bones. I remembered the rumour about secret vineyards on the island. I read comments online — tourists claiming to be treated to glasses of wine made from the Tajni Otok grapes by corrupted locals. I wondered if the wine I drank at the party in Trogir originated in those secret vineyards.

We were now at the shore where the boat was picking us up. It was windy, more than just a breeze. None of that stifling heat of yesterday; today was breathable and fresh. I wondered if I had enough to report back. The island had many charms; there was mystery to it even if you took the ghostly appearances out of the equation. A typical visitor — daring but still worried about safety — would feel some anxiety, and it would be heightened just by knowing what happened on the island. A typical visitor would listen for sounds, look at the ground to try to find fragments of bones. The visitor would look into the broken rooms and try to make out the shadows. The visitor would scrutinize everything so that they wouldn't be surprised by *it*. What *it*? The *it* could be lurking anywhere; there was no way to describe *it*. Everyone has their personal *it*. The visitor would interpret the island through the prism of its past notoriety, through their personal *it*.

My mother told me once that she used to be afraid of witches as a child. If she felt particularly scared, she could stay up most of all night trying to decide which way to turn — toward the window or toward the door — to make sure she'd catch a witch before the witch could catch her. She said she never caught a witch but that didn't mean the witch didn't show up to look at her when she finally slept. Maybe she would finally see a witch here. Maybe she would see sticks, strands of long grey hair caught in branches, chewed up carcasses of unidentified animals. This could be my write-up. I could promote the island as something that could bring to life people's personal demons and then tame them.

I hadn't known what my demon was, but I knew now. He wasn't harmless, but I could contain him within this story. I watched as he lay in the shadow of a tree, his straw hat over his face as usual. Near him, there was another little triangle structure made out of rocks, leaning against a trunk of a tree. The bushes behind the little structure were thick, and behind the bushes the forest was dark, the sunlight couldn't penetrate it.

I heard the motorboat coming from around the point. I looked away from the structure. The guide was pulling up to the shore. It was nice to finally see another human being. I liked the contrast of the lavender sweater against his dark tanned skin. The guide killed the motor and waved. I walked, got inside the boat that rocked once, and I held on to the little bench to steady myself. Once seated, I looked behind me. I said Luka's name.

Coming, lady? the boat guide barked.

Come on, I yelled toward Luka.

I watched him get up and walk toward the boat, jump in.

The motor coughed once and we zipped through the water.

I turned to face the island. I shielded my eyes from the sun. The bell tower was visible above the forest, some of the roofs, too. The building appeared more menacing now, as if there was a cloud above the place, yet the sky was blue, cloudless. I blinked. There was nothing wrong; it all looked fine.

But there *was* something wrong. Luka was gone. He was not in the boat.

He's gone, I shouted at the boat guide. Stop the boat!

He looked at me.

The motor is too loud, I shouted. Stop the boat!

The guide killed the motor. What?

My friend, I said. As I was saying it, I suddenly knew that Luka had never been in the boat.

The guide said nothing.

What should we do? I said. I was saying this to myself, as if I needed to convince myself that I should go along with my own story. What was there to do? I felt laughter coming on, my nerves short-circuiting into the wrong reaction. What was the right reaction?

The guide stared at me. The way he stared at me now was the same kind of stare I used to see on people's faces in grocery stores when my mother would talk to them about high exposure to nitrogen oxides from traffic exhaust causing cervical cancer, and how you could protect from it by wearing a magnetic belt across your pelvis and administering nightly douches.

Let's go, I said. Never mind.

Yes, the guide said. No time. He started up the motor.

The wind was giving way to the heat. It was going to be as hot today as it was yesterday. I acknowledged the heat. But I couldn't feel it now. I was cold. Starting from my toes, all the way up. It was ridiculous. But the more I thought about how cold I was, the colder I felt.

I looked toward the island. On the shore, there he was, Luka, with his arm wrapped around the shoulders of a dark-haired woman in a long coffee-coloured dress. He raised his hand and waved once, slowly. I waved back.

31

I DIDN'T KNOW how to process it all right away. Even with my and my mother's past sightings of ghosts and my own encounter with Luka, I was now back in the city with its insistence on my being a regular person — one who exists in reality where her day is divided by sleep, work, family — I had a hard time suspending logic and reason. I walked around in a daze. I stopped driving to work. Covering distance in a metal can seemed just too absurd, whereas my feet made sense, the feeling of the ground through the soles of my shoes. I touched things — trees, brick walls, leaves — as I walked. It seemed necessary to feel myself be in the real world. Lovers made me feel alive, and since I no longer had a lover I had to find alternatives. The touching and the walks calmed me but not for long; the restlessness would present itself as soon as I sat down at my desk.

I had already written the official report where I talked about how to get to the island, what it looked like, and what to do in Trogir. As for Tajni Otok, I knew I couldn't write the truth, I didn't want people to think I was turning into my mother. Whatever I'd end up writing would remind only me of what the truth was — people would read a story that I had fabricated while using some of the elements of my experience. I was going to normalize it. I felt that once it became a story, I could get what everyone wanted when it came to traumatic events: closure.

I pitched the idea to my boss as a new feature we could use in our marketing package. It would be a personal story. Like in a magazine: *It happened to me.* We could post it on our Unusual Places website. I would tweet it, send it out — maybe it would go viral? A first-person account of visiting a haunted island — how I met a handsome local who told me a tragic love story of a young man and a woman who died on the island. We could have it come out in the winter when people are especially reckless about splurging on vacations.

My boss asked me to send him a draft as soon as I was done with it. He said, Just don't go too heavy on the haunted stuff. We need some credibility, but write about your Croatian boy first, sure, my boss said and patted my chair as usual.

I didn't remember saying anything about the boy being mine. It must've been the way I said it.

My boss left my desk to phone his wife, who — a happy coincidence, he said — used to work for magazines and sent him a few links to magazines she liked reading online. He forwarded me the links and said to see if I could get the tone. *Make it breezy,* my boss wrote.

I thought of the breeze that I felt on the island, the smell of the sea. I visualized the small beach where we landed and

298 / JOWITA BYDLOWSKA

where I later saw Luka with Anna. I missed him. I missed her. I missed *them*. What a silly thing. But I missed them — the way one misses a nice couple one met and had dinners with on vacation — *Guys, we really need to get together when we're back in the city!*

I started to write my breezy story. In the beginning, I felt hostile toward it, but after awhile I gave myself a makeover in my mind and became the sort of character who gets a pale-pink manicure, regular hair blowouts, and who wears a pussy-bow blouse. Chic black ankle-length pants. Kitten heels. Kate, like my popular high school friend who'd grow up to look like that. She would own a funky Kate Spade purse, and she would make some kind of joke about sharing the name of a fashion label.

Near the end of my shift, my mother called to complain about the house being too empty. She had been complaining about that ever since I'd returned, and I wondered if she was referring to the presence being gone, not to the fact that I was away at work and the caseworker wasn't keeping her company.

Right now, she said, did you know the sitting room lamp-stand is made out of lead? It'll give me a tumour in my hand. It grows bit by bit every time I switch it on or off. I should get a dog, she said.

You can't take care of a dog. I can't take care of a dog.

What else do you have to do besides going on trips?

I work, I take care of you, I said, lowering my voice to a whisper as a pregnant blond colleague walked by with a raised eyebrow. I'll be home soon. Goodbye for now.

What? Said my mother.

We can talk later about some ideas, I said, although I couldn't think of any. Maybe with a small raise I could afford someone to come in and keep her company. But I didn't want to spend the rest of my childbearing years wasting my money and energy on my mother, even though it was the right thing to do.

Aside from the ongoing anxiety about my mother, I felt lighter and almost happy. For now, it seemed that my desperation about men had been quelled, and I became confident I could be fine on my own as long as I stayed on the move — I wanted to experience more.

A Girl in Trogir or What I Learned About Ghosts

I don't know about you but I find these winter months particularly taxing on my good mood. I miss the long, lazy days! I miss the heat! I miss the sun kissing my shoulders. (And, oh, how I miss bikinis — on that note, gotta get this bod beach ready.)

This is why, sitting here in my dark office with the gloom of February lurking outside, I decided to put my summer hat on.

I booked a trip to Croatia — a place I once planned to go with my ex-fiancé, Mike, for our honeymoon. And because Mike and I didn't work out — long, typical story involving an intern — I was always too apprehensive about going there. I thought I would have a bad time on my own because I would be constantly thinking about that relationship.

Still, unlike Mike, Croatia kept calling me and calling me … and, finally, I caved in. I went to the gym [Fix-Me Fitness], got rid of a few extra pounds (I had gained over winter, thanks to my mama's famous

macadamia cookies), and booked my trip through my
trusted travel agent [who do we plug?].

It went on like that for another five hundred words as I
described my single-gal trip where I met a man (*Hot tip: always
Facebook-stalk (and verify) peeps you meet on vacay!*) who took
me to a party. I described his ghostly beauty, the dark eyes that
pinned me as we danced together. I waxed on about the city of
Trogir that was like something out of a fairy tale.

I plugged hotels, I plugged boat tours I didn't go on, and I
plugged the waterfalls in Krka National Park, which you could
only access with a professional guide.

This is really good so far, my boss said after he'd read it.
This is really fucking good. Sorry, he chuckled.

He had never sworn before. I could now, finally, picture
us together: his paleness, his hand on my ass. I would have to
tell him to slap it, and he would, and I would say, *harder*, and
he would do it, uncertainly, a little harder. *No, harder*, I would
say and he would try to, but it would be the same kind of slap,
and it would be too frustrating to keep instructing him, so I'd
just let him finish pumping away. I imagined us going to some
golf-course inn with a heated pool, far enough away so that we
wouldn't run into anyone who might know him or his wife. He
would order the five-course couples special dinner for the two
of us and would mispronounce *amuse-bouche*. He would insist
I'd call him Samuel, not Sammy. He would pull the bedsheets
over his legs because he'd be ashamed of his legs being too
skinny, and he would growl at me if I'd try to peel them off to
look at them.

Josephine, are you okay? He leaned over more, his hand
closer to my shoulder now, the outside of his thumb brushing

against it. I took a deep breath and exhaled loudly. He moved back.

I looked up as Kelly got up, rolling her eyes at me, and making a gesture that implied gagging. It was the first time that I'd seen her behave so mischievously.

32

I WORKED ON my idiotic story in coffee shops all over down-town near my workplace. I couldn't seem to go home straight after work anymore; I dreaded having to be with my mother, and I wanted to be among people even though I didn't interact with them.

I still noticed bathrooms and paid attention to their locks — if the locks looked trustworthy to stay locked once you were inside, leaning against baby-change tables, your lover bending you over. I could even feel the phantom of Sebastian's body behind me if I thought about it all hard enough, but the memory wasn't at all powerful. I could allow myself to stay in the memory long enough to explore its permutations — my panties around my ankles, his hand gathering my wrists — without worrying about self-harm. Before, such explorations would fill me with the pain of longing. But now, for the first time, I was able to observe where, before, it was as if I was being observed.

There was all this space in me, a sponge meant to soak up all my toxic refuse, him included. The space in me came from a series of wounds. I thought of the first one by me, at me: I was looking in the bathroom mirror, looking at my four-year-old self after I fell off my bike. I had a nosebleed, and my knees were two red craters with grit embedded in the delicate torn-lace skin. I was not an angel like my grandmother said I was. That's what she called me in her language when I was little: *mój aniołku*. But I was flesh. I slapped myself hard across the face and screamed when my fingers made contact with my hemorrhaging nose.

My mother rushed into room and shook me, screaming at me to stop. Her glorious cloudy hair flew out of the thick black band, and her cat eyes were wild, darting all over my face, unable to focus. She had no control over either of us, but she grabbed my hands and held them in hers and screamed for me to quit it! And I quit it, but her violence didn't stop the bleeding that I felt bubbling up inside me — it just made it worse. Nothing spilled, however, as my surfaces were dry, my eyes opened wide trying to anchor hers and failing.

I wondered if I would've learned the world differently had she hugged me or immediately put Band-Aids on my knees. Instead, what I learned was that there was always a way to make things hurt more, and it was only through hurt that you could distract yourself. Those were terrible lessons, but now that I was back at home I finally understood what happened. My mother had no idea how to calm me down. I had to be my own mother or accept being motherless.

§

The ghost of Luka never came back. I wondered if our encounter was as crucial to him as it was to me and if he was freed now to give into death for good. Did he get his happy-ever-after ending with Anna in the afterlife? Was she at peace, too, finally, with him at her side? For a while, I thought about him before sleep, wanted to see if I'd be able to conjure him again, but other than in my dreams, he never showed. In my dreams Luka was my companion, but more like a brother than a lover. Often we were teenagers, a boy and girl of eighteen. We explored the island. We ran through the bushes till we'd hit secret vineyards, and we would pick grapes and eat them. I could taste their sunny sweetness and tongue-puckering sourness in my dream. Sometimes we'd dig into the little earthy hills, dig up bones. We arranged the bones into shapes of rectangles, diamonds, hearts. It wasn't a morbid thing we did — we were playful about it, and we giggled as we'd arrive at different configurations. We chased each other all over the mental hospital. We ran through empty rooms, rooms with broken metal beds, with stained mattresses that lay exhausted and contorted against the walls of small cells.

We ran into the kitchen, then the basement, then, suddenly, we would be in front of the same windowless room as in other variations of this dream, the room where Luka probably died. I would look down and see bloody footprints on the floor. And then the mood would change — the temperature would drop, and every sound was suddenly exaggerated and supernatural, water dripping in the wall turning into animal hissing that would, in turn, sound like a person shrieking but, oh, so quietly, like they had their vocal cords severed. A subtle terror would wash over me, and I'd find myself unable to turn around. Luka was no longer next to me, but there was *something* behind me, a black mouth, opened, slowly inhaling everything around it, me included. *Wake up, wake up*, I would shout in my head, aware that this was a dream and I didn't have to experience it. And I would wake up but I wouldn't be quite awake. I would lie in the darkness, trapped in my own body. I would scream and no sound would come out.

Eventually, my voice would pierce through that last barrier between the dream and consciousness. I was awake. I was in my bed. I was always surprised by the stillness and the silence and my sleepy mouth that didn't feel like it had opened at all.

Other nights I dreamt that Luka and I were in tunnels, running toward a light, calling each other's names, the light getting dimmer and dimmer, our feet stepping on giant slugs, squishing them between our toes, the light disappearing entirely. Then we were in complete darkness. The air would get thinner and thinner, and we took big gulps of air ... there was a sound of a heartbeat all around us.

I would wake up with my own heart beating hard.

In the morning after one of those dreams I would be almost certain that what I had dreamt had really happened. I'd spend most of my day trying to convince myself that I wasn't remembering a real event.

I tried to talk to him in my mind — ask where he was, tell him I missed him — but it wasn't the way it had been with Sebastian. With Luka I knew there was no reception, zero, nothing, and not that there was with Sebastian, but he was real. After some time I forced myself to push the Luka thoughts away before going to sleep, and the dreams stopped.

∽

I finished my dumb story, and my boss said I should think of a side career in magazines.

I'll think about it, I said. I thought of the essays I used to write and how I no longer felt indignant enough — about work, dating, eating disorders — to publish my displeasure.

He wasn't leaving. I smiled at him. I had nothing else to add.

He was in a talkative mood. It didn't happen often, but when it did it was bad. I'd yawned into my mouth. I didn't even have it in me to come up with my little scenarios where he and I go away on a secret fuckation to a golf-course resort. I had to wait for the talking to pass. There were words being said, full sentences, paragraphs, and it was dreadful. Last time, maybe around Christmas, he talked about a shed in his backyard: Should he remove it to make more space and maybe install something, like a small fountain? But if he were to remove it, he would have to store all those things, and should he pay for storage? Et cetera.

This could be the rest of my life: me sitting in my cubicle, having to listen to this drivel, listening to other drivel on the phone, writing professionally happy emails, and obsessing over whatever man came next.

As my boss went on, I became convinced that I needed to go on another trip.

You should just ask for things you want, a voice said in my head. It was Luka's voice. It was the first time I had heard him since the island. I shouted his name in my head, but there was nothing else.

Hello? Is this on? my boss tapped his ear.

I read his face. He looked happy. I risked it: Yeah, I think that's really amazing.

He seemed pleased.

I'd like to go on another trip, I said. To research another location. I think this is the direction that the company should be going in. Actual research where I can report and write articles about it if you think that's something I'm good at. More places like Tajni Otok, like Ecuador. I could look into all those leads we've been getting. I could find a bunch of other spots for us to explore. And I would like to be in charge of that. I'd rather that than a salary increase. I think we should take that risk.

My boss took a step back and nodded at me somewhat theatrically, which went really nicely with his bald head, like he was a butler. He said, I'd like to wait and see how we do with Tajni Otok first —

Maybe it was the way he was waggling his eyebrows, but I lost my patience with him. I felt a rush of assertiveness. Sure, I said, but it would be good to have something lined up right away. I have a good feeling about it. People will want to know what else we have to offer. I could go to Ecuador and then somewhere else. Our followers are increasing, and there's momentum building. We can't let this go, *Sammy*. This could be a game changer. This could be huge.

I was saying things I had heard people say in TV shows about business deals.

I would have to look into our budget, my boss said. His eyebrows were back in place.

I said, My point being, you can't travel online. It has to be experienced. I just want you to think about that. I'll write out a plan. Expenses, all of the rest. I've been with the company for how long?

I don't know. You tell me. He leaned closer to my computer screen, my face, and, yeah, of course, he wanted to fuck me.

Ten years, Sammy, I said and turned my face toward him. I rested my hand on his arm briefly, but it was long enough for him to flinch and smile and say that he would see what he could do.

Leaving work, I had another idea. Now that I handed in my article, I had nowhere to go but home. I dreaded it. I stopped at a park bench and took out my phone and downloaded the Airbnb app.

33

I TOLD MY mother I would be moving out. I said it on the way out to work the next day, casually, as if I was telling her I was going to be a little late. For two days she said nothing about it. She took long baths that I had to rescue her from every night, but she said nothing, even when I was towelling her off — her typical time for being chatty.

I wished she asked me why because then I would be able to tell her, but this was, again, just my old fantasy of communicating with my mother as if she was a normal kind of person, the sort of mother a daughter confides in.

I loved her, but I couldn't live *for* her because if I were to do that, I wouldn't be able to live my own life properly. Already, too much of my time had been handed over to others who didn't reciprocate my efforts in any significant ways.

There was an email from my boss telling me he'd assigned me another account — almost as good as Ecuador, he wrote. There was an active volcano in the Cordillera Central mountain range that seismologists have been getting excited about lately and, knowing hipsters, we worried people might be tempted to climb it for Instagram photo ops. I was thrilled about getting the new travel assignment, and at first I wondered if I had attracted good luck by standing up to my mother.

Wrong. I was finally asking for things I wanted; this was not about good luck. I recalled when Luka asked me if I believed in fate — now that I was becoming assertive, believing in fate struck me as too much of a copout. I didn't want to be passive any more.

Kelly had found a village in Lithuania with a small birch forest near which there was an unusual number of suicides — people travelling from faraway places to off themselves. In pictures, the ground of the forest was almost entirely covered by red moss; the white trees looked like bones surrounding the red patch. This time, Kelly didn't ask to consider her for the account. She was in love. I learned this after Sammy left my cubicle. Kelly was standing up at her desk, her face eager and bright.

Who is it this time? I couldn't tell those things. Everyone wore loose clothing and could potentially be pregnant.

Kelly laughed. Oh, God, not that!

This wasn't about pregnancy — this was about Kelly going out to a pub and meeting a man named Dave or David, who owned either a window-washing company or a truck with a hose, and who not only bought his own bungalow when he was still in his twenties but who also owned a tiny condo he was renting out for stupid amounts of money to tourists. Being a double homeowner was an impressive feat considering prices in the city, but Kelly didn't have any specific information about that. I suspected David or Dave must be in his fifties. What was a man that age doing in a pub? I guessed Dave was newly divorced or an alcoholic or both.

And get this — he has a brother who's single. R*eee*ally cute, Kelly said, tilting her head.

I shook mine no.

You're not still hung up on —

I shook my head again.

Okay, okay, sorry, she said, and picked up the folder with the Lithuanian village details and passed it over the grey wall. Behind her was an 8 x 10 printout of a man's face in a baseball cap tacked to the wall beside a much smaller picture of Kelly in a pink wig and a pair of fairy wings. That was the only picture she left hanging from her entire cosplay series. I felt sad that she let Dave's big face replace the other pictures.

She saw me looking and shrugged. I just thought they would look kind of weird next to each other. Like all of them together and then his portrait? She blushed.

No, for sure, I said, and quickly focused on the picture behind her head, but not for too long as to appear creepy although long enough to hopefully memorize him. I tried to memorize the face in case he started to come into work to pick her up, the way Matthews and Gregs came to work to pick up my other co-workers, and I had no idea who was who and which one they were picking up, and it stressed me out.

You know, I think our staircase workouts helped, Kelly said. Such a silly thing, but I've been feeling so much better. In my body. Men pick up on that.

I smiled back. I'm glad to hear it. We should have lunch soon. He seems sweet, I said, and pointed to the picture on her wall. Now, I genuinely felt happy for her. She deserved a nice boyfriend even if he was middle-aged and possibly an alcoholic. As long as he treated her well and made her beam like that, he was perfect. I felt guilty about not catching if he preferred to be called Dave or David.

∽

Two days after telling my mother I was going to move out, she left her bed when I was asleep, went outside, walked into the street, and stepped in front of a car. She was wearing slippers and her favourite stained nightgown with dark-pink flowers. She stepped in front of a car because she said she was told by the Lord to stand in the middle of the river — the street — to part it so that people who couldn't cross would be able to. She didn't explain what people. She had very little detail and claimed the questions bothered her so much, it was as if there were a drill inside her head.

I didn't believe her story but said nothing about that to the caseworker or the attending psychiatrist. I wondered about the crossing-guard vest and why no one had commented on it. A person who wants to die doesn't put one on. She must've obtained it from the church, maybe when she went on her sleep-away trip. The vest was the only reason she was still alive. Although she didn't put it on properly — it was inside out — still the fluorescent flaps flashed in the dark, and the car managed to brake, so it only grazed her instead of slamming into her body.

∽

Out of habit, I called Victor and asked him to meet me at the hospital. He knew about my mother, and I felt I needed someone there to whom I didn't have to explain.

He met me in the hospital lobby. He looked a little smaller than I remembered him. I was always shocked by his small stature after we'd break from one another for a while. In my mind, he occupied a lot of space although he occupied less space now.

It was a real miracle, Victor said. You can tell her that her praying paid off. The Lord doesn't want her to die — he was just testing her.

It's not funny.

No, it's not. I hope your mother is okay.

I hope so, too. I hope that's what he was doing, or the Lord won't want her anymore. It's a mortal sin to take your own life, I said.

Well, if that's the case, she didn't succeed. So she can repent. She just broke her ankle.

Thank God at least she broke her ankle. A bruise wouldn't be worth the guilt trip.

Victor said, I'll just wait here. Go back and see your mother. His thumbs softly wiped the tears off my face as if we were playing out a scene. I pressed against him. He was hard, his cock insisting on announcing itself. I stood on my tiptoes, and he pulled me closer to him, and for no good reason I raised my face to his, and for no good reason he kissed me on the mouth. He tasted strongly of whisky. Why was he drinking in the morning, or had he been up all night drinking? Was he drinking with a girl? Did she look like a younger me or was she completely different?

I could ask him. If I asked him, he would tell me. We would be invested in each other again.

I didn't ask him, didn't say anything.

I liked the smokiness of our whisky kiss. I couldn't taste another woman on him so that was good. The whisky was the right thing to drink before meeting with me. We looked into each other's eyes: *I missed you* and *I missed you*. He tried to kiss me again.

I pushed him away gently. Thank you for being here.

Can I have a hug?

Anytime, I said and counted to twenty, and released him.

I went back inside my mother's room. She was asleep now. I no longer wanted her. She was careless when she stepped in front of that car. She was careless when she took her baths. And she was careless when she asked me to care for her. I couldn't fake it anymore. At night, I didn't lock the front door, nor did I install a lock on the bathroom as I'd planned.

Right now, I watched her. Sleeping, she seemed smaller than she was. Her skin felt very delicate. Like you could puncture it, easily, with your nail. I took her hand in mine. She made a beautiful sleeper — an old woman who looked younger. They should let her stay on Valium all the time. I would talk to her doctor about that next step. There were many more next steps to take. For now, I just held her hand. I kissed her on the hand.

∽

Victor was still in the waiting room when I came out. I watched him. He was sitting in an orange chair next to the vending machine, fingering his phone: looking up old girlfriends on

Facebook or maybe playing online poker with teenagers from Russia and Mexico. I knew he liked to do both. There was a weariness to his face, skin on bone with just a microscopic skew. I felt tenderness for him as if he were a child — the kind of tenderness that's dangerous to feel about a lover. The kind of tenderness that lives next to pity. Victor, too, was someone I would have to leave behind. We would remain friends, of course, but I would no longer feel angry about not having a future together.

34

NOT LONG AFTER I moved out, my mother was admitted to a full-time care facility. There was no other way after her case-worker had said I would have to get someone full-time or do it myself. I picked the first home from the list she provided, a place called Caress and Care, which was both a creepy and reassuring name. The building was downtown, with a subway station right outside of it, which I liked because it was busy, and I imagined a lot of tenants spent their time looking either at the television or outside the window. My mother's room looked out onto the stop. My mother had a room to herself, which was more expensive than shared accommodations, but I could afford it now that we both moved out and could rent out the house. It was Kelly's boyfriend who helped out with that; he set me up with a company that offered places to academics visiting the country with their families on tenure. I cleaned the place the best I could and called its nauseating decor "old-world charm" in the ad I placed, hoping someone French or Spanish would buy my bullshit. Someone did, an elderly academic couple from Belgium.

The Airbnb apartment I rented was furnished, with tall ceilings and a floor-to-ceiling wall shelf. My bedroom was in the middle of it, in a fish tank-like enclosure where I could move the glass walls to separate it from or open it to the living room. There was a big black jet chandelier, which was the only object with any personality. I moved in some of my clothes and a few books and some electronics. I planned to travel a lot more and didn't want to commit to a place too seriously.

I wondered what it would be like to fuck a new lover in this space, so on my first Friday night there, I put on a tight dress and heels to go out and sit at a bar just like they do in the movies, and just like in the movies, soon there was a guy and he was buying me a drink. He reminded me a little bit of Victor, the same distractible manner, the same cockiness that was put on. He listed his accomplishments; he once won a gold for service journalism.

I asked how old he was and he was older, too. We talked and he told me about the company he'd started, something in advertising. The word "content" came up a lot.

I told him about Tajni Otok, how I went there and had sex with a ghost.

Interesting, he said and laughed, and I laughed with him. I told him we would've been considered insane in the past had we laughed so much, and he laughed again. We had more to drink, and his hand landed on my thigh, and then his mouth was on my neck.

Your place or mine? he said, just like in the movies, and just like in one movie, I suggested an alleyway. He looked unsure, suddenly younger-seeming. His shoes were so white. He was also on the smaller side, so there was no way he'd be able to hoist me up. That was the fantasy I had in that moment, of a man hoisting me up, slamming me against a wall.

He needed more drinks, so we had more drinks. At some point his face metamorphosed into Victor's and I called him that, and he didn't mind. He said, Victor? Okay. You can call me whatever you like.

I'm sorry.

No need to.

We tumbled out of the bar; he caught me right before I fell. He was stronger than I thought he'd be.

I bent over in an alley and he fumbled, and then I could barely feel him, and he grunted, and I wasn't sure if I should continue to lean against the brick wall or if I could afford to bend all the way down and touch the ground with my finger-tips, which struck me as odd but perhaps more comfortable.

He growled that he was going to come, and as he did, I called on God loudly, and he shuddered and surprised me by turning me around after he slipped out, finally kissing me. The kiss turned me on and I tugged at him, and he said, It's Patrick, not God or Victor.

Then we went back to my place, and the next time I said, Oh, Patrick, as he made me come with his sprinty little tongue and his mouth, like a little snake.

∽

I offered Patrick a drive home the next morning. Even though it was the weekend, I needed to get started on researching the Lithuanian village, but, truthfully, I just needed an excuse to get him out of my apartment — he had fulfilled his function of being a lover in a new space. He complained when I told him to get up and have a shower. In the car, his energy was low, and the way he asked for my number sounded rehearsed, just something he felt he had to do, although he quickly added he really wanted to see me again. I gave him my number with one digit off. I didn't care. He talked about his advertising agency again. I couldn't pay attention, but I had no heart to tell him he should stop talking because none of it mattered. I was in that two-dimensional state of not being quite hungover but not being able to treat life seriously because I was possibly still poisoned by all the alcohol. I didn't feel any guilt over the encounter — instead I felt giddy, like a person with a secret. I liked the brutality of how instantly it all happened between us and how clichéd it was.

Patrick lived close to the neighbourhood where Sebastian used to live before he moved in with his parents. Now that I was here, I had a thought to drive to the little coffee shop where I first met him.

The coffee shop was calm on Saturday morning, free from weekday women with ironed hair and sensible heels and men in suits, all on their way to offices. A mewing, folky song played on the stereo but quietly enough that I could tune it out. There were only a few people typing away on their laptops and plenty of empty tables, so I grabbed one in the far corner.

I ordered a large latte, set up my laptop, and got to work. I typed in the name of the Lithuanian village, Krasna Gora, and a bunch of articles popped up. As with Tajni Otok, I read the official stuff before moving on to Reddit threads. During the Second World War, a barn containing sixty people of Jewish descent had been set on fire, outside of the village. I had to see if anybody was old enough to remember the fire. I wondered, too, if the barn was near the small birch forest where people travelled to kill themselves and if there was a supernatural connection.

As usual there were some videos online, narrated by hushed voices of excitable young men who panned their cameras slowly over the white trees. Sometimes the videos were filmed at night with morbid music playing in the background, but none of it was useful to me. There was no reliable information as to how many people had died in the little forest or in what way.

Birch trees were too feeble to hang yourself from. I found some material on Reddit forums about two teenagers who drank poison à la *Romeo and Juliet* and were found at the site, but before long, the comment thread dispersed into insults between commenters about American politics, and the trail ended.

The front door banged loudly, startling me, and I looked up, and there he was — same self-assured walk and same strong build, not too tall but bulky. I liked the bulk; my body had a memory of that kind of weight pressing into me, collapsing on top of me. His hair was in a similarly messy style, similarly dark. Even his clothes resembled Sebastian's, a pair of sweatpants and a distressed leather jacket. I watched him go up to the counter. He leaned over and said something to one of the baristas. She flipped her hair and laughed too hard.

The man turned around, scanning the room as if to check if the audience was watching how he made her laugh. I was sitting behind a rack of T-shirts for sale, next to a shelf with mugs and paper bags of beans, and he didn't see me.

My entire body kept reacting to this man, to the arrangement of his facial features, the same teasing, predatory smile as Sebastian's; he seemed like the kind of man who might come up to you and demand your number.

I tried to listen to him talk. He had that almost-lazy cadence in his voice Sebastian did, the slight rasp. I couldn't hear the actual words. I moved closer, standing right by the shelf with all the coffee merchandise. He said something about a cake pop, asked the girl if they were fresh.

I ran my fingers over the overpriced T-shirts with a drawing of a pigeon on them advertising the coffee shop, as if I was thinking of trying one on.

His face was like a puzzle that scattered, then rearranged itself. A glimpse of Sebastian there, then gone. His voice vibrated in my ears, but it wasn't a voice I knew after all.

I turned around and went back to my table.

Overall, the whole experience was akin to trying to capture elusiveness itself: How did the melody go, or the words to the song, or the name of the film, or the name of the kid from Grade 1, or that thing we had for dinner; what was it?

I forced myself to focus on my screen. Soon, I found a curious Facebook post about a possible sighting. It was of a woman, not a young one or an old one. She was wearing a black dress and had long dark hair. The poster said she was there one moment and gone the next. She didn't seem like a person from the past, like a ghost, but the way she appeared and disappeared was disturbing, the poster wrote. She bared her teeth at him, too, like she was some kind of animal. I pictured myself doing that, baring my teeth at some asshole who was filming the site for the purposes of his blog.

Underneath the posting, people commented about other alleged experiences, whispers right in their ears out of nowhere, mysterious giggling in the forest, and eerie howling somewhere deeper in the small mountains surrounding the village. There were strange symbols carved in tree trunks; there was a drawing of a hanged man on the crumbling wall of the burned-down barn.

I copied the text, pasted it into the body of an email, typed in my boss's address, and hit Send. I tuned out everything around me — the voices, the flirty laughing at the counter.

I was in Tajni Otok again, the tip of my nose wet, tingling from the salty air. I was on the pebbly beach — there were pebbles, I forgot — waiting for the boat to come and claim me. Then I was on the boat. Luka was waving on the shore, a pale ghost of a pale girl next to him.

Josephine.

I'm fine, I said out loud.

I was back in the coffee shop. The counter was empty now. At the table next to mine, there was the guy, and he was just some guy. He pulled a laptop out of a briefcase. I heard a vague beat of electronic music. He took out a thin white ribbon of headphones and plugged them in and stuck the earbuds in his ears.

My laptop pinged. I scanned the email. *Great research. Booking tix*, the subject read.

A news alert popped up on my screen. The first lines read, "I love my kids, and I don't know why I feel that I want to decapitate them," the patient said. She had experienced only mild physical symptoms of the flu, but months later, she heard a voice that first told her to kill herself and then told her to kill her children."

I scanned the article. There was a new strain of flu, originating in Asia, that sounded like something made up for a zombie novel. It attacked people's respiratory systems, but in some patients the virus attacked their brains, as well, causing loss of sensations, such as smell or taste, and in a few hundred reported cases, psychotic outbreaks. The patients became violent and attacked their families or checked themselves into psych wards, afraid of their murderous thoughts.

I wished the explanation for my mother's illness was a mutation of a flu strain instead of genetics. Then again, I guess with the flu we were all at risk. A pandemic would be good for humanity. We were all so bored.

I looked to the guy, and he looked back at me and smiled distractedly.

I looked away. He was just some guy, and there was nothing I wanted to say to him, so I closed my laptop, got up, and left.

It was sunny outside, and I took off my sweater and wrapped it around my waist. I watched myself as if from outside as I walked in the direction of the parking lot. I felt light, my head filled with cotton and clouds. I touched a brick wall as I walked. The air was crisp, and there was a sweet, earthy smell of walnuts and rot all around me; it was mid-September, the leaves were turning orange and bloody red.

acknowledgements

I couldn't have afforded to be a writer and create had it not been for the help of the Canada Council for the Arts and the Ontario Arts Council writing grants. Thank you — I am forever grateful for your support. Also, massive thanks to the Woodcock Fund Grant for helping me through a health crisis.

My deepest thanks to the following people who made this book possible:

Sam Haywood
Barbara Gowdy
Megan Philipp
Jenny McWha
Julie Mannell
Russell Smith
Kwame Scott Fraser

Laura Boyle
Kathryn Lane
Mary Ann Blair
Robyn So
Rachel Spence
Ashley Hisson
Maria Zuppardi
Heather Wood
Elena Radic
Sara D'Agostino
Chris Houston

The following friends and family were also instrumental in making this book possible:

Jules McCusker
Hugo Smith
Brian McDonald
Naomi Gaskin
David B. Bohl
Victoria Hetherington
Cat Black
Bunmi Adeoye
Lisa Hannam
Agata Miszczynska
Neil Dev Sharma

"When you're living so intensely in your head there isn't any difference between what you imagine and what actually takes place. Therefore, you're both omnipotent and powerless," on page 4 is from *I Love Dick* by Chris Krauss. "Respect your efforts, respect yourself. Self-respect leads to self-discipline. When you have both firmly under your belt, that's real power," on page 136 was said by Clint Eastwood. "Could you really love somebody who was absolutely nobody without you? You really want somebody like that? Somebody who falls apart when you walk out the door? You don't, do you? And neither does he," on page 137 is from *Song of Solomon* by Toni Morrison.

about the author

JOWITA BYDLOWSKA was born in Warsaw, Poland, and moved to Canada as a teenager. She teaches creative writing and has worked as a journalist for the past two decades, covering the topics of health, especially mental health, as well as culture, arts, and fashion. She is the author of the controversial, bestselling memoir *Drunk Mom* and the bestselling novel *GUY* and has published many short stories in various literary journals. Jowita lives in Toronto.